IN THE TIME
OF TROUBLE

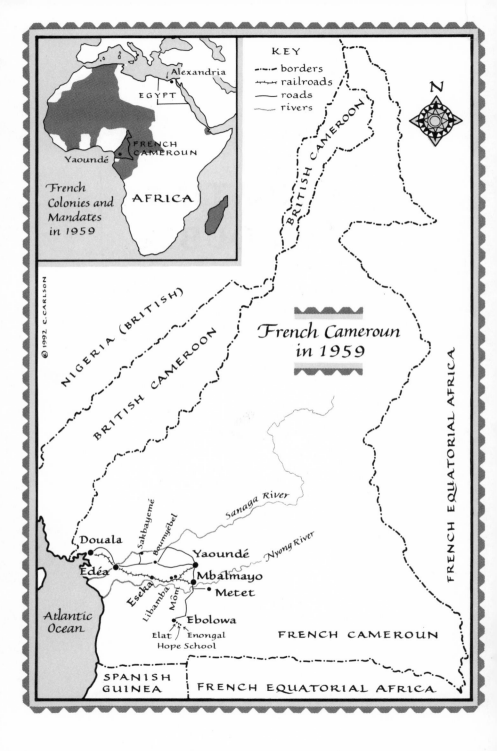

KEY
- - - borders
+++ railroads
— roads
— rivers

N

French Colonies and Mandates in 1959

AFRICA

Alexandria
EGYPT
FRENCH CAMEROUN
Yaoundé

© 1992 C.CARLSON

NIGERIA (BRITISH)

BRITISH CAMEROON

French Cameroun in 1959

FRENCH EQUATORIAL AFRICA

Sanaga River

Nyong River

Douala
Sakbayemé
Boumyebel
Yaoundé
Edéa
Eseka
Libamba
Mom
Mbalmayo
Metet
Atlantic Ocean
Ebolowa
Elat   Enongal
Hope School

FRENCH CAMEROUN

SPANISH GUINEA

FRENCH EQUATORIAL AFRICA

Charlotte Weaver-Gelzer

IN THE TIME
OF TROUBLE

DUTTON CHILDREN'S BOOKS
New York

Although this story occurs in a time and a place
that existed, no character in it is wholly based on
or intended to represent anyone living.

Map by Claudia Carlson

Copyright © 1993 by Charlotte Weaver-Gelzer

Published in the United States 1993 by Dutton Children's Books,
a division of Penguin Books USA Inc.
375 Hudson Street, New York, New York 10014

Library of Congress Cataloging-in-Publication Data

Weaver-Gelzer, Charlotte.
In the time of trouble / by Charlotte Weaver-Gelzer.
p.   cm.
Summary: Fourteen-year-old Jessie, daughter of missionaries,
finds her life and her relationship with her siblings changed by the
worsening political strife in Cameroun during the late 1950s.
ISBN 0-525-44973-6
[1. Cameroun—History—Fiction.   2. Missionaries—Fiction.
3. Brothers and sisters—Fiction.   4. Twins—Fiction.]   I. Title.
PZ7.W3625In   1993   [Fic]—dc20   92-11146   CIP   AC

Designed by Amy Berniker
Printed in U.S.A.
First edition
1 3 5 7 9 10 8 6 4 2

for Elisabeth and David Gelzer,
who in faith took their children along
on their own African adventure,

and for
Rachel Elisabeth Weaver and Susan Eyenga Mebanda Engo,
Daniel Calvin Weaver and Paul Bamela Engo,
because they have roots in each other's countries.

Soli Deo Gloria

CONTENTS

Kon me ngoo, a Nyambe, kon me ngoo,
Inyule ñem wem u nsolbene i weeni;
Ñ, m'a solbene isi titii i bipapai gwoñ,
Letee bilim bi tagbe.

HIEMBI 57:1

Be merciful to me, O God, be merciful,
for I have taken refuge in you;
in the shadow of your wings will I take refuge
until this time of trouble has gone by.

PSALM 57:1

1

Danger and Calling

It was Sunday morning, the second one in November, and the first Sunday of Advent, 1958.

Jessie decided she would write the date that way on her letter home today. She brushed her teeth, thinking about this while she looked out the large screened window in the back hall bathroom. An early-morning breeze lifted the fronds of the three palm trees she could see off to the left. The sky was a clear, bright blue, with lots of white puffy clouds riding high. There might be rain this afternoon. In Egypt would the sky be so deeply blue? It was the same sky there and here, in Cameroun. There were palms in Egypt; that would be familiar, too.

Jessie tapped her toothbrush against the second of the two sinks and took the brush with her into the dark, narrow dormitory hall and back to the large sunny room she shared with the only other girl in the eighth grade at Hope School.

She followed the trailing ends of her usual daydream about next September, when she and her twin, Joshua, and the other two boys in her class would be going to a Presbyterian missionary school in Egypt as high school freshmen. They would travel across the continent of Africa by themselves. Jessie would have her own passport. The idea of it—the thin green booklet with the gold seal of the United States engraved on the front—filled Jessie with deep excitement. Her own; a proof of her independence; a mark of her being, belonging to her alone and to be used by absolutely no one else. Jessie wished she had it now, to look at, to touch and lift her hopes once more toward the future, when she would be done with life at Hope School. She wouldn't have the passport until next term was over.

Dad had said he would make an appointment with the American consulate in Yaoundé for Jessie and Joshua to go in and sign the finished paperwork in March or April. Everything in Jessie leaned forward to that moment, and then her imagination leaped ahead to the long airplane journey— three days' and nights' worth—from the Cameroun port of Douala to Lagos and Accra and Tripoli and Khartoum and then Cairo, and finally, Alexandria. "Yippee!" Jessie wanted to shout, with the blood swirling in her and filling her wrists till they tingled with excitement. But Jessie did not shout.

The bedroom was quiet. Martha was already downstairs,

being the sort who was always on time. Jessie was not very often right on time.

"Jessie Howells!" the teachers or the houseparents would say. "Bring your mind to bear on the subject at hand." And Jessie would start to think about bringing her mind. How was that possible? By hand? And what about bringing it to bear? To bear what? Then she'd have a mental picture of a bear—an animal she'd never seen in person—lumbering toward the teacher's desk, and the next set of possibilities would make Jessie giggle. Then there would be trouble.

Jessie sighed with exasperation, partly aimed at herself; if she could just accept the grit work of organizing herself, or make herself concentrate on whatever it was that everyone else was doing, she'd stop feeling as though she were about to be caught making a mistake.

For example, it was Sunday morning, and that meant thinking about Sunday school. She would rather have been thinking about high school in Egypt. Or about danger. Instead she should have been remembering last week's lesson about the apostle Paul, who was a missionary—the first Christian missionary. This was a missionary school—she lived, ate, breathed, and slept school, so the lesson was more to the point right now than a passport and plane trips, and certainly safer than remembering the fighting going on in a distant part of Cameroun. That particular distant part of Cameroun was where home was, where her parents were at work.

Sometimes Jessie would help herself forget what she knew about that strange sort of war back home. She would rush out and join a field game with the other boarders, playing hard to keep her thoughts from resting on her fears. Other times she would swallow one quick-read mystery after the next, barely stopping when she closed a book, so as to keep her imagination occupied with other places, in other times, far from Africa. And there was always the passport daydream, in which she was dressed in an elegant linen suit, carrying a leather purse, wearing heels (not very high; Mom wouldn't even think past black patent-leather flats), standing by a desk where an airport official looked at the visas stamped in her elegant green embossed booklet, which she would draw out of her purse as if she were the most sophisticated traveler ever known.

But there were times when she made herself give up the candy distractions of daydreams. After all that self-indulgence, she sometimes had to force herself to think about the dangers that moved in the night, the dangers gathered invisibly even outside the house where Mom and Dad lived. Jessie dared these thoughts when she felt herself going numb in the heart, after a week or so of avoiding the memories and the questions about the French soldiers and the Africans, struggling against each other every day, right now, in the Bassa territory. Jessie knew the Bassa did not call it war. At least among the missionaries like her own parents, who were sympathetic to the Africans, the Bassa called it "the time of troubles."

Now and then Jessie remembered the troubles without intending to, and without any protection of her own daydream or someone else's story. She would find herself too deeply in the thought to pull away before she felt confused or frightened.

Early today, before it was light, she'd woken to an owl calling twice from the edge of the forest around the dormitory. At home, in Libamba, village men hiding in the forest from the French army signaled to each other with the owl's call.

She hadn't always known this.

One night last summer, Jessie had been folding clean clothes in the kitchen, and she'd heard the sound of owl calls repeated over and over, coming closer and closer to the shuttered windows in the room where she was working.

She had called out, "Mom? Do you hear those birds?" Imagining a line of them on the nearest tree branch, she'd started to open the kitchen door, when Mom had rushed in and said in a quiet and terrible voice, "Don't!"

Jessie drew her hand back from the handle as though it might burn her. Mom had stood still, listening, so Jessie stood still, too. Then her mother beckoned with her right index finger, and very quietly, Jessie followed her out of the kitchen and into the office, where Dad was sitting at his desk. Dad, Jessie had noticed, was not writing or correcting papers. He'd put down his pen and was sitting with his head raised, eyes on the wall, as if he could see through the paint and the cinder blocks to the campus road beyond. He, too, was listening.

Jessie still didn't hear anything but wind moving through the palm fronds and the hibiscus hedge, and then the sound of owl calls.

"What is it?" she whispered; her whisper was a loud noise in the office. Out in the living room Joshua put down the *National Geographic* he'd been reading, and when he got up from the chair, the wicker's creaking was like a pistol shot, startling them all.

When Joshua came into the office, Jessie felt safer, because he was with them, although she couldn't have said why being together made the family secure. Cassie, the youngest in the family and then only seven, was already asleep in the back of the house, four rooms and three doors away from the rest of them; to Jessie it seemed that her little sister had been cut off from the strength of the family, lost to the power moving in the darkness outside the house. She wanted Mom to tear through the house, grab Cassie from bed, and be instantly back in the office with everyone else.

The twins and Mom and Dad held completely still.

Then Joshua said, "What is going on out there?"

"Listen," said Dad, very quiet and low. "You can hear men on the road."

By holding her breath, Jessie could hear a sound different from the other, familiar night sounds. It was a long, sustained sigh, a low swishing, the dry, light sound of many bare feet moving over a dirt surface. If it had been one man walking, she'd never have heard him. If it had been several men just going by, she'd have heard them conversing together. There were no voices now. The ground gave back a muffled beat, like drums far off in the forest.

When the breeze passed through the hedge, Jessie imagined in it the sound of the men breathing as they passed the house, no farther away from her than Cassie was, asleep in the room the sisters shared.

If she could have seen them, there'd have been starlight gleaming on the long, thin stretches of metal the men carried—stars shining on the sharp edges of their cutlasses. And that blue light would move softly along the barrels of guns. This was not part of her imagination. Jessie knew those men were armed.

And yet she also knew that the bullets and the sharpened blades were not meant for her or her family. It was not the missionaries at Libamba who threatened those African men from the forest. The men, villagers by day and fighters at night, were sworn against Frenchmen, who now controlled Cameroun, a country that did not give them birth.

Dad breathed in a huge amount of air and let it out softly. "The college roads aren't patrolled by the French army," he said, still in quiet tones, as if ordinary ones would alert the men in the dark and call them back, unwanted. "The Maquis—that's the French name for political resistance fighters—cross the school land at night when they want to move large numbers of men to different parts of the forest here."

"Will they hurt us?" Jessie asked.

"No," said Dad, shaking his head briefly. "We didn't see them, and we can't report hearing them. What did we hear? Owl calls? The wind? And we wouldn't report them even if we did see them."

"No. We wouldn't report them to the French in any case," said Mom, with a steely, determined sound in her words.

So Jessie knew that her parents agreed with the Maquis. That seemed like a good thing. The French weren't going to hurt American missionaries, that seemed sure no matter what. And the Cameroun Maquis wouldn't hurt them either, if the missionaries agreed with them and let them alone.

It was these men that Jessie thought about early on Sunday morning, while she brushed her short, straight, very dark hair and tried to tuck the front strands behind her ears. She leaned into the mirror to see if she could admire herself yet, but she still had as many pimples as she'd had yesterday—more, probably. It was depressing to consider. Her nose was still too fat. That would never change. Her gray eyes looked good, though. She had nice thick dark lashes, too. Her eyebrows, darker than her hair, were too thick. If she was looking at a Bassa man who was in the

Maquis—who was a guerrilla fighter—would he make her afraid?

The bad-dream memory of the silent Africans marching past her house in the night with weapons ready (for what?) had almost no power here in the morning sunshine pouring through all three windows in the dorm room. Jessie felt quite sure of her courage; it had something in it of the calm, determined rightness she'd felt in Mom that night in the office.

Jessie's boarding school in Elat was a long ways from home, a long ways from the fighting around Libamba. There was no such fighting in the part of Cameroun where the missionary boarding school had been built. When Jessie met her eyes in the mirror, looking quickly at their quiet gray blueness and away again, she knew it was just a little too easy to feel brave.

Vacation was closing in on the school term. Counting from this first Sunday in Advent, there were only three weeks left before everyone went home. There were no Nancy Drew or Cherry Ames mysteries at home. At home even the thought of the passport and the coming adventure of going to Schutz, the high school in Egypt, would not be a strong distraction from the danger all around her. There would only be Joshua and Cassie to play with, and Jessie didn't think the three of them would feel like hide-and-seek at home.

She snatched up her thick red Revised Standard Version

of the Bible and whirled away from the mirror before she could meet her eyes again and see what going home meant this time.

Jessie ran through the dormitory halls and pounded down the old worm-eaten wooden staircase, going three steps at a time and nearly falling to the cement floor at the bottom, stumbling over her own feet in the speed of her flight. Her little sister, Cassie, and Cassie's roommates, Elissa Janeway and Lorayne Ware, all of them in the third grade, were just coming off the staircase, too, and Jessie barely missed colliding with them and knocking at least one of them to the ground.

"Sorry!" she panted, dashing off. Even in her hurry she heard Cassie calling, "Morning, Jess!" but she didn't bother to answer her sister's greeting.

She had to hurry. She was late. Uncle Don's usual work was up on the hospital station, as one of the missionary doctors. He always gave the eighth-grade Sunday school class the impression that he never really had all the time he was taking for them. He smelled of disinfectant no matter when Jessie was around him, even on Sunday afternoons at the vesper service, which all the missionaries on the school and hospital station attended together.

It was as though he never quite left the precise work he'd been called to do for God, here in Cameroun. One of his precise works had been to deliver Jessie and Joshua. As often as she saw Uncle Don, she knew this fact over again. Here was a man who had known her from the beginning, and knew her still. That disinfectant had probably been one of her first smells. This made Jessie begin to smile, but then she remembered she was late, and so she pushed the thought away for later.

As she slid into her seat at the study-hall table, she glanced nervously at the part in Uncle Don's thick white hair, wondering if he would scold her this time. He never had yet, but she knew that being late was rude, and she could have tried to be on time at least once this term. Sundays, though, were the only days here when time was mostly her own.

Uncle Don looked at her from under his dark eyebrows without remark. His eyes went back to the open page in his Bible. Jessie tried to peer discreetly at her roommate's Bible to see what passage they were studying today. Martha was looking at a map of the countries around the Mediterranean Sea, as they had existed in the first century A.D.

Marvelous! Maps today! Why had Mom and Dad given her and Joshua Revised Standard Version Bibles without maps? Joshua, who was not much like her for all that he was her twin, didn't care what his Bible looked like or what it had in it, as long as it was there when he needed it. But Jessie loved maps. And her Bible just had words in it.

"Jessie," said Uncle Don, and in the single word of her name was all the weight of greeting, scolding, and affection. "I've told the others that if they don't have maps in their Bibles, they are to look up the passages in the Acts of the Apostles, which tell us about Paul's calling, his being cho-

sen by God for specific work, and also the first of his missionary journeys."

Jessie flipped the tender, crackling pages of her Bible
back and forth, listening to everyone else around the table
doing the same thing. Together they made the sound of
leaves moving in a light breeze. Joshua was at the end of
the table opposite Uncle Don. He had found his place, and
now, with both elbows on the table, he was leaning his head
on the heels of his hands while he read. His long fingers lay
against his cheeks, and their tips, every fingernail neatly
pared and very clean, touched his temples. Now and then
his fingers moved in rhythm, as though he were playing the
piano. That was what Joshua did best, and as often as he
could. Although he didn't say so himself, everyone else said
that Joshua would be a concert pianist when he grew up.

Across the table from Jessie, Wheat Janeway was leaning
back in his red metal chair, turning the pages of Acts with
one finger, which he wet before touching the paper. Wheat
was the tallest eighth grader, and the one Jessie and Joshua
had known the longest. Wheat had been born up at Enongal
hospital the month before the twins, and Uncle Don had
been there for that birth, too. Wheat said he wanted to be
a doctor. He sat next to Uncle Don on Sunday mornings—
"so I can get used to the smell of disinfectant," he said.

Next to him, Sam Ware tried leaning back in his chair,
too, but Sam didn't have long legs to keep the chair balanced, and it fell toward the table again with a loud thunk.
Sam blushed. "Foiled again," he muttered, and Jessie

grinned at him. She liked Sam's way of laughing at himself. He probably had already found the passage in Acts he was going to talk about, because he was the fastest reader and the smartest of the eighth graders. He planned to be a banker, he said, or else a circus manager. Maybe both. Jessie had the feeling that Sam could do anything he decided on, and she knew he'd only decide on what he liked.

Jessie didn't feel that brave about herself. She had no idea what she was going to do—when she grew up, or on the Christmas vacation just ahead. She could imagine *being* grown-up, in a new place, but that wasn't enough. When she thought of the others in her class, she felt herself longing for as much certainty as they seemed to have about themselves and the future. She wanted to have her direction settled. She wanted to be grown-up *now*, with the important questions of who she'd be answered; she fiercely wanted to be doing something necessary and important *now*, instead of being in school, forever, it seemed, eternally waiting to be ready for something she didn't know about yet.

On Jessie's right, Martha doodled in the top margin of her notebook page. From the corner of her eye, Jessie tried to figure out what Martha was drawing. For a moment she was puzzled by all the lines and rectangles, and then she recognized the picture of a piano keyboard. Of course.

Martha thought she was in love with Joshua. She was also very good at drawing, whether it was a sketch of things on their dresser table or an old tennis shoe or people's faces. Drawing piano keyboards was as close as she ever came to drawing Joshua's face, thought Jessie, and smiled with affection for this friend of hers. She had been keeping the secret of Martha's crush, going on for six months already. It was a great sorrow in Martha's life that she would not be going to Schutz with the others in the fall. Her parents were due for furlough back in the States, and she would start high school in a small town in western Pennsylvania, instead of in Alexandria. Jessie agreed with Martha and felt sorry for her, having to go back to America.

"Well, are we nearly ready to start?" asked Uncle Don. His voice, deep and gravelly, was a sudden intrusion on Jessie's mental wanderings. Late again, even in my own head! she thought, and hastily read the section headings at the top of the page she'd been staring at all this time.

"The stoning of Stephen." She shivered. That story interested her and repelled her. Stephen had been young and full of life—"Stephen full of grace and power," said the verse. Jessie imagined him to be tall and dark-haired, with a gentle, laughing mouth—like Joshua's—but brave and strong, because he hadn't tried to get away when the angry crowd threw stones at him until he was dead. What a horrible, slow, hurting way to die! Was it worse than having your head cut off, or being stabbed in the heart, or being shot somewhere? Jessie didn't quite know how to imagine what bullets did.

Martha could. Martha's father, Uncle Charles MacLeod, was another missionary doctor, but he was a hunter, too. He hunted elephant, which was difficult and very dangerous.

Up in the dorm room she and Martha shared was a waste-basket that Uncle Charles had given Martha a long time ago, made out of an elephant's foot. Jessie tried not to look at it when she went by their dresser.

The elephant foot had been in their room since the second grade, but about a year ago, Jessie had begun saving her wastepaper and putting it in the ordinary sort of wastebasket the other dorm rooms had: large, square fifty-pound flour tins with the tops cut out and a bit of cement poured in the bottoms for ballast. The printing on the sides of the tins had been obscured by rust spots or worn away with use, but on some of the newer ones Jessie could still read the blue and red lettering proclaiming "Pillsbury's Best Fine White."

Fine white what? Jessie would sometimes ask herself. She knew that Pillsbury, whatever it was, meant flour, but it irked her that the word itself didn't appear on the sign. Fine white sheets? Fine white paper? Fine white people? That last bit of the word game made Jessie laugh, because she could see missionaries shrunk to Lilliputian size and all packed into flour tins, standing up next to each other and loaded into boats, shipped across the Atlantic, stopping at Southampton (where the tins would be brought up on deck and everybody would take some foggy air and exercise), then sent on to Bordeaux (where they'd be given sunny air and some fine red wine—imagine! Missionaries drinking wine!). This made Jessie laugh again. Her parents drank wine sometimes; this was one of the things that made them different from the other missionaries Jessie knew. Finally the tins of Pillsbury's Best Fine White People would be unloaded in Douala, where the forest wall was densely green and thick, and the smothering heat and humidity made the Best Fine White People clump together so they had to be shaken vigorously to get them out and separated and sent off to work in the jungle.

"Jessie, read us the passage you've picked," said Uncle Don in a dry voice.

"Um, uh . . . ," said Jessie, seeing the words she was looking at and knowing right away she was in a jam. She'd have to bluff this one. "This part comes just after Stephen has finished that long speech in his own defense at his trial, about God and the prophets, and he's said that the chief priests are wrong to have rejected Jesus, and that he sees Jesus in heaven at God's right hand. They think he's blaspheming. And then it says, 'But the council cried out with a loud voice and stopped their ears, and rushed together upon Stephen. Then they cast him out of the city and stoned him. And the witnesses laid down their garments at the feet of a young man named Saul. And as they were stoning Stephen, he prayed, "Lord Jesus, receive my spirit." And he knelt down and cried with a loud voice, "Lord, do not hold this sin against them." And with that he died. And Saul consented to his death,' " she read, at the end of the story about Stephen.

Sam laughed derisively. "What's that got to do with Paul's calling?" he said. "You're one chapter too early. The light on the road to Damascus and the great conversion is chapter nine, not seven. His name is still Saul in the part you read. He hasn't changed his name or anything in this part." It was Jessie's turn to blush, and she didn't have a quick answer for herself.

Uncle Don didn't say anything. He looked right at her, as though he were seeing the whole journey she'd made up for missionaries packed into flour tins on their way to Africa. He said slowly, "Can you defend your choice of passage? Can you explain why you started before the actual call is described in the text?"

"Give her a minute to make it up," said Wheat, and the others laughed. Jessie laughed with them, because she was going to make it up, after all.

"I was wondering," she said, "what it would be like, to stand there watching somebody else get killed, and be glad about it."

There was complete silence in the room. Jessie knew, immediately, that she'd got their attention. They were all looking at her question for the first time, even Uncle Don. Something moved deep inside her, a queer, brief flush of joy she didn't recognize easily. Without even trying, she had been able to give the others an idea they thought was interesting. How had she done that?

While she was still amazed, Uncle Don began talking. "I never thought of that before," he said.

Pride and wonder streaked through Jessie, making her chest tight.

"I always thought how wrong Saul was, and how magnificent Stephen was as the first martyr," said Uncle Don. "But you're right. This witness of Saul's must have been important to the way he behaved toward Christians after his conversion, loving the Church as strongly as he did. So, what do you think it would be like, Jessie, to be Saul there at Stephen's stoning?"

"Scary," said Jessie right away, without having to think. "And I think it would be exciting."

"That's terrible!" exclaimed Martha.

"Yeah, well, Jessie's the one who says she'd like to watch a house burning down," said Sam.

"Not if there are people inside," said Jessie quickly.

"Why would it be exciting?" asked Uncle Don.

"The fire or the stoning?" asked Jessie.

"Either. Both," said Uncle Don, and Jessie could feel the thing in her suddenly moving again, reaching up for the conversation, for the idea, wanting to get hold of the words to knead them into understanding.

"It would be exciting because of the danger," said Jessie, the words coming without any difficulty at all. "The danger of being responsible for another person's death. And because of the courage you'd need, I think. The courage to do what was right."

"Do you think courage comes only when danger is dramatic?" asked Uncle Don, leaning forward on the table, his blue eyes looking hard at her. And suddenly everyone in the class was watching and listening to her talk with Uncle

Don; Jessie found that she didn't care what they thought. Uncle Don thought courage was for more than life-and-death sorts of dangers. Like what, for example? Jessie wanted to go on with this conversation, following the thoughts until they came out into the open, where she could know them all at once, have them and decide about them. She opened her mouth to answer the teacher.

And then the dorm's xylophone rang its limited five-note tune, signaling that Sunday school was over. Jessie was beginning to tell Uncle Don that she'd been thinking about danger just that morning, and the sound of the bell was like a hand clapped over her mouth. She looked down at her Bible, feeling cut off and lonely, and even a bit foolish. Why should Uncle Don care what she'd been thinking about, anyway? Besides, she'd have next Sunday, and one after that, too, for more talking with him.

"You've given me a lot to think about, young lady," said Uncle Don. Jessie went all still, listening to him. Was he just saying that, or did he mean that her thinking had really been worth his time? "There's a lot in the idea that sensing danger and being called are connected. You are right. God calls us into the unknown, but we get comfortable and don't want to risk answering Him. I'll have to work hard on next week's lesson," he said, "to keep from disappointing you!"

Jessie stared at him, delighted and astonished by the compliment. She found herself longing for next Sunday. Somewhere in the background she heard a car pull into the roundabout in front of the dorm, and she heard other kids

begin to yell excitedly, calling out the way they did when
term was over and parents started arriving.

Uncle Don turned his head toward the sound of running
feet and shouts of greeting, names obscured in the tangle
of voices. The words sorted themselves out as the voices
got louder. "Jessie! Jessie! Joshua! Your parents are here!
Your parents are here!"

Jessie froze, her gray eyes meeting Joshua's. Something
terrible must have happened. A chilly blankness spread behind her ribs, and she knew that one of the terrible things
was happening right now. She ought to have been perfectly
delighted to see her parents, after four months away from
home. She'd imagined and longed for this sort of surprise
visit and early term's end often enough over the years of
boarding school. Now that she'd got it, it was all wrong.

"Come on," said Joshua grimly. She followed him out
of the study hall, and there they were, true enough, standing
on the front porch. Cassie was already with them, her arms
flung around Mom's waist, jumping up and down in the
first hug. In Mom's face Jessie saw two things: Whatever
was dangerous at home was not just a nighttime thing anymore, and Mom was disappointed that Jessie wasn't running
gladly to meet her.

2

The Mud Sea

It was still Sunday, the first one in Advent, 1958. The whole Howells family was in the Libamba carryall together, bouncing and bumping over the deeply rutted dirt road connecting Elat with Yaoundé. In all her life, Jessie had never known Dad to drive as fast as he was driving now.

Jessie saw the road in her mind's eye, putting it where it would be on a map of Cameroun. She saw the road itself, too, and glared at the red dirt and the ridge of little red stones that crusted its edges. She did not feel safe and content to be with her family. She was very angry indeed.

"Get packed, right now," Mom had said. "Pack everything. Just put it all in the suitcase. We have to be on the road again before lunch."

"Did you guys fly here?" Joshua had asked. It was normally at least a five-hour trip between Libamba and Elat. Mom and Dad had arrived at the dorm a little after ten-thirty in the morning.

"We left as soon as it was light," Mom had said, pushing Cassie up the dorm stairs ahead of her. Cassie kept turning around to hug Mom, and Mom smiled at her and kissed the top of Cassie's head and tapped her gently on the shoulders to keep her moving. Jessie clumped along behind them, her heart as heavy as her feet. Behind her thick, determined anger was a small trembling thing, which Jessie could not ignore. She was afraid. Mom was afraid, too. So they both were angry.

Martha had helped. Martha had helped a lot, piling clothes on Jessie's bed, actually packing the huge green musty suitcase that belonged to Jessie, while Jessie ran herself frantic all over the dorm. She was looking for the things she'd normally have collected in a leisurely way during the coming three weeks before the term's end: overdue library books, her good English fountain pen, barrettes, a sweater, her Bible (she'd left that on the study-hall table this morning), all the graded and returned school papers she'd stuffed into her book box week after week.

Lugging armfuls of junk acquired mysteriously during the nearly fourteen weeks of school, Jessie had run up and down the two flights of stairs at least five times, each trip making her tremble and sweat with fury as much as with the effort it cost her. When she met Mom in the front hall, coming out of Cassie's room, rage at the sight of her pleasant heart-shaped face made Jessie gasp. Then she made a tight, wordless sound in her throat, a sound like a growl. Mom looked as though she'd been hit, and hurt.

Now Jessie had a fierce headache. She closed her eyes, and in her aftersight, the side of the road still whizzed along and the red-dust-coated leaves and grasses of the forest blurred sickeningly. In the front seat, Mom was unwrapping the waxed paper from the peanut butter sandwiches Aunt Pearl had put together for the Howellses. Aunt Pearl was the housemother at the dorm. She and Uncle Walker had been quick to help Mom and Dad get the twins and Cassie ready to leave. Uncle Walker had taken the carryall into the town of Ebolowa to fill the tank at the only gas pump in the area, while Dad helped Joshua pack. Aunt Pearl had made lunch for the road and tried to get enough conversation from Mom to find out what was happening in Bassa territory to make the Howellses take their children home early.

"There's trouble coming," Mom had said, and that's all she would say to Aunt Pearl's repeated questions and concerns. Dad hadn't said much more. In a voice not as taut with anxiety as Mom's, he had explained gravely, "We don't know how long the roads will be open. We want to take the children home while things are still . . ." And Jessie had wondered if he meant to finish there, or if he had been about to say something else: "while things are still calm" or maybe "while things are still safe."

It was more like driving straight into fire, she thought.

What a stupid thing. Why not just leave Libamba for a while until everything got better? But they couldn't do that. Mom and Dad supervised a dormitory at Le Collège Évangélique de Libamba, a school for African students who came from all parts of Cameroun. As long as the students were on campus, Mom and Dad had to be there, too. That was part of their work. And their calling?

The memory of Sunday school—not even three hours ago—made Jessie grit her teeth. Next Sunday's pleasure and excitement was lost to her now. Her glance of resentment was hot and slow. She would like to have burned a hole in the back of Mom's seat. Why not Dad's? Wasn't this his decision, too? Of course it was. Her parents made decisions together. Dad didn't seem to be as angry as Mom was, or as worried, even though he was driving so fast that the car shimmied when the road was smooth. The rattle and bang of all the metal parts in the carryall was constant. It was as if all of them were holding pot lids and kettles and clashing these things together every other minute.

Joshua sat on the other side of the car, behind Dad, looking out the opposite window. Cassie sat between Mom and Dad in the front seat. Nobody said anything. Mom handed the sandwiches around and everybody ate in silence. Jessie took small bites and ground them between her teeth with vengeance in her heart. Grimly she comforted herself with thoughts about passports, airports, and high school in Egypt, once she was six thousand miles beyond her parents' reach, independent and free for nine whole wonderful months.

Then, about two hours on the road, just south of Otélé, everything came to a complete stop. Jessie guessed that, as usual when cars began stringing together with no traffic coming the other way, the road had washed out somewhere ahead of them. They were on a stretch where two-ton cocoa trucks and four-ton logging trucks passed every day on their way to the Otélé train depot. The heavy vehicles often ground the road down to a washout. If only it wasn't a real mud hole, thought Jessie, biting a tiny piece of skin from inside her lip and letting it go as soon as she felt the pinch.

Dad sighed slowly, almost groaning, when he saw the line of trucks and the two autobuses stopped dead in front of them. Jessie could only see the side of his face, but now his mouth had the grim, set look that had been on Mom's all day. He let the motor idle for a minute or two, as though trying to believe the line of vehicles would start to move soon. Then he sighed again, all his breath coming out fast and impatient. He turned the motor off and sat still. His fingers tightened on the steering wheel.

The gesture made Jessie give up her anger. Dad was afraid, too. They were all in trouble. They had to keep moving to get home before dark. It was absolutely imperative that the family not be on the road after nightfall.

This was something Jessie had known for two years. The Maquis made the roads dangerous for any white person, and particularly dangerous for white people in cars. Who could tell who you were in a car at night? Americans and French looked alike, were alike, were good targets for the anger in the people who had waited too long already for white men to acknowledge Camerounians as free and responsible for their own affairs.

In Bassa territory, farther north than Libamba, American Presbyterian missionaries had been caught on the roads in daylight. The Maquis would cut down trees so the trunks fell across the road, and could do it with such precise timing that last March, Uncle John Witmer had been trapped in his car between two great logs falling one hundred feet apart.

Then the Maquis had dragged him out of his car and into the forest. Jessie wasn't quite sure what had happened next. Her ears stopped working, or her attention froze on the picture of the African men wrenching the car door open, branches and leaves of the new-fallen trees still quivering all around them. Uncle John had been at Mission Meeting in August, when all the missionaries gathered for their annual time of work and play together. He'd gone back to America, though, the next month or so.

Uncle John had worked in the hospital on the station where Wheat Janeway's parents lived, and Wheat had told her and Joshua that Uncle John had asked for it. He had gone around saying that the Maquis were nothing but Communist agitators without enough sense to see that the French had the best interests of Cameroun in mind all along.

Mom and Dad agreed with the Maquis. The two of them weren't asking for anything. Well, no. They were asking to get home in time.

"Let's get out," Dad said in a flat, resigned tone.

Once she had climbed stiffly down to the road, Jessie stretched and leaned against the warm, dusty carryall, listening to the usual high, shrill sound of the insects and birds filling the forest. Now, beyond that placid humming, she heard shouts and the thunk and ring of ax heads biting living wood. And beyond that was the unpleasant grinding, throaty whine of an engine trying to haul itself out of a mud hole. There was a stink rising in the air, a rotting smell mixed with some sweet odor going sour.

"Come on, let's look," said Joshua, rounding the back of the carryall. As Jessie followed him, she looked down the road they had just come and saw a glint of sun on the steel grille of a truck. The high canvas tenting on the back of the cocoa truck flapped as the huge machine snorted to a crawl, driving up behind the Howellses' car. It came so close that for a moment Jessie feared it would drive into the carryall and crush the suitcases and trunks, Jessie's papers, Joshua's music books, Cassie's dolls.

The driver shut off the motor and opened the door in one motion, and was out of the cab and running past the twins before they had got beyond the carryall themselves. When they reached the edge of the mud hole, the driver was already down in it, helping the men who crawled and slipped in the morass, laying fresh-cut logs next to each other side by side. They were making a bridge over the ground itself. Only there was no ground; it had all turned liquid.

"Wow," said Joshua. "This mud hole is bigger than most villages we see on the road. I can't believe it!"

Jessie stood next to Joshua in the full noonday sun, squinting at the sight. It seemed to her that the earth had been wounded; she was looking at an immense open, running sore. Now she recognized the stink: fetid oozing mud mixed with fast-decomposing leaves and branches, all heating in the sun. And there was something familiar about this place where they were stopped. Jessie looked around, puzzled, trying to make out what her recognition was telling her, but she'd never seen anything like the ruin in front of her.

On the far side of the huge orange-red mud hole, probably two hundred feet across by now, a cocoa truck was being hauled up the slippery bank by a line of men, at least twenty of them, pulling on great thick ropes fastened to the front and sides of the truck. The men were placing the logs so as to go around the two other trucks hopelessly mired above the axles.

Jessie saw that Dad had gone down in the hole with the other men. He and another driver, an African, were dragging a young tree by the branches. Dad slipped twice while Jessie watched and came up covered brown; mud coated his arms, dripped from his shoulders. As soon as that tree was in place, he and the other man tugged and rolled another sapling over the ground. The mud was so nearly liquid, the ground so soggy with recent rain, that the loose branches and the men's feet sent up soft, thick splashes.

Now Dad staggered up the bank, wiping mud from his arms and wrists with his splayed fingers, shaking mud from his hands. Tear-shaped splashes marked his face, clumped in his hair. "We're going to go around," he said to the twins, breathing hard. "You'll have to walk after the car. If I need you to help push, I'll tell you. Otherwise stay clear. Alida!" he called, and Mom came around from the other side of the truck that was first in line, holding Cassie by the hand. Two French women peered after her.

"We can't wait till they've got this finished," Dad said, waving down at the work and the log path. "It'll have to be put back together after every vehicle goes over, and we'll be here all day. The driver of the truck behind us will help me get the carryall around the edge of the hole. You drive," he said to Mom. "I'll pick the way out and push when we need it."

Without being asked, Jessie reached out to take Cassie's hand. "Wait here until we're across," said Dad, looking from Jessie to Joshua. "Don't come till I wave, and be careful of the falling trees."

Jessie looked up at the sun and then down to her shadow, just beginning to lengthen off to the right. It was about one o'clock in the afternoon. If this had been an ordinary trip, they would have about three hours left after Otélé. The roads always got worse after they turned west, and Dad would be forced to drive more slowly.

Cassie said nothing, but she tugged on Jessie's arm, pulling her sister close to the edge of the washout so they could see Dad making his way along the edge of the hole. Where he walked it was not road at all, but newly cleared jungle, all stubbly with stumps of saplings and brush just sliced off at the tops. Jessie watched village men swinging axes and machetes at thin, silvery tree trunks.

Dad waved toward the carryall. Jessie looked back and saw Mom sitting behind the wheel. The engine turned over, and Mom pulled out of line. Her face was set, her eyes measuring the distance between the edge of the road and the vehicles she had to pass. She drove right by Jessie and Cassie without looking at them.

People who were waiting for the log path to be finished watched Mom's progress, pointing and exclaiming with disbelief. The two French women Jessie had noticed earlier came out for a clear view. Either they didn't think she could understand them or they didn't care. "That woman is crazy," said one. "Americans think they can do as they please," said the other. "We have to wait our turn. They should not be allowed to go by themselves."

Jessie turned her head to give the women a good, long look, so they would know she'd heard them. Both women stared back. The first one went on, quite loudly, as if she were sure Jessie wouldn't understand French. "Look at those children. Look at them standing there alone. The poor things. The big girl doesn't look like the other two at all, does she?" Jessie turned her head back again, quickly. She most certainly did not want this scrutiny to continue. While she stood waiting, though, she looked over at Joshua's profile and then at Cassie's. It was true.

They both had the same heart-shaped faces, the same curving line from cheekbone to jaw that she did not have, and wished for sometimes. And their hair was the same, a straight sandy brown color, unlike her own, a good dark brown, nearly black. People often thought Joshua was her older brother, which was certainly not the case, and they often said, "Twins? Why, the boy and the younger girl are more like twins, aren't they?"

The African truck driver who had helped Dad clambered out of the mud pit to join Dad, already way on the other side. They were ahead of the car, waving their arms, pointing out the places to avoid, as Mom bounced in the seat, steering over uncleared land. And as the car inched along, Mom and Dad seemed to get smaller and smaller. Something, perhaps the combined forces of waiting and hurrying in and around the mud hole, pulled Mom and Dad away from her.

Soon they were so far off that they couldn't have heard her if she'd yelled for help. The carryall stopped for some reason she couldn't make out. Then Dad disappeared behind it, was swallowed by the bush, and after a moment, Jessie couldn't see Mom either, even though the car was still there.

"Where are they?" asked Cassie. "Where's Dad? Where'd he go?"

"I don't know," said Jessie, more to herself than to her sister.

"He's around the front," said Joshua, pointing. "He's tying a rope to the bumper."

"Can we start over to them yet?" asked Cassie, and Jessie shook her head.

"Now can we go?" asked Cassie, moments later, and Jessie answered aloud, with irritation.

Everything went so slowly that Jessie wanted to scream. Her shadow was merging with the shadow under the truck at the front of the line. The sun went down at five o'clock, and darkness would be complete half an hour later. And there they would be, she and Joshua and Cassie, standing alone by a cocoa truck, with Mom and Dad and the carryall beyond sight on the other side of the mud lake.

"He's waving!" yelled Joshua, even though Jessie was right next to him.

"Hurray!" shouted Jessie. She let go of Cassie's hand and looked hard at the tangle of broken, crushed jungle they would have to cross. The carryall wasn't quite around the mud hole, and neither Mom nor Dad could come back to guide them. They would have to find their way by themselves.

Joshua went first, with Cassie in the middle. Jessie could see every misstep Joshua made, and so she got around with less mud on her than he did. Cassie fell most often and got scratched once so badly that her leg was bleeding a little when they got to the other side. Jessie was hot; her feet squelched in her tennis shoes, and muddy water bubbled up through the canvas over her toes. The mud on her legs made her skin itch. Her throat was dry with thirst, but there wasn't any water to drink. When she finally reached the carryall and stopped, all her muscles began to tremble.

Dad was taking Cameroun money out of his wallet, paying all the men who had helped pull and push the carryall around the hole and onto the road. He held his wallet and touched the money with the tips of his fingers; mud was caked and drying in every crease of his skin. He didn't seem as annoyed by it as Jessie was by the small amount on her. He had something else to do, to take up his attention.

Mom had opened the rear doors and was rooting through Joshua's suitcase, looking for something Dad could change into for the rest of the trip. "Here," she said to Jessie, who came back to see what was going on. "Wipe off as much as you can with this." She handed Jessie some of Joshua's socks and underwear. Jessie dabbed at the blood and the mud on Cassie's leg, and Cassie complained because Mom wasn't doing it.

"Shut up," said Jessie, tired and pressing enough to hurt Cassie just a little, on purpose. Cassie screamed. "Don't be such a baby," said Jessie between her teeth. Cassie kicked Jessie in the knee with her good leg. "All right, do it yourself!" said Jessie savagely, throwing the slightly bloody mud-soaked sock at Cassie.

"Girls, that is not a help," called Mom in no-nonsense tones. "And for heaven's sake, Jessie, get the two of you into the car, now. We've got to move." She slammed the back doors to the carryall and glared at Jessie as she came around to open the front. "Get in, Cassie. I'll look at that in a minute."

Why do I have to get the blame for that little runt? thought Jessie. "Why couldn't you have taken care of Cassie?" she said to Joshua, accusing him. Joshua was already in his place in the car, leaning out the window on Dad's side, looking back at the truck first in line, just now driving down into the mud hole on the logs. He didn't answer Jessie. Maybe he hadn't even heard her. He didn't want to hear, thought Jessie, and knew she was right.

At least they were driving again. Catching a glimpse of Mom's watch, Jessie saw that it was two o'clock. They might be close enough to Libamba by dark so that they could get home safely.

What was she thinking about? The closer they got to Libamba, the more dangerous the darkness.

"Do you want to turn off at Metet?" asked Mom. "I'm sure the MacLeods would welcome us for the night. We'd be there by four o'clock."

"I don't think we can stay away even for one night," said Dad. "That was the only possible holdup," he added, meaning the mud hole behind them. "I think we should be at home tonight. You know we can reach Libamba by dark, if not by sundown."

Mom had wanted to get to safety while it was still light. Mom had not wanted Dad to insist on going all the way home this afternoon. Mom thought Dad was wrong. She was angry with him. Jessie got this far before she closed her eyes, shutting out Mom's set jaw and the silence in the front seat. It spread and made the air seem solid and cold, pushing Mom and Dad apart, blocking Jessie from their presence.

"What was it like when you came through this morning?" asked Joshua. He had to lift his voice over a rise in the metallic racket in the car. Jessie was amazed. Not only hadn't he heard her when she'd been angry, but he didn't seem to know that Mom and Dad were angry with each other. It seemed to her that she and Joshua and Cassie were heavy stones in a bag that her parents were carrying between them as they raced over a difficult road. Joshua should have just kept quiet. Instead, he was asking a perfectly reasonable, normal question, just as if this were a normal trip home from school.

Looking around at the stretch of road they were on, Jessie suddenly recognized it by the tiny village they'd just passed, whose distinctive feature was a massive bright red bougainvillea, larger than any of the three houses in the clearing. She'd once seen a girl about her age next to that bush, playing a clapping-and-dance game with a younger girl. Both girls had waved at her.

Before today, that place back there where the mud hole was now had been a little valley stream. The road had gone down a gentle incline, crossed the water on a small wooden bridge, and come lightly up the other side. Everything familiar in that place had been lost when the bridge washed out and trucks and cars went right on crossing anyway, grinding through the fragile, sandy streambed, crushing the plants and the earth that maintained the stream's proper shape. In one morning, the whole road had been changed, even though it still came from and went on to the same places.

"The bridge must have washed out last night," said Dad. "The boards were still there when we came by this morning, and the road wasn't too bad going up the other side. There's a lot of traffic on the road today," he remarked to Mom. Mom turned her head away, looking out her window instead of answering.

Come on, said Jessie silently. Say something. Be friends again. Do what you tell me to do. Don't let the sun go down on your anger.

Mom looked down toward Cassie, snuggling in against her. Cassie reached out toward Dad's wet, mud-stained shoulder and touched him with the tips of her fingers. Dad glanced over at her, smiling, and met Mom's eyes. They looked away from each other. Jessie thought she might not ever get her breath back. Dad looked back at Mom and said, "It'll be all right." And then Jessie saw that Mom was crying. She was biting her lower lip, and her nose was reddening. Dad took his right hand off the steering wheel—his left hand tightening its control—and reached over. He touched Mom's knee, and she put her hand over his.

Jessie felt loved and held close in the same warm act that melted the silence between her parents. She drew two deep breaths and stretched the muscles in her neck and shoulders. Without doubt, they'd get home before dark.

Shadows from the forest crossed the road ahead of the carryall. Dad couldn't keep up the speed he'd made before the mud hole. There were smaller, shallower mud holes to slow down for, although none was as serious as the first one. Jessie found herself leaning forward, as though she could help push them to Libamba and safety with her body. Mom held Cassie with one arm and held on to the car's armrest with her right hand. Joshua sat bolt upright, watching the road ahead of them as though he expected something to happen, something that would stop them from finishing the trip tonight. He tapped the fingers of his right hand against the window frame, thumb to pinkie, as though practicing scales.

In the dusk, Jessie recognized trees by their peculiar shapes: the trunk with a nose on it halfway up to the top, the treetop with two long branches sticking out, looking like a woman running with her arms in the air. By these trees she knew they had about an hour left to go.

They drove that last hour in inky darkness. The carryall's headlights shot two long stretches of yellow into the night, and when the car swung around curves and passed villages, scattered rays of light would catch in the eyes of goats and sheep sitting on the hard-packed bare earth of village commons. Jessie would see eerie ovals gleaming blue and green, staring at the family as the car hurtled past. Using tatters of the bravery she'd felt that morning in front of her mirror at school, so long ago already, she imagined men's eyes watching her family race home, watching them through the long high grasses, looking for them and waiting in the darkness among the trees of the forest on both sides of the road, watching and waiting, their fingers testing the sharp blades they held.

"Let's sing," said Mom's voice in the dark.

After a long moment in which Jessie's mind went blank, hunting for something to sing that would be right, Joshua began an Advent hymn. They all sang with him. Jessie couldn't see anybody clearly, but she felt them through their voices joining in the song. They sang it in unison.

> *"Let all mortal flesh keep silence,*
> *And with fear and trembling stand."*

For Jessie it seemed the perfect choice, in a minor key, with words shaping themselves to the truth of that moment in the car.

> *"Ponder nothing earthly minded,*
> *For, with blessing in his hand,*

Christ our God to earth descendeth,
Our full homage to demand."

She sang, and then held her breath. The words took their own course, and by singing them, she fitted the moment to their meaning. She saw her own made-up fear of goats' eyes and men's eyes in the dark as a foolish thing. There was yet another fear, having nothing to do with how much someone could hurt someone else. It was a right fear, a clean, fiery thing, a knowing of the truth that was like knowing lightning.

They sang all the rest of the way home. They sang one Christmas hymn after another. After a bit Cassie's voice dropped out, and Jessie guessed she had fallen asleep. By the time the carryall crossed the last bridge, over the Liege River, Jessie herself had begun drifting off. They had just finished "It Came Upon a Midnight Clear." She jerked awake, hearing Mom say with curious intensity, "There's no soldier there tonight." Jessie looked wildly through the window into the darkness, as though she'd just seen a fierce face staring in at her.

Then Dad slowed the car, turned left, and Jessie saw the looming narrow bulk of the college dispensary building off to one side; a lamp was lit in the room where the nurse slept. Home! home! home! everything seemed to call, as the carryall purred its way along the narrow campus road, passing one familiar building after the next. Home again, and at last.

Getting out of the car and into the house looked like it would take forever. She was stiff. Everyone was stiff. Cassie barely woke up enough to be taken to the bathroom before being bundled into bed. Jessie found she was ravenous and ate four slices of bread without stopping. She had thought she could stay up for a while—it was only seven o'clock—but as soon as her stomach was satisfied, an irresistible fog seemed to close over her brain.

She stretched in bed, waking up slightly to the delicious feeling of lying down. She stared into the darkness of the room, because with her eyes closed she still felt the shake and rush of the car, as though she and the bed were in the carryall, as though nothing had stopped since the great moment this morning—could it have been this morning?—when she'd had that conversation with Uncle Don. For a moment Jessie tried to bring the Sunday school lesson into sharper focus, but her mind refused, and everything blurred gently. She told herself to listen for owl calls, but then she thought, Never mind that. We're home, and nothing else matters tonight.

3

Courage

Being home before the term was over at Hope School meant being home before the term's end at Libamba, too. So in the morning, Mom and Dad had class to teach, and they left the house by seven-thirty. In the evening, they had papers to correct and lessons to prepare. Jessie couldn't remember a vacation when her parents hadn't been free to spend time with her and Joshua and Cassie. Usually the three of them came home on vacation after Libamba's classes were over. Of course, in the days when she and Joshua had been too young to leave home for Hope School, when they were younger than Cassie was now, Mom had hired an African woman to take care of the twins while she was in class.

Jessie could remember her. Nléla had been young and pretty and she'd laughed a lot, and easily. Every morning she had walked to their house from her village, and she often brought them food she'd made that would be interesting to eat as a morning snack; sometimes it was peppery bobola, the fermented cassava stick that the Bassa and the Bulu tribes used as a staple, like bread or potatoes. Sometimes Nléla brought a mango or a few perfect ripe guavas, pale yellow on the outside and a deep rose color on the inside, sweet and fragrant.

Nléla would take the twins on long walks around campus while Mom and Dad were teaching. In her mind's eye, Jessie saw Joshua running ahead of her and falling, and Nléla running past her to pick him up. Joshua was wearing a pair of green coveralls; it had been a pair that Jessie thought belonged to her. Joshua's pair had been red. In the corner of the same memory, Jessie saw a snake, hanging from a tree branch.

She blinked. The twins were sitting in the living room; Joshua was flipping through the pages of a four-month-old *National Geographic*. Jessie had already looked at it; she'd already looked through the whole pile of magazines that had arrived while she'd been away at Hope School.

The breakfast table wasn't cleared yet, because Cassie was still asleep. Although this bit of housekeeping was the twins' chore, by mutual agreement they had begun the morning in procrastination. "Hey," Jessie said.

Joshua looked over at her briefly before picking up the next magazine on the pile.

"Remember Nléla?"

"Of course," said Joshua. "What about her?" He sounded bored, and he probably was, just as Jessie herself was, three days into this enforced vacation.

"I was thinking about her," said Jessie slowly, "and I remembered a snake in a tree. Do you remember that?"

"Yeah. It was down by the Liege." He looked up at Jessie, then out the window, concentrating.

Pressing her memory, Jessie tried to see more of the place where the tree was standing. Instead, and against her will, she saw blood on the snake, and then she remembered the snake's head, cut off, on the boards of the bridge over the Liege. When she saw the snake's head, she saw her feet in sandals. In the back of her throat she made an involuntary sound of revulsion and felt a crawling between her shoulder blades.

Joshua looked over at her and gave a laughing grunt. "Remember the head?" he asked, his eyes challenging her.

"Yeah," she said shortly. "But there's something else I can't see that bothers me."

"It was the man," said Joshua immediately, and at that moment Jessie's heart began to thud in alarm. She remembered the man, too. He had frightened Nléla. Joshua had been running away from the bridge and the snake and the man with a machete.

"We went to look over the railing," said Joshua thoughtfully. "That's what I remember. We stood there watching
the water," he added, and stopped, narrowing his eyes to
get the memory to clear.

"Looking for crocodiles," said Jessie.

Joshua nodded. "Where was the man before that?" he
asked. "I only remember him behind me."

"He was standing there at the end of the bridge, holding
the snake," said Jessie rapidly, remembering everything in
a rush. "It was still alive. It was a big one, a python, and
Nléla started shouting at him. Remember that part?"

"Oh, yeah," said Joshua, leaning forward. Jessie leaned
forward, too, looking at him, looking through him, rubbing
the tips of her fingers lightly over her thumbs, as if running
the memory through her hands. Then she held one hand
still, fingers closed, having caught the thing she needed.

"She shouted at him, 'Go home to your mother.' Remember that? I thought she was shouting at us, because
she was behind us. And then—and then—"

"He came up to us on the bridge, dragging the snake . . ."
And Joshua stopped.

He must have been seeing the five-foot snake, whipping
and writhing in the man's impossible one-handed grip, just
as she was. Fighting a sensation of nausea, Jessie remembered holding on to the rough board railing of the bridge so
tightly that she felt the splinters going into her fingers.

"I must have been closer than you," said Joshua. "I think
its tail touched me."

"And then he cut off its head," said Jessie, forcing the memory into words. With a swiftness that was all part of the snake's desperation to get free, the man had put its head against the top railing of the bridge and with his other hand brought the machete up into the air—Jessie remembered the blade flashing—and then it thunked against the wood, and the snake's severed head had leaped backward onto the bridge and fallen, mouth open, at Jessie's feet. And blood had pumped out of the snake's body, pouring over the man's arm.

Joshua ran; Nléla ran after him. Jessie watched her brother running, watched Nléla run past the man and the snake, and knew she was alone. She hadn't been able to move, though a part of her imagined she was running with Joshua. The other part kept very still, watching the man, who was now watching her. She hadn't let go of the wood railing; as she met the man's eyes, she pressed her shoulders into the boards and wondered if the railing would give way; she would fall backward into the river, where a crocodile would be.

In front of her the man gestured with the hand that still held the snake's body; its blood dripped from his wrist. A drop of the blood fell on her arm. She had only known this because she felt its warmth on her skin and had looked down to see the dark round splash. "You," the man had said, his eyes strangely gentle, "you, little sister, you have courage. You hear its voice."

Then he'd gone off the bridge, trailing the limp, dusty

body of the snake, its blood splotching the boards she had to cross to reach the place in the road where Nléla now crouched over Joshua, sheltering and comforting him. Trembling, Jessie had watched the man and determined not to move until he was away beyond reach of her.

He had walked along the road between herself and Nléla, toward a tree the twins called the Singer because of a crooked branch that gave the treetop the look of an open mouth. He'd hung the snake in the crotch of a low branch, putting the severed end carefully on the other side of the tree, almost out of sight. The snake's black body stretched down full length against the gray tree bark, shining where the little stream of its blood coursed. Then he'd wiped his machete on the grass at his feet and gone off the road into the forest. Jessie knew there wasn't even a path at that spot. It was a crazy thing to do. It meant he was going nowhere.

"He wasn't right in the head, was he?" said Joshua. "That's what Nléla said."

Jessie remembered that, but what the man had said to her was more important than what Nléla had said about him. Even today, when she was old enough to recognize that the man had obviously been deranged, she couldn't undo her terror and her fascination with the clear, quiet way he'd looked at her while he told her that mysterious thing about herself. She hadn't wiped off the snake's blood but hadn't liked it on her either. It had cooled against her skin.

"I can't remember getting off the bridge," said Jessie,

lacing her fingers together and kneading them restlessly. "All I can see is the snake's head down by my feet and the rest of it in the tree."

"We came back, don't you remember?" said Joshua, breathing deeply. "I didn't want to go, and I didn't want to stay by myself on the road either. Nléla kept calling you and calling you, and you wouldn't move. Finally she took me—probably dragging me—and we came back for you. I had to go by that thing in the tree twice." He swallowed hard, all the skin over his lower jaw and neck moving backward.

"She picked up the head, remember that?" Jessie's voice was soft with wonder; the memory amazed her. "She just bent down and picked it up and threw it over the railing. I was thinking that I had to walk over it, but she got rid of it first."

"She hated snakes," said Joshua. "Remember her telling us that was the only thing she was afraid of?"

"She made me wash my arm," said Jessie, almost to herself. "We stopped at the first mud puddle, and I washed it off there."

"Washed what?"

Jessie hesitated before answering. She'd never told anyone what the man had said to her. Only Nléla knew the blood had fallen on her. The man's words probably had meant nothing, but she'd wondered about them occasionally in the years since, when she was able to think of their meaning while holding the whole memory at bay. She'd always been reluctant to really open the secret; this was true even now with Joshua, who had more reason than anyone to believe her. The whole thing would sound ridiculous, and then she would never understand it.

The snake's blood was like a mark that sealed the man's words. Nléla hadn't touched it, although she'd poured the yellowish muddy water from the puddle through her own cupped hands held over Jessie's arm, while Jessie rubbed the drying stain away. Later, when Jessie had dared to look down, in place of the little reddish splash there had been the larger, faintly brown mark of dried dirt. The sun had sparkled on the fine layer of mica rubbed into her skin.

"I had a splash of the blood on me," said Jessie finally, with some effort. Joshua grimaced in disgust and, to her relief, left the matter at that.

"We never told anybody, did we? I don't think Nléla told Mom and Dad. Even though it used to give me nightmares, I never did either," said Joshua. He stretched his arms above his head and yawned without covering his mouth. "I wonder why."

"I bet we knew they wouldn't have let her take us all over the place, down to the river and along the railroad tracks and to her village and all."

"Do you really think so? I think Mom and Dad are pretty calm about things like that. You know: Here's where we live, and that's what can happen. If they're going to get their own work done, they can't be worrying about us every minute."

"We don't worry about them," said Jessie. "Even-Stephen." She sat up tall and stretched her ribs, lifting her arms out side to side. "So what are we going to do today?" she asked. She took a deep breath, as if just waking up from a bad dream.

"Holy cow! Here comes Mom!" Joshua exclaimed, slapping his magazine onto the pile on the coffee table and leaping up from his chair. "We haven't even begun heating the dishwater!"

"I guess we'll do chores," said Jessie, already busy at the dining table, grabbing the dirty cereal bowls.

"We'll be lucky if she doesn't make us wash the kitchen floor and sweep every room," he called from the kitchen.

Mom came into the living room at a slight trot. "I'm between classes," she began breathlessly, and saw Jessie belatedly stacking dishes. "Oh, for heaven's sake!" she said, disgusted. "I might have known. Get that done now. I need you to make dessert for this evening."

"Why?" called Jessie on her way to the kitchen. Mom had gone into the office, and Jessie couldn't hear her answer. She rushed things from the table to the kitchen counter, in her hurry clearing away Cassie's unused place setting, too. Joshua rolled his eyes at her and took the clean bowl and spoon back out to the table.

"Jessie!" called Mom, and Jessie ran out of the kitchen, bumped Joshua into the table corner, ignored his loud complaint, and came to a stop, panting, in the office doorway.

"Yes, Mom," she said, with a long sigh of impatience. "What?"

"Don't talk to me in that voice," said Mom severely.

"Sorry, Mom," said Jessie, forcing the apology. She knew quite well that her own anger was rising because she had been caught goofing off. It took a real effort of will to hold her temper in check and admit at the same time that Mom was right to be irritated with her. At the dorm, she would have let go with her anger and felt somehow that Aunt Pearl deserved it, just because Aunt Pearl wasn't Mom. Lots of kids got mad and yelled and acted up because Aunt Pearl wasn't mom. But once back at home, it was easy to see that Mom's irritation (and Aunt Pearl's, too) was justified. Jessie sighed again through her teeth, grimly holding on to this understanding. Without it, she would fight Mom the whole vacation long.

Mom looked up from her desk, unexpectedly smiling with excitement as though she were about to give Jessie a wonderful present. "Today," she said, "a new family is coming to Libamba. We're getting our new mathematics professor."

"That's . . . good," said Jessie carefully, not sure why Mom thought this was important for her.

"Yes, it is," said Mom firmly. "Monsieur Essam will be our second Cameroun faculty member. We've been waiting for him to finish his advanced degree at the University of Strasbourg. He's bringing his whole family today on the eleven-thirty train, and everybody on the station will go to

Aunt Polly and Uncle George's for dessert tonight, to welcome them."

"Including us," said Jessie. This was going to be about
cooking. Dessert was a pleasure to make. "Okay. What do
you want us to make?"

"I think we've got a coconut in the food cupboard," said
Mom, stacking notebooks on the desk. "Make some coconut cookies."

"Nothing chocolate?" asked Jessie, wheedling.

"There's no more cocoa," said Mom, gathering the notebooks and coming to the doorway where Jessie stood, flapping a dish towel against the wall. "Don't do that," she said
automatically. "It marks the paint. I don't think we can get
cocoa again till the next time someone goes up to Yaoundé,
and no one knows when that will be a safe trip. We certainly
can't go on a whim just for luxury food items."

Jessie backed away from the door as Mom came toward
her. "Okay," she said. "Coconut cookies, then."

"Don't waste eggs," called Mom, crossing the living
room. "Their price these days works out to twenty-five
cents apiece. Incredible! And Jess," she said, stopping at the
living-room door. Jessie had begun flapping the dish towel
against the nearest dining chair and stopped that quickly.
"The Essams have a daughter just your age."

Jessie watched the double screen doors in the living
room swing back and forth and settle against each other. A
little hardness formed itself in her, pushing against the thing
Mom had just said. The idea of getting to know someone

new her own age, so late, said Jessie to herself, so close to the end of being here, wasn't fair. It wasn't nice. It was too much work.

"Come dry!" called Joshua from the kitchen.

Jessie took the dish towel in, snapping it against walls, the door, and Joshua's shoulders as she went by him.

"Cut that out," he warned. "What did Mom want?"

"We have to make dessert," said Jessie glumly. "There's a thing happening at Aunt Polly and Uncle George's tonight, to welcome a new teacher."

"Really?" Joshua was interested and looked sideways at her. "Is this the African guy Dad was talking about? He was in Germany getting an advanced degree. Dad says he's a genius."

"I guess so," said Jessie. This information made her curious, but she didn't want to know much more. The less she knew, the farther away she could keep herself from the new girl. Why did she insist on that when she had nothing else to do in the barren weeks of vacation ahead? The reason hid from her but pressed her resistance, too. Jessie tried standing up straight to get rid of the discomfort. "I'm supposed to get all friendly with the daughter, who's our age," she said.

"I wonder if she was in Germany, too," said Joshua.

Jessie couldn't keep from thinking about the new girl as she did her share of the cooking and Cassie care. She smashed the coconut open on the back porch with a hammer and grated the wet, white coconut meat, scraping every one of her knuckles raw as she worked. With every cut, her resentment of Mom's unspoken assumption bit deeper. How could she think that friendship was easy to accomplish? Just a thing of how d'ye do and now-we'll-like-each-other-won't-we! This girl and she would have nothing in common, except the obvious: Their parents worked at Libamba, for the Church. And even that fact wouldn't make ground between them, the way it had for Jessie and Martha, say.

Jessie had always seen African kids around and knew some by name when she went to church at home, but she didn't have any as friends. She had no idea how to talk to one, even though she had spoken Bassa like a Bassa child since she was two. It wasn't language that made the connection, but what you could share with the other person. And aside from the ground they all walked on together, and the trees they looked at, and the air they breathed, Jessie couldn't imagine anything to overcome the fact that she was American and would always be, and this other girl was Camerounian. That fact between them was as plain and immense as the Atlantic separating the shores of their continents.

So the work, really, was in getting to know an African girl. And that was the hidden reason against doing the work—and a pitiful one, too, admitted Jessie with fine scorn for herself. If it had been an American family, or even a French one, she could see spending the effort. It would be practice for the rest of her life: at school in Egypt and wherever she went to college, and later on, living in America or, if she was lucky, in Europe somewhere. But Mom was obviously expecting her to open up to this new girl, and Jessie had no intention of doing that. She would be polite, of course, but that was all.

Occupying Cassie was her job for the day, and Joshua's tomorrow. Jessie let Cassie stir the cookie dough after the addition of each ingredient. While she dumped more wood into the firebox to heat the oven, she scraped the knuckles of her right hand against the cut edge of a log and stared at the blood welling up from the skin already opened on the grater. What had the snake man meant? What did the voice of courage sound like? Like trumpets? Like drums? She didn't hear anything but her fear of changing and being different. And when did you need courage? Only when your life was in danger? What had Uncle Don meant when he asked her if there were other kinds of danger than losing life at the last minute? Oh, she wished she could talk with him right now! The blood glistened and grew rounder on her skin, and then broke the surface tension and ran down between her fingers.

"Jessie, what am I going to do?" wailed Cassie. "I dropped an egg!"

"I didn't say you could put them in," yelled Jessie. "Now Mom's going to be furious with me!"

Cassie cried and Jessie stormed at her, wiping the shattered egg from the red tiles of the kitchen floor and rinsing away the little rivulet of blood from her fingers as she washed off the thick yellow yolk, too. Behind them, on the piano in the living room, Joshua changed from the monotony of scales practice to the mad galloping music of Grieg's "In the Hall of the Mountain King." The louder and faster Jessie and Cassie screamed at each other, the noisier Joshua was on the piano. Suddenly Jessie gave it up in a short, fierce sigh.

Joshua brought down lightning and thunder on the Mountain King's dwarfs. Cassie laughed nervously and jerked her head to the left and the right, flicking her long brown braids behind her shoulders. Looking at her sister's round clear eyes and anxious smile, Jessie was sorry she'd visited her own frustration on Cassie.

"It's all right, Cass," she said, pushing herself with difficulty over the hump of worry about Mom's irritation. "We've got three more eggs and we only need one. Here's how you crack it."

She gave Cassie a fresh egg. Between them they only burned eleven cookies, and Joshua moved on to statelier music, by Brahms.

When the family set out after supper, walking in the dusk toward Aunt Polly and Uncle George's across campus, Cassie carried the basket with the plate of three dozen fragrant cookies wrapped in a clean white napkin. She reached out for Jessie's hand, and Jessie was surprised to be warmed and comforted by this. She'd gotten used to the numbing sense of dread that had grown in her all afternoon.

Then what was this tight feeling that seemed to take up

more and more room in her chest? What was this sense she had of knowing more than she understood, and this slippery anxiety that ran along with her, like a shadow at her side?

"Dad," she asked, her voice sudden and loud in the peaceful bluish green light of dusk.

"Mmm?" He turned his head back over his shoulder to hear her.

"How come we're safe walking across campus at night like this?"

Dad drew breath; Jessie could hear it filling his nostrils and his chest. "Well," he said, letting the air out with the word, as if letting his concern escape lightly. "We don't know that we are, but we aren't likely targets for the Maquis." His voice was soft and dropped down on the name. "We have our work to do, our lives to live, and we do that in trust. To live otherwise is to make ourselves prisoners of fear."

And the truth shall make you free, thought Jessie. What was the truth here? "Dad," she said, and he turned his head again, but it was harder to see, because the light had already faded from blue to deep purple. "You mean there's nothing to be afraid of?"

"No, I didn't say that." He slowed his pace to walk beside her. "We live by what we can do, by choosing to risk. We aren't very much alive when we keep ourselves safe at all costs."

"So we're like Stephen," said Jessie impulsively.

"I beg pardon?"

"You know, 'Stephen full of grace and power,' " Jessie explained.

"Ah, yes," said Dad. "Yes. Stephen who gave life for witness."

Jessie heard voices. Ahead of her family, laughter floated across the darkness, sounding louder than it would have by day, she thought. They were meeting the other faculty families walking to the party at the Goods'. Although Dad and Joshua carried flashlights, her family walked the road without turning them on. There was a confidence in that that Jessie liked.

Ahead, from the right and the left, where there was a campus crossroads, the other families converged on the Goods' house. Beams from their flashlights skittered over the road and slipped up toward the sky. Splinters and flashes of yellow light from the windows of the house showed through the openings of the hedges and palm branches growing at the corner where the road turned right. In moments there would be many people with them on the road, and Dad would stop talking to her.

"What's witness? What's a calling?" she asked, trying to hurry him, hoping he would go on talking until they were in the Goods' house and she could lose herself in greeting the missionaries whom she hadn't seen since starting school last term.

"Witness is showing what you believe. Calling is hearing your gift," said Dad simply.

"Everyone has a gift," said Mom. This was one of Mom's

favorite sayings. Imagining Joshua was doing the same thing, Jessie rolled her eyes impatiently up at the night sky and saw the Milky Way poured out overhead, thick and wide and white. Mom went on talking. Jessie knew she was being addressed, but she deliberately concentrated on the great span of stars, whose beauty lifted her heart in spite of her preoccupations. "You know that, don't you?" finished Mom.

"Um, yeah, yeah," said Jessie obediently, certain that Mom wouldn't press her for a more specific response.

"*Bon soir, famille Howells!*" called Oncle Pierre Carras. His voice was reedy and high, but his words were warm. Jessie called her answer to the greeting with the rest of her family. Within moments other missionary voices were raised in greeting, and the sound of footsteps crunching gravel mixed with laughter and light conversation. Jessie walked silently on the side of the road, listening to them and glad of their familiar company but not able to let go and be among them, as she might have if this had been an ordinary evening gathering.

If she held back, stayed on the front porch, perhaps she would stop feeling so peculiar and edgy. But if she held back, someone would notice she was missing and come out to find her. Then Mom would be angry and disappointed with her. Jessie wanted to shout at Mom. Why had she talked about this girl? Why hadn't she left it all alone so Jessie could meet her without any expectations or dread beforehand? That would have been so much easier.

Short of breath because her thoughts were running so fast, knowing all this worry was stupid anyhow, and with the sense of her stomach falling away from her, Jessie entered the cheerful, laughing mix of forty voices conversing in three different languages.

Over there, Aunt Lou and Aunt Norma were speaking French in broad Philadelphia accents with Tante Berthe, whose accent was fast, sharp Parisian. Immediately to Jessie's left, Aunt Caroline and Uncle Max were talking in English about ordering parts for the repair of some office machinery. And to her right, Jessie heard Bassa, without foreign accent, spoken soft, like the high and low tones of water running over stones. "Sometimes you must be the guest," said the voice, and Jessie turned her head to see the speaker.

A tall darkly brown woman about Mom's age was standing in the corner, talking to a girl—it must be *the* girl, thought Jessie—whose back was to the door. But Jessie knew by the set of the shoulders and the upward tilt of her closely scarved head on her long neck that the girl didn't want to be here any more than she herself did. The hardness that had settled in this morning now flopped queerly in Jessie's chest.

Following Joshua to the refreshments table, she was greeted by the faculty members, who, according to the custom among Presbyterian missionaries in Cameroun, had been aunts and uncles to her since she was a baby. She smiled and said hi to Aunt Polly, standing behind the table.

Jessie took four of Aunt Polly's excellent crumbly peanut butter cookies in her left hand and chose a tall dark green metal tumbler full of lemonade with her right. Joshua said, "Pig!" to her under his breath, and she gave him a withering glance, hardly thinking about what she was doing. If she gave it thought, she'd put the cookies back.

Holding everything carefully, Jessie made herself straight and thin and slipped between people until she came back to the corner by the door. Aunt Peg and Tante Berthe and Mom were all talking there now, holding the Bassa woman in conversation, exclaiming over the cute little girl and boy who hung on her arms, right and left. Jessie looked beyond the woman's shoulders and met the sullen gaze of a girl—the girl—who was standing with her eyes set straight ahead of her, as though saying, You can't make me.

Jessie grinned at the girl. They can't make me either, she thought. She held out the stack of cookies and the tumbler of lemonade in a gesture so vague it might not have seemed like an invitation. The girl looked at her warily. Jessie inclined her head slightly, gesturing with her chin toward the door to the front porch, and avoiding Mom's stern eye, she edged in that direction. Let Mom think she was skipping out.

On the porch, she sat on the broad cement ledge topping the brick railing. She set the cookies and the tumbler carefully beside her and leaned against a pillar. The night was beautiful, clear, warm. Someone had cut the Goods' grass that afternoon, and its sweet, spicy smell rose up to mix with the dry tang of dust from the road. A light wind wove into the evening the fragrance from Aunt Polly's frangipani tree. The stars in the Milky Way seemed to sing.

There came the sound of a light scraping step behind her. Jessie turned a little, not too much, and said, *"Meyega a."*

"Me nyoñ," said the girl, polite and quiet, waiting.

"Me nlona bini inyu yés," said Jessie. I brought these for us. She waved at the cookies, visible to both in the light from the large square living-room windows. The girl came toward her and moved so she stood in shadow. She had a sweet, light, lemony scent. Perfume, and a nice one. Mom didn't wear perfume very often, and Jessie had never had any. She said, *"Parfum yoñ i numb loñge,"* beginning the sentence in French because she didn't know a Bassa word for perfume. You have a good perfume, she'd said.

The girl came to the railing. *"Tata a bi lona yo ngéda a bé i Jaman,"* she said. My father brought it from Germany.

"You didn't go with him, then?" asked Jessie, still speaking in Bassa.

"While he was gone we lived in my mother's town," said the girl.

"Is it far?" asked Jessie.

"Five days' walk," said the girl. "We came by train. The village is closer to Edéa." She sat on the railing across from Jessie.

They ate cookies and looked into the darkness. Jessie listened to her own chewing and then listened to the girl's chewing, too. She swallowed and asked, *"U nyo?"* Did you have a drink?

"To," said the girl quietly. No.

Jessie suddenly imagined all the people between the corner of the living room and the refreshments table as strangers, not as the family she knew them to be. Their number would have flattened her against the wall, too.

"I'll go and get one more. This one is for you," she said.

She was in the room and out again before anyone stopped her, bringing four more cookies and a yellow metal tumbler with her. The two girls sat on the warm cement railing in companionable silence. When the cookies were finished and Jessie had drunk the last of her lemonade, she said carefully, *"Jôl jem le Jessie."* My name is Jessie.

The girl laughed, making a light, rich sound. *"Me nyi. Ba nkal me le wa loo. Jôl jem le Mendômô."* I know. They told me you would come. My name is Mendômô.

Each one leaned against a pillar, facing the other. Mendômô's expression was obscured in the dim light. After a while, Jessie mentioned that she went to school in Elat. Mendômô laughed, an unexpectedly warm sound that delighted Jessie, and said her father's village was close by there, up near Enongal. Now Jessie laughed and said that she and her twin had been born at Enongal. Mendômô said, *"Kii me."* And so was I.

At this, Jessie and Mendômô began to laugh as though they had heard the greatest joke of their lives. And after that, everything they said made them laugh. They only stopped when, suddenly, they became aware of their mothers standing in the doorway, listening. It seemed to Jessie as though a gust of wind had nearly blown out a candle. In Bassa, Mom said gently, "It's time to go home," and Madame Essam said the same thing. "Yes, it's time to go."

Jessie felt cramped. Mendômô waited until the women had turned back into the living room to collect the families, and then she said, "Where is your house?"

Jessie made a map in her mind's eye, thinking of the directions she would give Mendômô, the trees and stumps and buildings to describe as landmarks. "No, it will be easier at first if I come to you," she said.

"Come in the afternoon, then," said Mendômô. "I am finishing the classes of the term here."

"I will come in the afternoon," Jessie responded, and she laughed with relief. The evening had turned out unbelievably right. She heard the same sound in Mendômô's laugh. On the way home, she felt almost sick with the strange, excited anticipation of beginning something new, beyond anything she'd known before.

She heard a night bird call and knew it was not an owl.

4

Mendômô

At the table during lunch the next day, Jessie asked, "Dad, where are the Essams living?"

"Right now, in the second to last metal house," said Dad, sawing at the tough cut of beef. "Uncle George is nearly done with the new house they'll have before next term, down the road from the Goods'."

"Why?" asked Mom, looking at Jessie.

Jessie remembered the slight breeze from last night on the candle flame. She filled her mouth with pôga so she wouldn't be able to answer right away.

"I want to play school after lunch," Cassie announced.

Joshua groaned. It was his turn for Cassie care. "We did that day before yesterday," he said. "Why can't we play something else?"

"Like what?" Cassie said, challenging him. Joshua had no answer.

"Are you going to visit the Essams?" asked Mom, passing the squash to Joshua, who made a face but helped himself.

"She invited me," said Jessie briefly, helping herself to the squash also.

"How nice," said Mom. Jessie merely nodded. Mom having been right about Mendômô made Jessie resent her approval. She was unprepared for the next remark. "I need you to change the sheets in the guest room before you go," said Mom casually, and turned immediately to some academic topic with Dad.

Change the sheets on the guest room bed? Had somebody been here before they came back from school, and Mom waited all this time to change the sheets? Was somebody coming to visit? "Why?" Jessie asked, bluntly curious.

"Because I say to. And that's all you need to know."

After lunch, while Jessie was washing up, Mom came into the kitchen and said quietly, "The clean sheets are on the end of the bed. Don't worry about it, Jessie. Just change them for me, will you? I would do it myself if I didn't have two meetings following my afternoon classes. And be home by dark, all right?"

"I will." Her lack of resentment surprised her. There was clearly something Mom couldn't tell her, something happening in the guest room she wanted Jessie not to ask about. So when Jessie first went in, she looked around the clean, quiet place for clues. The red waxed floor was striped in yellow bars of sun slanting through the closed shutters. A new curtain had been tacked over the screen against the louvers in the outside door. When Jessie and Joshua were about ten, because of that outside door they used the guest room for games of make-believe involving airports, offices, and hotels. Maybe Joshua would remember that and play the same thing with Cassie.

Not only did the outside door have a curtain—there hadn't been one on it before, had there?—but it had a new lock above the handle. Jessie went over and turned the long-barreled key in the hole. It clicked softly and moved; Jessie pushed the handle down several times, but the door stayed shut fast. The handle moved noiselessly. She remembered it having the sound of a double click-and-tumble. She turned the long key back again. Nothing else in the room showed a difference, but the sheets had been slept in. With the idea that she already knew more than she wanted to, Jessie quickly made up the bed in clean linen. She went out and closed the door without changing anything else.

Ten minutes later she climbed the wooden stairs leading to the green metal front door of the green metal house the Essams lived in now. She knocked, knowing the sound would be a hollow thunk and that her knuckles, still sore from grating the coconut yesterday, would feel the door's warmth. She heard every footfall of the person coming to open the door. Mendômô looked out and blinked in the bright sunlight. Jessie smiled at her.

"Meyega a," she began, and Mendômô answered, *"Me nyoñ."*

"I've come," Jessie went on, shot through and trembling with that strange excitement she'd known last night; she hoped Mendômô hadn't forgotten.

"Jôp," Mendômô said softly, inviting Jessie in with a sweep of her right hand. The house smelled hot, like an iron heating up. In the air was also the rich, heavy smell of ngont, one of Jessie's favorite foods, and the strong, high tang of bobola made with palm oil.

Madame Essam came out of the back part of the house. Jessie knew the two rooms she'd come from were like the living room, with the windows long and narrow and set high in the walls, almost at ceiling height. The door Madame Essam opened had no handle but only a keyhole, high up near the top. Out of old habit, Jessie almost leaped to keep the door open behind Madame Essam. Then she saw Madame Essam slide a stone into place, to hold the door ajar.

The whole conversation was in Bassa. Madame Essam needed to have a set of cooking pots returned to a woman in the village across the Liege bridge; the woman had loaned them to her until her own kitchen things arrived on the train today. She wanted Mendômô to take them back, but Mendômô didn't know the way. Did Jessie?

Jessie asked if this was the first village after the bridge —the one called Njok Bôô, the Village of Nine Elephants. Madame Essam nodded. *"Bi nke ndap Ngo Masé,"* she said. The pots go to the house of Ngo Masé.

Jessie bit her lip and had to take a deep breath before she said she knew the way. Madame Essam gave Mendômô the package of bowls wrapped up in an old piece of cloth. When the girls went out of the house, Mendômô closed the door and shook the fingers of the hand she'd used. "Why is this house of your people so hot?" she asked, settling the package on her head and starting down the stairs.

"It was made by the American army for its soldiers who went sick in their heads while they fought in the desert in Egypt and Libya," Jessie answered, "in the Second World War." Jessie named the war in French because she knew no Bassa term for it. "Uncle Ted Cozzens, who built Libamba station for the school, needed housing for the faculty, and the American army gave the houses away, for the price of bringing them from the desert to the jungle."

"Soldiers," said Mendômô, and spat, neatly, on the side of the road. The package she carried on her head was not dislodged with the motion she made.

Jessie didn't have an answer for this. There was a sound in Mendômô's voice of rage and sorrow combined.

"We lived in one of the metal houses," Jessie said, to keep the conversation alive, "until my little sister, Cassie, was born and the first men's dormitory was finished."

"They are not good houses for the forest," said Mendômô with some scorn. Once again Jessie had no reply. She agreed with Mendômô. Mom had often said the same thing. When they came to the fork in the road, Jessie kept to the right, wondering what to say next. The girls passed a single mud-

and-wattle house with old rain-rotted thatching collapsed and sagging in from the roof beam. They looked at the house and then at each other and laughed.

"You speak good Bassa," said Mendômô.

"I've lived here since I was born," said Jessie. "The house we are going to was the house of a woman who took care of my brother and me when we were small."

"Ngo Masé?" asked Mendômô.

"Her daughter, Nléla," said Jessie. They had come down the sandy track to the main road between Yaoundé and Douala, and in a moment after turning off the Libamba property, they would see the Liege bridge. Jessie fought with a rippling dread of walking across and squelched it. "Nléla was married three years ago and moved to a village about half a day's walk from here." Now they were close enough to hear the water and see pebbles on the boards. Now they were on the bridge.

"Then she is not far away," said Mendômô.

"She is dead now," said Jessie.

They were halfway across the bridge. Jessie looked ahead. Through the wooden slats she could see the brown water rushing and turning in against itself as it ran away, six feet below her. Mendômô turned her head to look at Jessie. Jessie had meant to say in an ordinary voice, "On her way, bringing her new baby to her mother's, she was crossing a stream on a log bridge, and they fell in," but her throat could only squeeze the words out, and once started, she had to gulp down air before she could finish. Mendômô reached out and linked her arm in Jessie's. Like this, they walked to the other side of the bridge.

The girls climbed three dirt stairs cut into the bank. When they reached the beaten-earth common, Jessie saw right away that nothing had changed in the little village, set some ways back and high above the road. There was no one in sight. Most of the women would be in the forest, cultivating their fields. Some chickens scratched and clucked softly around the posts of the palaver hut in the center of the common. Smoke rose through the thatch of the third house from the left. Jessie led the way to it. She paused outside the open doorway, looking into the dimness of the main room.

"*A mama, Ngo Masé!*" she called. "*Dinyega a!*" We greet you! Silence, except for the persistent low cooing of hens and the shrill tiny sounds made by a flock of chicks scurrying after them.

Jessie called again, listening harder for an answering call out back. The girls waited in the drowsy quiet without speaking to each other. Finally they heard a voice raised in greeting, and then, calling out words of welcome, Ngo Masé came into the house through the back door and hurried toward Jessie. Putting her hands on Jessie's elbows, she drew her into an embrace and kissed both cheeks. Still holding Jessie, she leaned back to see her better.

Ngo Masé looked the same. Her deep brown face was lined with soft wrinkles, but her cheeks were smooth when she smiled. Her short gray hair was bound in an old faded scarf, and she wore a caba, the village women's long loose dress, which matched the scarf. Her eyes were glossy and dark, bloodshot from the smoke of many cooking fires. Jessie found herself trembling over tears, being so warmly held by this old, brown, wrinkled woman who smiled happily at her. Between them was an ache; they met over the memory of Nléla. Jessie had not been back to this village since Nléla's funeral.

Then Jessie introduced Mendômô, who gave back the borrowed pots with her mother's thanks. Ngo Masé expected them to follow her through the dark room, past some low armchairs and a low table, and out to the kitchen, a second, smaller building behind the house. There she drew them into the smoky, dim little building and called out a woman's name. Jessie saw her, sitting by the open wood fire, plucking a chicken. She was heavily pregnant. A pile of feathers was on the ground to her right and a plucked chicken in an enameled basin to the left.

Jessie and Mendômô sat when Ngo Masé motioned them to the low log bench along one wall. She brought them some pieces of fresh sugarcane, and they chewed and sucked on the juices while Ngo Masé explained who they were to the other woman. When asked, Mendômô talked about her family, but after mentioning the odd and different fact that her parents came from two separate tribes, she spoke only briefly about her mother's home near Eseka. The conversation lagged a little then, and Jessie wondered if she and Mendômô could go soon without offending Ngo Masé.

But the old woman enjoyed Jessie's company and told her so. She said that it reminded her of Nléla and the times before now, the times when Jessie and her twin had been this high and Jessie had long braids like her little sister now, and they had often come to the village with Nléla to help gather fruit or firewood or pound corn in the mortar; did Jessie remember all that? Jessie did. And did she remember learning to balance water on her head?

Immediately Jessie recalled the soakings she'd gotten, trying to balance a bucket of water while going uphill from the riverbank. Joshua had refused to carry water, but he'd learned to balance loads of wood on his head. Carrying water was a woman's thing. So was carrying wood, but Joshua hadn't minded it as much as getting wet.

"The whole village came to see," Ngo Masé said to the other woman in the kitchen—a daughter-in-law, Jessie was sure—"and no one could believe that the white girl was doing a village girl's work, but she was able, she was very good."

At the memory of Nléla laughing with pleasure when Jessie finally balanced the water bucket on her way up from the Liege, Jessie smiled. For so long Jessie had kept herself from remembering Nléla's death, and now the thought of Nléla happy and alive twisted in her.

Ngo Masé fell silent, as if the same had happened to her just then. "She moves in my heart, and then it is hard to carry the loss of her," said Ngo Masé. Jessie listened; the other woman spoke a single word. "Yes," she said, and somehow this kept the memory of Nléla open and warm instead of shutting it aside. In silence, Jessie said it, too. Yes. It was hard to carry the loss, hard to remember, but she did.

When the girls said good-bye, Ngo Masé accompanied them to the edge of the village. As they set off on the road toward the bridge, neither Jessie nor Mendômô spoke. Just before the bridge, Jessie's shoelace came untied, and she sat down on an old mossy log to do it up again. Mendômô sat down next to her. The silence had gotten long, and Jessie didn't really want to talk about Nléla. She looked up and pointed to the orange-painted iron railroad trestle not far upstream.

"I saw the dead train," she said. "It died two years ago, on the day after we came home from school."

"But that was in December," said Mendômô.

"Yes. How do you know that? Were you here?"

"No," said Mendômô. She went quiet, as though going away from Jessie and the moment there in the shade of the palm. Then she sat up straight on the log. "It was a great victory, that train," she said. "It was the last one. After that, there were more soldiers, and everything was harder for us."

"Us?" asked Jessie, a chilly sense of understanding coming with the question.

"Of course. Who is not for the men who fight for our own country? We don't have to be in the forest to be with them," said Mendômô.

Jessie began longing to be safe at home in her living room.

Mendômô showed no signs of getting up to go. "What did you see that day?" she asked, clearly wanting from Jessie what she herself valued and did not have.

Jessie was glad to have something to offer. She remembered the day almost perfectly. Breakfast had been suddenly interrupted by a student who came to the front door to call Dad. Instead of unpacking their Hope School trunks and suitcases, Jessie and Joshua had rushed out with Mom and Cassie, joining the three hundred–odd students and villagers beyond count, filling the road and the paths leading down to the bridge over the Liege. The crowd was enormous.

The morning train from Yaoundé to Douala had been derailed on purpose by the Maquis, who had loosened the ties on the curve just before the trestle so that the train would have slowed down anyway before the accident. No one had been hurt, but the damage to machinery and the French schedule of connections had been considerable.

"People were excited. It was like a—" Jessie wanted to say a fair, but that was an English idea that didn't translate into Bassa. "It was like a big market, with everyone pleased and happy to be there. We laughed and there were girls dancing, and I saw the front of the engine on its side down the bank, and all the trees and grass crushed around it. We stood on the bridge and climbed on the railing, and everyone celebrated as though something great had happened."

"I told you. We don't have to be in the forest to be for them. They proved to the French that the territory was their own," said Mendômô. "But afterward the danger came," she added in a low voice.

"Do you . . . do you . . ." Jessie hesitated until Mendômô encouraged her with a little questioning noise in her throat. "Do you know people in the Maquis?" asked Jessie, and sensed right away this was a mistake. No one asked, no one claimed to know, no one spoke about knowing what might cause someone else to be hurt.

They were just rising from the log. A large convoy truck roared around the curve in the road beyond Ngo Masé's village. When the girls leaped backward, Jessie lost her balance and fell behind the log. The truck had passed by and clattered hotly across the bridge before she was on her feet again. Even so, she saw the several dozen soldiers wearing camouflage—Africans all—in the back, all staring at Mendômô, and now at her. Mendômô stood straight and stared back. Jessie saw that Mendômô's shoulders and arms were trembling, but the soldiers could not have known that, because she stood tall and unyielding. The intensity of Mendômô's anger made Jessie afraid of her.

All that was companionable between them evaporated. Jessie walked along beside Mendômô but could not begin to understand the silence in her. It was like that moment earlier in the afternoon when Mendômô had spoken of soldiers and Jessie had no way into her full meaning. When they had crossed the bridge and were coming to the turnoff for Libamba's campus, to Jessie's relief Mendômô began talking. "Do you know the name of the big man?" she asked.

"Yes. You mean Um Nyobe," said Jessie, naming the political leader of the Bassa uprising against French control of Cameroun.

"He was killed in his home, his village, in a trap made by the army, last week," said Mendômô, her words like stones she was throwing, hard, at people Jessie could not see, at people standing behind the soldiers, she thought. "And then, because the French wanted us to feel his death," said Mendômô, her voice full of rage, "they took his body from village to village and made people come look at it."

Immediately and in horror, Jessie wondered if this had happened to Mendômô, in her mother's village. She did not ask. They passed the ruined mud house by the roadside and in unspoken agreement took the right-hand fork in the road, so they would go on walking around campus rather than return to Mendômô's house. Jessie couldn't help but imagine the body of the dead man laid out on a planed board and people—men, women, and children—brought up close to see the hero, the leader, dead, dead, dead. Themselves, then, lost and alone and defeated.

"We did not go," said Mendômô. "We were in the city, in Sakbayemé, with my mother's sister. She works in the Presbyterian hospital there. But they came to my village and forced my grandmother—" And Mendômô made a sound with her tongue and her voice all at once, which was a little like a sob, a sound without being a word, which said everything that her grandmother had suffered. And Jessie understood this suffering without knowing it precisely.

"My grandmother had three sons and two daughters," said Mendômô. They were walking by the Goods' house now, and Jessie looked over at the broad sheltered porch wall where she and Mendômô had sat last night in the dark. "One son died when he was a boy, from a hunting accident in the forest." Her voice softened. "The other daughter still works in the hospital. And there is my mother. The daughters are alive." Mendômô tightened both hands into fists, and then, as Jessie watched, deliberately stretched her fingers out again and held her palms up to the sun. "My uncles were good men. One was a teacher of young children, and the other had begun a business in the same city. They were not as old as my mother. They both had children of their own."

Jessie listened to the past tense in Mendômô's story with a growing dread. She kept her eyes forward. The road was familiar, even to the mud puddle in the middle around this curve ahead and the long stretch of forest and bush on the right after the chapel; there was no building on this stretch, and people were far away from them as they walked.

Up ahead was the college garbage pit, where a herd of pigs snorted as they rooted about the edges. Jessie didn't like those pigs. They had run at her and Joshua once, surrounding them when the twins were much younger and shorter. Sometimes village hunters came after the pigs for a feast. Dogs wearing bells ran the roads of the campus, barking fast, and the hunters ran after the dogs and the pigs and threw their spears when they came close to a pig the right size, and the pig lay in the dust on the road, screaming and bleeding, screaming with spears sticking up out of its body, until a hunter came close and cut its throat with a machete. Jessie had seen this happen.

"Both of my grandmother's sons joined the UPC," said Mendômô, her words coming fast now, as though she'd waited a long time to be able to say all this. Jessie nodded. The initials stood for the political party founded by Um Nyobe in 1944. It was the source for resistance against the French. "Last year, one of my grandmother's sons was killed by French soldiers in their police prison, in Sakbayemé. They said he had killed himself in despair, but we know they lie. My uncle was a strong man who believed his choice was right. He would not have finished himself that way. It was the soldiers and the police who beat him and broke him and killed him."

This was sickening. Jessie didn't want Mendômô to go on, to say any more. She thought of running away down the center spoke of the campus road system, leaving Mendômô alone with her story. Then she thought she would just tell Mendômô to stop talking. But Jessie could not do either of these things. She kept her mouth closed and walked slowly, watching her feet and Mendômô's keeping pace together.

"Last month, when we knew my father was coming

home after three years and would be with us in a week, we were with my aunt in the city, preparing to come here, buying clothes, making arrangements. And a man came to the door. We thought it would be news about my father, or perhaps even my father himself come early. The man said that my grandmother needed her daughters in the village that night, so we paid a taximan much money to drive us there before dark. And when we came to her home, there were many people in front, the way it is for a funeral. The way it had been the time before—with the son who was in prison. And inside, there was the body of her third son."

It seemed to Jessie that there was too much of her there on the road. Her presence seemed huge and hollow. Because she had nothing to say, her longing to comfort Mendômô seemed useless and empty. Because she could not imagine such a thing happening to her own family, her sympathy seemed cold, like that of a stranger. Jessie struggled to re-member that she'd only met this girl, this friend, last night. She'd known Martha since they were seven years old, and she'd never felt as much of Martha's life as she understood of Mendômô's in less than a day. Jessie made a sound be-hind closed lips, a sound for the pain.

"They do a thing on the forest paths," said Mendômô, her voice low, "a thing the French learned to do in some other part of the world where they are also fighting to keep land not their own."

French Indochina, thought Jessie quickly, picturing the

place on the map between Thailand and the Pacific Ocean. She'd read about this other fighting in one of the American newsmagazines.

"Some men from there came to make their traps here," Mendômô went on, waving her left hand as if pointing to that far-off place. "I saw them in Sakbayemé. Small men, straight black hair, not your color skin," she said, looking over at Jessie, who blushed. Mendômô reached out with her right hand and stroked Jessie's arm from elbow to wrist with one brown finger.

"On the paths in the forest they dig deep pits," Mendômô went on, but now she stopped to breathe deeply before she could go on. "And they set in sharpened stakes, with the points like spears, up in the air. They cover the pits, and when men—or women; it could be women on their way to their fields to work—when they hurry along the paths, they fall in, and they die like pigs waiting to be cooked. And that is how they killed my grandmother's last son."

Jessie began shivering and had to press her hands against her midriff to make the shivering recede. She looked around and saw they were standing by the foundations of the new house for the Essams.

That night, while Cassie was taking her shower, Jessie went and stood next to Dad's desk until he looked up at her and said, "What is it, Jessie?"

"Dad, I have to know. Is Um Nyobe dead?"

"Yes, Jessie," said Dad sadly. "Yes, he is. He was caught

in an army ambush in his own village, in Boumyébel, the day before we came to get you at Hope School. We could not tell what would happen here afterward, whether there would be wholesale revolt or massive army invasion and all means of travel cut off. So we brought you home while we could. How do you know about Um Nyobe?" he asked curiously.

"Mendômô told me. She told me—" And Jessie saw two bodies lying together on that plank she'd imagined in the afternoon, two men, one shot many times over, the other pierced in the neck, the shoulders, the chest, the groin, the knees, held up by spikes to die as a warning to others moving in the forest. "About a trap on forest paths," Jessie whispered, tightening her lips so she could say what she meant to say. Then she changed her mind. She could not talk about the other thing—about Mendômô's uncle. "She said the army brought Um Nyobe to the villages and made people come and look at him, dead like that."

"I've heard that, too," said Dad, rolling his yellow pencil a little ways back and forth on the desk. When he spoke again, it was as if to himself. "Um Nyobe was not a big man in physical stature, but in his ability to call people to their rights and strengthen them to resist injustice, he was a great man. And courageous." Dad looked up; his tone of voice had become definite. "He was a quiet-spoken man, but clear in his ideas. He came here once, almost two years ago, for a private meeting with those of the staff who were sympathetic. I met him," said Dad. He looked down at his hands again. "He was about my age. He had escaped so many times before, Jessie, that the French must think the Bassa will go on believing him to be alive unless they are forced to see the body. And the French believe the resistance will be broken by this." Dad shook his head.

"It won't," said Jessie. "It won't, will it?"

"I don't know what will happen, Jessie."

"It's wrong to do what they do," she said fiercely, straining against a burning in her throat. Mendômô had wept openly, there by the new building that would be her home. She had talked with tears running down her face. "I want it right!" Jessie said, almost shouting. "Why can't someone make them stop!"

"Well, we can only try," said Dad. "A little at a time, even when it doesn't seem like enough."

It was late at night. Everyone in the family had gone to bed, and the generator in the hangar had been turned off. The only noise was the normal sound of the wind making leaves touch each other, and night birds calling as they settled on nearby branches. Then there came another sound, a low pulse and throb, far away.

Jessie woke up suddenly, sharply, and lay trembling in bed, trying to remember that the room made four strong walls around her. The darkness without and the darkness within was the same, so that the walls might not have been there at all. Her bed might have been in the road, and she lying there, stabbed and bleeding to death alone.

She heard a motor chugging through the dark, at some distance, coming closer, on the main connecting spoke of the road leading from the classroom buildings to the dormitory where her own house was, coming right toward the house, on and on, like that truck on the road home the other day, driving up so close it could have crashed into them. The motor belonged to a Land Rover—Jessie and Joshua both could identify cars by the sounds of their engines. It drove right under her own window. The engine was cut. Then there was a long silence swelling with the sounds of the birds. Quite suddenly Jessie recognized the steady shrilling of insects, though that had been in her hearing all along. Perhaps that motor had been in a dream, and she had only now woken from it.

Jessie's stomach ached. Keen stabs of cold slipped about in her gut and moved up into her chest. She thought she'd go deaf trying to hear what was happening outside. Then the wind rattled the stiff leaves of the hibiscus hedge, and at the same time Jessie thought—almost imagined—she heard a car door open and close. Quick footsteps crunched across the gravel under the eaves of the house. More long silence. She knew whoever it was stood right by the walls of the house. Right by the guest room door. The room next to this one that she and Cassie shared.

Straining to hear, dreading any sounds, Jessie closed her eyes as though her ears would catch more that way, even though the darkness in her room was so thick that it hurt to try and see anything at all. Faintly, faintly, came the sounds of a key in a lock, and then the noises of someone inside the house, moving about in the guest room. Jessie imagined the person coming through the door into the hall and suddenly leaping upon them all, spear and machete in hand, stabbing, slashing, blood everywhere, Cassie screaming. Herself holding stock-still, as she had that day on the bridge.

There were quiet rustling sounds in the room next door and then creakings, unmistakable noises of someone getting into bed.

Jessie tried hard to stay awake all night, imagining for a while that her family needed her to be on guard. After giving time to that idea, she saw how silly it was, considering that Mom had known someone was going to use the clean sheets she'd asked Jessie to put on the bed. In spite of herself, she fell asleep.

In the morning, moments after waking, she remembered the person in the guest room. A chill clutched her stomach and a shiver hovered between her shoulder blades; with deliberate effort, she made herself get out of bed. As slowly, she went to the bedroom shutters and unlatched them, pushing them open to look outside. There was nothing there but the faint marks of a Land Rover's tires on the grass. By eight o'clock, when she went out for the first time that day, the grass stems had already struggled upright again. All that was left as proof of the stranger were crimped little chunks of dried red mud that had fallen into the grass from the tire treads.

5

Gifts

Jessie wanted to know who had been sleeping in the guest room. The question ran along beside her other thoughts all day. What would she pick out of the Christmas barrel as gifts for Joshua and Cassie? Who had a key to the outside door? If Mom didn't have any cocoa left, how could they make the Christmas fudge this year? They always had fudge from Grandma Howells's recipe for Christmas. Of course Mom and Dad knew that someone came secretly to sleep in the house. When sorting laundry, put the dirty socks with the dark clothes. If she asked them about the person who had come into the house last night, would they tell her anything? Would they tell her why the person came here?

Jessie thought not. She stood on the back porch next to the square white washing machine, feeding the guest room sheets she'd taken off that bed yesterday through the ringer into the first rinse. The washing machine was American, driven by a gasoline motor so loud and shrill the twins had to shout at each other to be heard. Cassie, whose job was handing Joshua the clothespins while he hung the clean washing on the line, screamed when she had something to say. And when the wash was finally done, Jessie bent down to shut off the motor. For a moment all of them were deafened by the sound of silence that followed.

She'd tried out every way she could imagine for bringing the subject up. "Mom," she could say, "I heard someone coming into the house last night through the guest room door." And Mom would look at her and look away, with an expression that said, Don't say any more. The same expression had been on Mom's face the day Jessie had wanted to know why the sheets had to be changed.

Or she could say, "Dad, I know someone slept in the guest room last night." And Dad would probably smile a little and say, "That's what a guest room is for, Jess."

She might get them both in the office tonight and demand to know. "I don't like feeling scared to death in the middle of the night when people with machetes and spears are marching by the house and someone, not in our family"—and here she would sort of lean toward her parents and speak most accusingly—"comes in whenever he feels like it."

And Dad would say mildly, "I'm sorry you are frightened, but there's nothing to be afraid of in the house." And

Mom would say, more emphatically than Dad, "Who is our family, Jessie?" And then everything would stretch into a sort of Sunday school lesson about life and love. Anyway, Mom would be right and Dad would be right and Jessie would end up knowing nothing more than she knew now.

And just what would she have if she found out who this person was?

A name—and something more, thought Jessie. She'd have knowledge that could hurt that person, and she'd be able to give it away if asked. Not that she would, of course, but that possibility came with the information she wanted. It was likely Mom and Dad could be hurt somehow if the secret got out. What could that person be doing in the house at night anyhow? Well, no one looking for him would expect him to be here. And who could be looking?

The army.

But that answer raised more questions, and more ominous ones, too. It raised the memory of the soldiers in the truck by the Liege bridge yesterday, and that made Jessie think of Mendômô trembling and standing straight in defiance of everything those men stood for—the deaths of her uncles, the sorrow of her grandmother's heart. Everything Jessie thought of increased the weight of her curiosity, making it a more difficult thing to satisfy. In the end she decided that she ought not to ask about the person in the guest room last night.

So she was shocked when Joshua caught Dad's attention as the twins were washing up the supper dishes and said,

"Hey, Dad, did you know that someone came in the house through the guest room door last night around midnight?"

Dad was filling the wood box by the stove. He stacked the split wood carefully, neither answering nor ignoring Joshua, because he looked up to meet Joshua's eyes in a long glance before he laid the last pieces of wood in place. He dusted his hands then and said quietly, "I didn't hear it last night, but I do know who it is. We gave this person a key so he could be free to come and go when need arises."

"Oh," said Joshua. "Okay." He swished a plate in the rinse water and held it out to Jessie. She rubbed it dry, looking back and forth between Joshua and Dad with amazement. Joshua squeezed the dishcloth and shrugged. "I just thought you ought to know."

"I do," said Dad. He looked at Jessie, smiling at her astonishment. "What is it, Jess?" he asked.

"Nothing. I mean, I thought—I heard, too, but I didn't—"

"Have you got a complete sentence in your head?" asked Joshua, handing her the next plate. She took it and flicked the draining water toward him. He made a rude face at her.

"I wasn't going to ask about it," she said to Dad, ignoring Joshua. "I figured you didn't want us to talk about it."

"I'm not going to talk about it," said Dad, "and neither are you. It isn't anything you need to know about, beyond what I've said just now."

"But what if—," Jessie began, wanting to know, feeling it her near-adulthood *right* to know.

"There are no what-ifs you carry responsibility for in this matter," said Dad, still quietly but now more serious than Jessie had ever heard him be. "You will have to control your curiosity, and you will have to do the same with your tendency to worry about everything."

Although he didn't name her, she felt he meant Jessie alone. Joshua took things and left them and, as far as Jessie could tell, didn't seem to carry anything but music in his head. She liked to know how things fit together, how people worked together, and why.

"It's *not* worry," she said, turning to Dad, both of her hands in fists so he could see that she was serious, too. "I only want to know enough so I don't imagine the wrong things." Jessie felt herself trying to explain it too earnestly. She should stop, but she didn't. "So I don't scare myself with what I don't understand," she said. "Don't you see?"

"Yes, I do," said Dad. He took the stack of dried plates, opened the cupboard over Jessie's head, and put them away. "I expect that you and Joshua alone among your peers have any clear idea of what's happening in this country now, but everybody, regardless of knowing any facts, has an opinion. I know that your understanding is only partial, and naturally you want to know more. In this case, knowing more is not going to make you safer, Jessie. This is a time for trust."

Dad paused, letting the thought come to rest in Jessie. Trust would mean living with the fear but not letting it run away with her imagination. And it seemed clear that trust was not going to be a comfortable, or even comforting, thing.

As he talked, Dad swept up the fallen bits of twig and bark around the wood box. Jessie spread the dish towel out to dry on the drain board, and then held the dustpan for him. "Thank you," he said, sweeping the woody bits toward her. "Everybody takes sides, and even among ourselves— meaning among the missionaries—we are able to hurt each other badly, in the name of being right."

Dad cleared his throat. "We know someone who carries authority and can very easily be hurt from either side," he said. "Mom and I are able to help this person, and when we were asked, we agreed that the risk involved was not as great as the person's need for shelter. We are able to help, and so we do."

"Are you ever scared about all this?" asked Joshua. "Is it hard to do?"

"Do you mean, are we afraid of being caught?" asked Dad, with a rueful half laugh. "Yes. That would not be a good thing, all round."

"Joshua," called Cassie from the living room. "Joshua, come play something for me before bed. Please?"

Joshua dried his hands on his shirt and went to the kitchen door, but he turned around there and said, "Dad, what would happen?"

"The French would expel us from the country, I think," said Dad gravely. "And this other person could well lose everything."

"Life?" said Jessie, all the muscles in her arms and shoulders, even her heart, tense, leaning toward his next words.

Dad didn't answer. He stared at some point in the air between himself and the kitchen counter; Jessie wondered what he was seeing. She herself carefully avoided the thought of the staked pits on the forest paths and the softer, somehow worse, mysterious death by betrayal in prison.

Later, in bed on her back in the darkness, with Cassie snuffling gently beside her under the great mosquito net protecting them both, Jessie wondered about Dad and what sort of person he'd been when he was a boy. What had he imagined doing as a grown-up? What had he known about himself that made him sure he was doing the right thing when he left the college where he taught in America and came to Cameroun to teach history? How did people know the right thing to do with their lives?

Actually, she knew the answer to that. There were rules, and where there weren't rules, there were people to tell other people what to do. Don't be mean. Do your homework. Be on time. Be considerate. Be neat. Don't lie. Don't steal. Don't hurt other people on purpose. If you hurt them by accident, you're still to blame. Don't sass your elders. Don't give up halfway through whatever it is you're doing. A job well begun is only half-done. Be patient. Be discreet. Be a good friend. Love your neighbor. Do good to your enemy. Bless, don't curse. All that stuff.

How did all that tell you whether you should play the piano or not, or be a banker or a doctor or study art? How would that tell you anything about deciding that your life was worth the idea of freeing a country from another country's control? How could you tell whether or not you were meant to be somebody special?

She had the questions down firm; she even knew people who might listen while she asked them: Dad, Mom, Uncle Don, Martha, maybe Mendômô. But everyone would look curiously baffled, and Uncle Don might say, "You know by living, honey. You know by putting it to the test." Dad would probably say, "It isn't the rules that give us the answers. The rules only help us get along the way. The answers come when we need them." And without doubt, Mom would say, "You should decide your direction by the use of your gifts. Your gifts have your purpose in them."

What gifts? Jessie wanted to know. What gifts were hers?

She meant to stay awake and listen that night, but she slept soundly anyway and did not hear if the stranger came again to stay in the guest room.

Three weeks later, on Christmas morning, everything began as usual. There was bacon and eggs for breakfast, the only time in the year. There was cinnamon raisin bread with fondant icing. And there was the basket of presents.

It was never a big to-do, that basket of presents. Jessie had picked out her selection from the Christmas barrel of things Mom had bought in the States during the last furlough and kept on hand since then for birthdays and celebrations like today's. She'd picked a box of paints for Cassie and a double set of playing cards for Joshua.

Joshua's gift to her didn't come from the barrel. When she opened it, Jessie didn't understand what she was looking at until she turned the six brown speckled disks over and saw the little hole carved in the back of each one. Joshua had made her buttons.

"Out of what?" she asked, holding the buttons in her palm and touching them gently with her right forefinger. They were beautiful, perfectly round, smooth, shiny. They filled her with wonder.

"Palm wood," said Joshua. He ducked his head as though shy with her, but then he said proudly, "They must be the only palm-wood buttons in the world. Uncle Nat told me palm wood was too soft to carve, but I kept at it. I couldn't have made anything bigger out of it, though."

"Let's see," said Mom, delighted. Jessie gave her two buttons, and Mom held them up to the light and turned them over, exclaiming with pleasure. "Oh, Joshua, they are wonderful! How did you think of this tapering in the back?" she asked. "It's so graceful!"

"What'll you do with them?" asked Cassie, ever practical.

"I don't know. Wait until I'm grown-up and have a dress made for them," said Jessie grandly. She held a button up to her cheek; the coolth of it startled her. By grown-up she meant this coming summer. She could see it now: a tan linen suit with a white blouse and these buttons on the suit jacket. And everyone, the officials and the other travelers in the airports and all the new kids she'd meet at Schutz, would admire her, and she'd be beautiful in it next September.

"That's forever!" said Cassie. "I'd put them on a necklace and wear them now."

"You'd lose them," said Jessie, deliberately holding the buttons out of Cassie's reach.

"I would not!" Cassie stretched her arm farther and swiped at Jessie's elbow.

"You would too," insisted Jessie, getting up from her chair, lifting the hand with the buttons high overhead.

"Oh, girls, not on Christmas Day, please!" sighed Mom.

"Let's have a picnic lunch," suggested Dad, just as Mom started on a long scolding lecture about peace and harmony and Jessie trying for once to control herself.

"That's a good idea," said Mom instead of all the other things. Jessie looked at her quickly. Something, some catch and tightening in Mom's voice, told her that Mom had, with difficulty, chosen not to get angry with Jessie. Jessie was ashamed of herself then for having egged Cassie into quarreling.

"If we clean things up without delay," said Dad, "we can be at the Nyong River in the bamboo clearing by noon." The work went fast, everyone at it together. Wrappings folded carefully for the next year, table cleared, gifts put away in the back of the house, picnic made and packed, and everything was ready in good time.

They borrowed the school carryall again. "Maybe someday," said Dad, when Cassie and Joshua both asked Dad when the family would buy a car. "We don't really need one of our own right now."

Jessie agreed with Dad. She liked sharing the car with other people. The car they all used was a thing that connected everyone at Libamba, that truly made them part of the same family. They drove toward the river on a narrow track after leaving the main Yaoundé–Douala road that paralleled the rail bed. This track was hardly used by vehicles. The way was greenly walled by forest for long stretches, and everyone looked out the windows, but nothing could be seen through the blurred screen of leaves.

"Oh, Mom," said Cassie suddenly, "we have to go back to school so soon, and I'm going to miss you." Mom hugged Cassie, and Jessie fought the rise of sorrow in her heart and throat. She didn't say things like that anymore, but she felt them just the same. In advance of going back to Hope School, the pain of separation was always bad.

"Well, school's still two weeks away," said Dad cheerfully, "and as a matter of fact, we've got a surprise for you." Jessie leaned forward a little, thinking they were about to see it on the road ahead, or maybe when they got to the picnic spot by the river. "We've been asked to do Bible Conference this year," Dad went on.

"Are you coming? Are you going to? Are you?" shrieked Cassie, flinging her arms around Mom and jumping in the seat between her and Dad. "Say yes! Say you are!"

Jessie and Joshua exchanged glances. This wasn't bad

news, exactly. It would be great to have Mom and Dad visit the dorm in midterm; they never did that, because the school term at Libamba always ran on the same schedule as Hope School's year. But to have Mom and Dad be Bible Conference leaders! To have them be dorm parents for a week! The idea had definite drawbacks. Sharing Mom and Dad with forty other kids was one. Having Mom and Dad talk about the Bible in front of everybody was another. It was just too . . . too . . . Jessie hunted for the word she wanted and could only think of *close.* Too near.

She wanted space between herself and them, and yet she wanted all of them together. It was more than she could think about, but she itched to get hold of what she meant and have it clear. Not that she didn't love Mom and Dad or wasn't proud of them . . . Well, she couldn't do all this thinking inside of herself; she needed to talk it out. Never mind about it now. Joshua had turned away to look out the car window again. She couldn't bring it up with him. The less she thought about it, the better. Still . . . how lovely to have Mom and Dad visit for Easter!

"Dad," she said, "have you made the appointment with the consulate yet?"

"I've written to them, but the consul hasn't answered me yet," said Dad. "These things take time, Jessie."

Jessie sighed with impatience. The plan was to go up to the American consulate in Yaoundé to apply for their passports when the consul had the twins' application papers ready. She knew Dad was right, that getting official documents took a long time. But that knowledge had no power to moderate the longing she felt whenever she thought of holding her own passport in her hand.

Dad slowed the car to just above a crawl as the track entered a large village clearing. Three women carrying babies on their backs stepped out of the road, watching the car curiously. Here people were moving about. Jessie had time to look at two men talking together in the shade outside the palaver house, to notice the preoccupied expressions of girls carrying pails of water on their heads, to watch a woman cheerfully carrying a chicken upside down by its tied legs. A crowd of barefoot little boys in shorts and ragged shirts raced hoops across the common, speeding them with sticks as they ran alongside, deftly avoiding the girls and the women in their way.

"That always looks like fun, but it's hard to do," said Joshua.

Jessie heard him, agreeing, but before she could say so, she saw something that took away her breath. The car had left the village and rounded the curve, just picking up speed, when Dad braked suddenly for a man who lurched into the road from the ditch. He staggered strangely, not crossing the road as any ordinary person would, but coming right toward the car. Dad stopped and waited patiently, watching the man. Jessie watched, too, her eyes frozen on him, her heart barely beating; she recognized the old, dread chill shivering down between her shoulder blades.

She knew him. He moved along as no one should, in a

jerking, shortened, side-to-side stoop, but she knew him. She didn't want to be sure of that, but she couldn't take her eyes off of him. When he shambled slowly, painfully around the front of the car, she pressed her shoulders against the backseat to get away, and once again she saw herself pressing away from him, her back against the rough-planed wood railing of the bridge, the rush of the river Liege far below her.

She had seen his feet when he shuffled in front of the car, and though she couldn't see them now, and was glad of that, oh, heart-glad she couldn't see them anymore, the heavy thing on his legs would be forever in her vision of him on the Liege bridge.

She felt herself in him, imprisoned as he was, with his feet forced through holes carved in a length of wood so he could only take one step and then another, each as short and treacherously balanced as the steps of a toddler. The man went by them, step after step, his head turned, looking in the car windows the whole time. He stretched out his left arm and trailed his fingers the length of the body of the car. He smiled at them all, but it was a smile for everything, people, chickens, trees, the sky, not a smile of one person reaching to another. Because of his smile—a sweet, unknowing one—Jessie could keep looking when his eyes met hers, but it took all her strength of will to face him.

Dad waited, holding the car perfectly still, until the man had dragged himself beyond the vehicle. At last, when Jessie's held-in scream to *go!* thickened her tongue and throat,

Dad let the clutch out and drove on. Jessie sat stiff in her seat, trembling, her hands folded tightly over a hollow between her palms, her fingers pressed hard against the bones of her knuckles. As soon as she released her hands, another violent shiver seized her.

Cassie said, "What was that thing on his feet?"

"That's the man," Mom began, and stopped to swallow. "That's the man who is . . . disturbed," she said, and sighed. "He used to come to Libamba years ago. Don't you remember him, Jessie? Joshua?"

Behind her back, the twins looked at each other quickly, and then away.

"His mother used to come with him," said Dad, glancing in the rearview mirror. "As long as she was alive, she went where he went, to make sure he was all right. But I suppose there's no one else in his family who will do that now, and the village has put him in that device to keep him from wandering great distances away and hurting himself."

"I wouldn't like that," said Cassie firmly. "How come he doesn't get splinters?"

"Oh, I'm sure they smoothed it before they put him into it," said Mom gently. "It isn't as cruel as it looks. He can still go where he wants to. He isn't shut away or kept from village life."

Jessie leaned hard into the seat of the car, arms folded over her stomach to keep it from flopping, eyes closed. She breathed slowly, evenly. Martha had told her once that it was the right way to calm down. "Don't yell, for pity's sake," Martha had said during one of Jessie's flares of temper. "Breathe first, then *think*. Don't get mind-diarrhea." The memory of this made Jessie grin a little. Martha said such odd, unlikely things sometimes. Thinking of her roommate brought Jessie a pang of loneliness. She missed being at school, talking and carrying on with Martha and the others in the familiar, unchanging routine of dorm life.

When they came to the crossing point at the Nyong, Dad parked the car to the side of the track, behind a row of canoes pulled up on the bank. "It was him, wasn't it?" said Joshua in a low voice, while they unloaded the picnic basket from the back of the carryall. The shiver snaked along her back again, and Jessie tightened her grip on the basket handles, as if holding on to something with all her strength would keep the horror from taking control of her. "It's funny," said Joshua without a trace of humor in his voice. "He doesn't look much older. We were five then, weren't we? Almost ten years ago." Jessie nodded. "I liked him better on the bridge," said Joshua, grunting as he swung the car doors closed.

Did she like him? Jessie didn't think it was a matter of liking. If a car could be proof of connection between some people, why couldn't an encounter like that old one on the Liege bridge be a real connection between her and the snake man? Would it make a difference that he hadn't known her then and couldn't remember that time?

"Mom," she said, "can people like that—that man on the road—tell the truth?"

"Oh, yes," said Mom without hesitation. "They see other sides of things, Jessie, even if they don't fit in life the way most of us do. In other parts of the world," she went on, spreading pâté on rounds of French bread, "or, in our own part of the world," she corrected herself, "we don't have time for such people anymore. Nowadays, people like that man are kept separate, so we don't struggle with their understanding. They can't make wholes of life, Jessie. They can tell the truth, but they don't know how to live with it."

"Oh," said Jessie, seeing darkness and empty places and no one touching. Mom handed her a sandwich, and Jessie knew a blessing in the casual brush of Mom's fingers.

"And do they have gifts?" asked Joshua, teasing Mom gently.

Mom gave him a wry grin, with a look from under her eyebrows. But when she said, "Of course they do," she was serious.

"Like what?" asked Joshua, challenging her.

"I don't know," said Mom evenly. "I don't know that man. I do know that God gives each one of us gifts to use in living with ourselves and each other, regardless of our state of mind or how society understands us."

Joshua met Jessie's glance, and between them was the secret of the snake man's powerful gift of fear. In Jessie alone was his gift of prophecy. It refused to be still in her, be just the words he had said, be something to happen in the future. The awful moment in which they had been alive together there on the bridge surrounded his words about courage in her, and all at once those words slipped loose from her memory, moving in the present moment, now like a light-filled bubble, now like a dark, ominous promise of trouble ahead. If the man had been whole, an ordinary sort of person who had made an ordinary observation about her, the words would have come back as a compliment, but they wouldn't have waited in her, like something living, biding its time, ready to leap without notice.

"Do you think they have courage? Those sorts of people, I mean," said Jessie, her trepidation making the words tumble together as she spoke.

"It takes courage to open our lives to what we can't control and don't understand," said Mom, looking at Jessie, considering her own thoughts. "It would take courage to live with such fractured life if we were his family, I'm sure. I don't know about the man himself. Maybe he has it without being able to think about it, as we do when we are whole within ourselves."

Jessie stared at a fluttering of small white butterflies dancing over an eddy in the brown, slow-moving river. They rose in a loose, ragged cloud and floated down again toward the glistening surface, and then made an unevenly spaced line over the water as they came to rest on the mud of the bank. She felt like the river, moving on and on within a set path, not free like the butterflies to go anywhere at will. The things she thought were like the butterflies, which could not land on the water.

"Mom," she said, without breaking her gaze at the shining surface of the river, "what's courage for?"

She expected Mom to say, "For bravery," and that would be a simple end to it. Being brave was just stiffening her resolve to get through something that was going to hurt. She'd done that every year of her life since going to Hope School, holding her heart stiff and making it angry so it wouldn't ache unbearably before, during, and after the separation from Mom and Dad. She'd done that whenever there had been the yearly round of shots and inoculations all the missionaries got to keep them healthy for another twelve months.

But Mom said, "Oh, courage is for being able to do what is right when you are afraid you can't. Courage is strength in your heart, I think."

"Do I have it?" Spoken very quietly, making herself completely still to hear with her whole being, and the river chuckling to itself as it flowed on by.

"Yes." Decisive certainty in Mom's voice. It seemed to Jessie that she ought to face Mom, but looking at the sun, skipping brilliants over the ripples on the river's surface, was more comfortable than giving Mom her attention. Mom said, "You have an interesting kind of courage, Jessie."

Now Jessie's glance swung across the grass and the green checkered picnic cloth to Mom's face, to the light glancing off her glasses, to Mom's brown eyes, looking thoughtfully at Jessie. "I've told you before that the three of you see patterns. Joshua sees them in music. We'd never have known that in time if we hadn't been able to buy Oncle Michel's piano. Cassie sees patterns in numbers. She's been able to understand higher math concepts from the beginning. She sees the arrangement and balance of objects the way an architect does, for example.

"You see patterns in people. You understand others. It's the least obvious of the three kinds of gifts, and the only one not evident in what you can do by hand. But you can't get proof of what you know. Your insight is harder to use than, say, Joshua's, because no one applauds you when friendships go well and last a long time, and no one can see the ties you make so easily as costing you anything."

"What do you mean?"

"When you made friends with Mendômô, was that easy to do?"

"Well, it was at the end," said Jessie, remembering how simple the work of friendship had seemed that night at the Goods', but how thick and unpleasant she had been during the day, trying to decide what she would do when she got to the party. Was that what Mom meant by using her gift?

"Everybody you meet is important, isn't that so, Jessie?"

Jessie tried to think of someone she knew who wasn't sharply in focus for her. There must be someone at Hope School, some missionary, some African teacher, someone. . . . And everybody she thought of was real. It was as though she met people on the inside, not just recognizing their faces but their peculiar differences. She could name people, and then she'd be listing hundreds, she thought. She

had a clear impression of everyone who came to mind—
except Cassie. Well, of course, Cassie was her sister and
didn't count in the same way. Cassie would always be there.
Annoying, but there.

"There's Cassie, of course," she said lightly, as if sharing
a joke with Mom. Mom didn't think it was funny.

"Yes. That's true. You don't want to make Cassie important, Jessie. You treat her as though she were someone
you will not know the rest of your life." Mom's voice had
a warning and a sadness in it.

Jessie toughened her heart and shrugged. Mom's lips
tightened, and she looked down at her hands in her lap.
Between them was a sense of discouragement, of all the
good things they'd been talking about come to naught. A
fairly big fish leaped up through the brown shine of the river
and plopped back in again. Farther down the narrow path
along the bank, in among the stand of bamboo, Dad's voice
called out and Joshua's answered, with Cassie's piping in
behind the two. Their words were indistinguishable.

Jessie thought that if she sat there any longer, Mom
would start talking again about paying more attention to
Cassie when they all got back to Hope School; it was a song
and dance she and Mom went through before each term
now. Jessie had always thought that one of the big advan-
tages of being in a boarding school—being at Hope School,
in any case—was that out of her parents' sight and super-
vision she could do as she pleased, wear what she wanted
to wear, ignore as she chose the requests and hopes Mom

might have that were not convenient or interesting to Jessie herself. Cassie care was definitely one of these requests and hopes. What Mom couldn't see, she couldn't control.

Mom said, "Why do you ignore Cassie at school?"

"Because I don't feel like having a little kid tagging along all the time! Because she cries so much! Because I can't do anything for her! Besides, I don't think I love her very much," said Jessie, daring Mom with her last thought.

Quick as a flash Mom said, "Love is more than a feeling, Jessie. Love is something you do. You're old enough to understand that."

Before they could start a sticky discussion on the subject, Jessie thought that either she or Mom should get up and leave, so she did. Rather than get into a fight about the right thing to do while she was at school, she would walk along the riverbank and look for crocodiles in the water. That was the sort of thing she'd want to be able to tell her grandchildren. "When I lived in Africa," she would say, in a creaky old voice, "on Christmas Day we would go to the great river Nyong and look for crocodiles. It seemed like an appropriate thing to do," she'd add, and everyone would laugh and admire her for her wit and her experiences.

While Jessie walked, she knew she was still silently arguing underneath the little scene she'd made up about being old. How rapidly Mom had answered her just then. And the idea that love wasn't a feeling. Of course love was a feeling!

She discarded the thought of Cassie and kept the thought

of going back to Hope School. That brought back the thought of leaving Mom. She'd have Cassie to work things out with later, but Mom she would only have for a couple more weeks. She didn't feel warm toward her yet, but by now, from so many leave-takings, Jessie knew that if she wasted this time at the end, she would remember Mom with a longing sorrow: I could have made up the argument, but I didn't, and now I can't. That was a horrible thought to have by herself, far away, in the middle of the night.

So on her return to the picnic site, Jessie made herself go help Mom clean up, and when she came close, a sense of duty mixed with impulse moved her, and Jessie kissed Mom suddenly, getting them both over the hump of discouraged loneliness. Mom smiled warmly and kissed Jessie in return. So there was peace between them at the end.

6

The Telegram

Martha and Joshua were arguing.

It was Friday afternoon. Jessie, for once ready before Martha, sat out on the cement porch with her stack of books beside her and waited. Real school was over for this week and the next one, too. Next week was Bible Conference. Already. It was the end of March; Mom and Dad were coming on Sunday afternoon, and Jessie didn't think she was ready for them to suddenly be houseparents.

It was more than just the problem of sharing their attention with everyone else. It was also the matter of having them be here, where she had her own life, separate from theirs. Jessie wasn't sure she really wanted them to come, and yet she was looking forward to Mom and Dad seeing her in that first moment of greeting. And there would be the lovely shock of going around a corner and finding Dad in the next room, or looking up at the teacher and seeing Mom, and the deep pleasure of saying good night to the houseparents and having that blessing reach Mom and Dad immediately. It was going to be all right, Jessie decided.

She listened idly to the fight going on inside the classroom. The classroom windows had no glass. The room would have been intolerably hot and stuffy if the windows had been glazed. The builder had put in a long piece of expanded metal grillwork, which filled the window space with open diamond shapes. Jessie drew this diamond pattern in the thin layer of sand on the cement porch, wondering what was heating the disagreement between her brother and her roommate. When the quarrel began, she'd been finishing her after-school chore of cleaning the sink and counters in the science room. Now they had reached the trap of the "I-did-not/You-did-too" stage. Jessie leaned against the sun-warmed school wall, wondering if she should interrupt them.

"Oh, you did too," insisted Martha inside the classroom. Jessie cringed for Joshua. "You said you would finish it by this Friday. Now I've got to go to the press without your page! It stinks. I'm going to have one whole page completely empty, because you didn't care about getting around to finishing what you promised you'd do." The steel of justified rage edged her voice.

"I told you I didn't want to do it in the first place. It's a stupid, girl thing to want anyhow. I bet you asked Aunt

Letitia to make me the assistant editor on the *Daze* just so you could hang around me. Well, you're right. I don't care about the paper, and I don't care if a stupid empty page embarrasses you."

"All right, then, I'll give them an empty page except for the words 'Joshua Howells was supposed to fill this space' written on it. How about that!"

Slam! Slap! Bang! Joshua was getting his books out of his desk, dropping the mahogany lid, whacking the books on top of each other, and shoving his chair around. Jessie heard quick footsteps, and then Joshua shouted, "Get out of my way!" Jessie looked sideways and saw that Martha had jumped into the doorway and was blocking Joshua's exit.

"Oh no you don't, Joshua Tyndale Howells!"

"Leave my middle name out of it," snapped Joshua.

"You stay right here until you write something for me to put in the paper. You promised, and I need it, and *now!*"

While they were carrying on like this, Jessie's back began to hurt, and then her stomach got tight. I know what the matter is with him, she thought. He wants to practice. He's grouchy because she's keeping him from the piano. He's embarrassed because she's goopy about him and he knows it somehow. And he doesn't want Mom and Dad to come and embarrass us either, she thought, knowing this as surely as she knew the sound of Joshua's voice from that of everyone else's. Jessie looked down at the backs of her hands and turned them over. I can talk them out of this argument, she thought. Should I? Would I just be bossy if I did that?

"Oh, just draw something," said Joshua, shoving at Martha. "I don't care."

"Fine. A picture of you maybe, saying 'I'm just a lazy bum!' "

"Just so it doesn't have a heart on it anywhere with our initials in it!"

Martha gasped. "You're horrible," she said in a choked voice, and Jessie knew Martha was about to cry, if she wasn't in tears already.

She got up and went to the doorway. "Hey, look!" she said, louder than the two of them.

They turned around. Martha held on to Joshua's shirtsleeve while she did this. She had begun to cry, and the effort to stop the tears had made her nose a splotchy red. Joshua was so angry he was white around the mouth. His Adam's apple looked sharp enough to cut through his throat as it slid up and down.

"Come on," Jessie said, looking at Joshua. "Take the paper into the dorm, get whoever is fooling around in the living room to write a couple of jokes on it and draw a picture of their dreams or nightmares last night or something, and you bike that down to the press before four o'clock. That gives you at least an hour on the piano."

"I absolutely *have* to give it to them this afternoon," Martha said angrily. "They're going to set the type on Monday."

"Okay?" said Jessie, looking straight at Joshua. "What's the matter with you anyway? I'm usually the one who's late with stuff like this."

"You Howellses are too much," said Martha, tightening her lips and shaking Joshua with the grip she still had on his shirtsleeve.

"Let go of me," growled Joshua, and he pulled his shoulder out of Martha's grasp. He breathed through his nose in short, furious snorts and made his eyes little and snarly when he looked back at her. "All right! I'll get your stupid page done." He stalked off across the grass toward the dorm.

"You'd better! By four o'clock! Do you hear me?" she shouted after him, her forehead and cheeks turning a dull red.

Kids on the playing field heard her and turned their heads to look at Jessie and Martha on the school porch. Jessie thought it was a good thing they couldn't see that Martha was in tears. They'd have begun teasing her right away. "Martha loves Joshua, Martha loves Joshua," they'd sing.

"I hate him! I *hate* him!" Martha gasped, wiping her eyes with the back of her hand. "It's so embarrassing to keep asking the men at the press to give me an extra day and having to tell Aunt Letitia why I haven't got the paper in. He's done this to me *twice* already! I hate being late, and I hate it when other people make me late, too. He doesn't have a good reason, Jess. He's just being ornery."

"Come on," said Jessie. She thought about putting her arm around Martha but didn't. Martha didn't like being touched in sympathy. "You know Joshua hates it when he can't practice in the afternoon. He'll be sorry later, and he'll do it. Anyway, you've only got three more of these things to get out, and then the year's over, and we're done with Hope School forever."

"Yeah, and then I go back to America, and you go off to Schutz in Egypt, and Joshua finds some other girl there, and everything's ruined."

"Joshua's not about to fall for any girl," said Jessie, laughing to herself, partly from Martha's dramatic grouchiness and partly because she woke right up to the reminder that soon they'd be getting their passports, soon she'd be there, in an airport, in that linen suit . . . brown maybe, or tan— Mom would never let her have a white travel suit. Maybe she'd have Joshua's palm-wood buttons put on the jacket instead of saving them for some later, more important time. She'd be standing in line, all the adults coming off the plane, wherever, Dakar maybe, or Lagos or Khartoum, and in Cairo, too. And she'd come up to the official at the desk inside the airport building. She'd reach into her purse—she and Mom would have to buy a real purse, an African snakeskin . . . well, maybe just dyed leather with leopard fur around the bottom . . . Anyway, she'd take her passport out and just hand it over, and the customs official would flip it open and look down at her picture and up at her to be sure the passport was hers, and he would look at the exit and entry visas. She'd have her health card showing she wasn't carrying typhoid or cholera; she'd carry her own ticket proving she was going to Egypt. Till now, Dad had carried all the tickets on their trips, and she and Joshua and Cassie were still on Mom's passport. Mom would have to get a new one, with only Cassie on it. In the airports, after this, the official would stamp a page in her passport, showing she'd come through Nigeria or the Sudan or Ghana on her way to Egypt. She'd travel all her life and fill her passports with visa stamps. Anyway, after she'd gone through the formal airport entry, she and Wheat and Sam and Joshua would make their way to the transit lounge with all the other passengers. They'd sit there, and everybody would look at her and wonder that she was the only girl traveling with the guys; the people looking at them would all wonder about those teenagers traveling alone, doing just as well as any adults could manage . . . no matter what happened.

Jessie breathed in deeply, enjoying the salty sensation in her chest, the sensation of stretching into the time of being an adult, enjoying it, because she was going to be good at traveling, being older, living on her own in a new place. . . .

Jessie leaned against the door frame while Martha went back to her desk and lifted the lid, looking for her homework texts. Poor Martha. Martha was going to miss the fun of that trip without any adults, flying up the African continent. Then Jessie reminded herself of the way Martha saw this thing she would miss.

"Nothing matters as much to Joshua as playing the piano," Jessie said, trying to comfort her roommate. "Besides, you'll come to Schutz the year after that. You can try again then."

"What would you know about it," muttered Martha, crushing an old homework paper and throwing it all the way across the room into the trash can.

"Nothing," admitted Jessie, feeling free and superior about her detachment from interest in boys. She could see a complicated and messy thing was happening to Martha's reason and emotions. Jessie tried to imagine what Martha was feeling like, but she kept remembering it was Joshua that Martha was going soft over, and he wasn't anything to inspire one. Jessie pushed her hair back behind both ears, faintly remembering the pleasure she'd had in contemplating her face the last time she looked in the mirror. It wasn't that she thought herself beautiful, only that she knew herself to be interesting in looks and inside herself.

She could persuade herself that Wheat or Sam was interesting as more than the kind of cousin-brothers they really were to her, but then, thought Jessie, she knew that she was persuading herself, whereas Martha apparently couldn't help the way she felt. She said carefully, "I don't know what your problem is, really. I don't think Joshua's about to fall in love with anybody, though. I don't see what you can do about it if he does. So I don't see why you should worry yourself sick."

"Let me alone," Martha growled, baring her teeth at Jessie.

Martha was going to be edgy and sour all afternoon if

Jessie didn't get her attention away from the fight with Joshua. So as they walked from the classroom building to the dorm, she said, "I began working an idea out with Wheat for a kind of neat project to do sometime before we graduate from Hope School. Something to do together on a weekend. What if we painted the back wall in the dining room?"

"What for? Anyway, no matter what color it is, the food will still be awful."

"No, I mean paint something on it," said Jessie, dragging her patience back to her intention to distract Martha. "A map."

"Oh, a map," said Martha. "Lovely. Great. Just what everyone wants to look at while we eat disgusting oatmeal and disgusting meat loaf and disgusting tapioca pudding."

"Martha, cut it out," said Jessie in sharp tones.

"Why? You think the disgusting meat loaf is as disgustingly bad as I do."

"Of course. Everybody does. But you're just being awful on principle. So cut it out. It's what you tell me all the time when I'm grouching on you."

"Okay, okay. I'll try to pretend some interest. A map of what? The Holy Land?" said Martha, in a resigned, mincing, and falsely jolly tone. She didn't want to be cheered up, but Jessie rolled her eyes to the blue sky, telling Martha she was ignoring that fact. "Oh, maybe a map of the missionary journeys of Paul! How nice! How appropriate!" Martha exclaimed, pushing hard on her sarcasm.

"Good grief, no. A map of Cameroun," said Jessie promptly. It was going to be okay. Martha's grouchiness was already a shade lighter than it had been a minute ago. "Wheat and I thought if we painted the outline, then we could get all the kids from each mission station to figure out something to stand for that place, and we could paint it where the station belongs on the map. You know, like the first church at Efulan or the hospital at Metet or the two classroom buildings we have at Libamba or something."

"Yeah? That's not a bad idea," said Martha, interested in spite of herself.

"I know," said Jessie modestly, pleased with the idea and pleased with Martha's return to good humor. "Anyway, thinking about it keeps my mind off Mom and Dad being here next week."

"Are you still nervous about them coming?" Martha lifted her right arm to rub an itch by her cheek. The top three books on the pile she was carrying slid off and fell into the grass. Jessie stooped to pick up the book nearest her. When she handed the science textbook to Martha, she looked over the pile and saw a small red car coming up the lane.

"Look," said Martha, pointing to the lane with her chin. Any car coming to the dorm was interesting. They might see one car a week besides Uncle Walker's own little gray Deux Chevaux. An unfamiliar car was interesting and un- usual. For a flashing moment Jessie thought it might be the green Libamba carryall, and swift delight flew up in her. She saw herself running over the grass to greet Mom and Dad, to hug Dad and see his face and hear his laugh.

Jessie and Martha knew on sight all the cars belonging to Presbyterian missionaries. This one was not a missionary's car. It probably came from Ebolowa, the town nearest the mission stations of Elat and Enongal.

The two girls stood still on the lawn, watching as Uncle Walker came out of the dorm and went down the front steps to meet the Frenchman getting out of the red Renault. Jessie knew he was French by his khaki shirt and shorts and the dark pointed shoes he wore. And besides, he had a self-important, officious air about him, the sort proclaiming that he was in charge. As he got out of the car, the man was unbuttoning his left shirt pocket. He shook hands with Uncle Walker and then took a long, thin yellow envelope out of the pocket and gave it to the housefather.

A telegram envelope, thought Jessie.

"Come on," said Martha. "Let's get four o'clocks, and then let's find Wheat and go ask Uncle Walker if we can plan that map project. It sounds interesting, the more I think about it."

"Yeah, okay," said Jessie, following Martha into the dorm by the side door. She couldn't bring her mind right back to the project, though. She was remembering a conversation she'd had with Mom two years ago, before coming back to Hope School for the second term. "What if something went wrong at home?" she had asked. "Letters take a week or more. How would you let us know?" And Mom had said easily, "Oh, we'd send a telegram, of course."

Well, Jessie was probably borrowing trouble. There were probably lots of reasons Uncle Walker himself would get a telegram.

When she went into the study hall through the side door, Jessie slowed a minute to let her eyes adjust from the brightness of the afternoon to the dim light inside. The dorm's bicycle racks were just in front of the doorway, and more than once Jessie had run right into a bicycle left hanging partway out of its stall, because she hadn't seen it in time.

Cassie was there by the book boxes, on the other side of the ranks of bicycles. When she saw Jessie, she called out excitedly, "Jess! Jess! Guess what!"

"What?" said Jessie without enthusiasm. Cassie asked her that every time she saw her and never had news Jessie thought worth the time it took to think up the three necessary wrong answers for the game.

"Look what I can do! Look! I can't wait to show Mom and Dad!" Cassie pulled a sheet of lined paper from her book box and held it out to Jessie. Jessie looked at it without touching the paper. In round, laboriously scripted letters, Cassie had written: "I can write cursiv! evry letter off the alyebet."

"That's nice," said Jessie. "*Alphabet* is spelled with *ph*, not *y*. And you left a couple of *e*'s out of some words."

"Let me see that," said Martha, and she took the page from Cassie carefully. "That's really good," said Martha.

"You really draw your letters. Look at those clear *e*'s and *l*'s, Jess." And Martha held the paper out to Jessie again.

"Yeah, I saw," said Jessie carelessly, standing on tiptoe to shove her books into her book box. It was on the top row, and Cassie was standing right below it, so Jessie had to reach over her sister to get everything in place. "I said it was good."

"When did you start doing cursive?" asked Martha.

"We've been learning it all week," said Cassie proudly, "but I'm the only one who can really do it right so far."

 "I'll have to ask Michael to show me his," said Martha. "We can't have a Howells beating a MacLeod." She and Cassie laughed together. Michael was Martha's little brother, also in the third grade. "You've really got something to show your parents when they get here," said Martha. "They'll be proud of you."

"I can't wait!" said Cassie, hopping from one foot to the other. Her enthusiasm drove Jessie's right out of her.

Jessie walked ahead of Martha and Cassie down the long back porch to the snack table by the tall brown ceramic water filters. She made faces to herself as she walked, little smiley goody-goody expressions to show what she thought of Martha being so sweet and sisterly to Cassie. Martha did it because she thought Jessie wasn't nice enough to Cassie, wasn't comforting and motherly enough, wasn't doing what she ought to as an older sister at the dorm.

Well, too bad for Martha. Too bad for Cassie, too. They

could please each other. Something about being close to Cassie made Jessie's neck start to swell on the inside. Her throat got tight, as though she'd eaten something too sweet or too creamy to swallow comfortably. No big kid had looked at Jessie's good spelling papers when she was in the third grade and said nice things to her, or wanted to see the A's in social studies and geography and composition she'd gotten since then. And no big kid had ever comforted her when she'd been a homesick little twerp in the first years at the dorm.

Cassie would have to learn just the way she had, thought Jessie grimly. It was boarding school from now until the end of college, and everything done would be achieved at a distance from Mom and Dad and from their deserved, desired approval. She was actually doing Cassie a favor by not giving her the attention. That way she wouldn't miss it as much later on. Jessie clenched her lips together tight over her determination.

"You sick or something?" inquired Wheat, helping himself to the cold buttered pancakes the dorm cook had put out for afternoon snack. When Jessie glared at him, Wheat shrugged and changed the subject. "Listen. I saw Uncle Walker in his office just now. Want to go in and ask him about doing the map on the wall?"

"Sure," said Jessie through her mouthful of pancake. She started to follow Wheat, the idea of the map on the wall growing more real as she went, but in the middle of the dining room she thought of the telegram. It was like seeing a danger sign in the roadway. Keep away, keep clear, it seemed to say. Bridge out ahead.

Oh, I am stupid, thought Jessie with fine scorn for herself. Really! If it was something about us, about Joshua, Cassie, and me, he'd already have told us. He'd have gotten us right away.

In the background, out on the part of the front porch doubling as the dorm's chapel, Joshua was practicing scales on the piano: One-two-three-four-five-six-seven-eight, eight-seven-six-five-four-three-two-one, *chum-chum*; and he changed key in chords and began going up again.

Wheat stopped at the door to the office and looked back for Jessie. She came around the end of a dining table, looking hard at the long-familiar pattern of yellow lines and gray checks on the oilcloth, trying not to show her reluctance. After all, she wasn't holding back because of the map project—she didn't want Wheat to think that and then quit on the idea. She couldn't have explained to anybody why she thought the telegram was bad news for her.

Wheat knocked on the doorjamb. Uncle Walker was sitting at his desk behind immense piles of papers and books that had been there so long they had gathered dust. He did not look up immediately. Wheat knocked again, and Jessie looked over his shoulder and between the book stacks to see what the housefather was doing.

He was staring at the narrow yellow strip of paper on the desk before him. When he looked up at the second knock, he met Jessie's eyes immediately, and Jessie knew by the shock in his expression that he'd been thinking about her.

"Oh! Jessie!" he said, although Wheat stood in front of her in the doorway. "I, uh, I was just . . . getting ready to, uh, call you. And your brother," he added.

"I can come back later," said Wheat. "If this isn't a good time, that is. Jessie and I have a thing, an idea, we wanted to talk to you about, but . . ."

"Later would be better. Would you please go and bring Joshua here, Wheat?" Something was the matter with Uncle Walker's voice. It was too soft, too tight and quiet.

"Sure," said Wheat, and when he turned around he shrugged and made an I-don't-know-what's-the-matter-with-him gesture with his eyebrows. Jessie smiled in spite of the chilly trembling in her midriff. But as soon as Wheat was gone, there was nothing between her and the telegram. Jessie's throat began to hurt; no, it was her chest that hurt, throbbing; no, her skin tingled on her back and down between her ribs and in her wrists. No, not even that. It was her bones that hurt in her wrists, her bones were watery. She shivered and leaned against the wooden door frame.

"Come in," said Uncle Walker, still using that voice of dead quiet. He looked terrible. He looked like something huge was pressing on him from the top of his head; his eyes had new thick, pouchy wrinkles under them. At least, Jessie didn't remember seeing the bags there this morning. And his cheeks sagged. His mouth was down at the corners. He sat hunched in the revolving office chair. Jessie had the impression the weight was something concerning him as well as her, but he was already feeling sorry for her.

She sat on the edge of the bench along the wall, which was also loaded with books, file folders, and stacks of papers. She waited, everything in her concentrating in a single small point in her stomach. She could feel the bits of pancake settling heavily in her gullet.

In the background, Jessie listened to Joshua's scales going on and on, and then Joshua stopped running the scales, abruptly, in midoctave. Somehow the sound of that interruption was more ominous than the sight of the yellow telegram Uncle Walker was now smoothing gently on his desk blotter.

Joshua came to the door of the office, breathing hard with suppressed irritation. Wheat was behind him.

"Come in," said Uncle Walker, and both boys came in. "No, well, I meant just Joshua."

"Oh, sorry," said Wheat. When he went this time, Jessie wanted to call out, Oh, don't leave us!

"I have bad news," said Uncle Walker in the ordinary voice he used to announce meetings of the stamp club or the new chore lists. "I need to ask you if you want Cassie here while I tell it to you or if you'd rather tell her yourselves later." Jessie noticed that when he stopped talking, his lips trembled. She thought about her heart. Her mind worked, but all her feelings were getting thick in the middle of her, shooting sparks of something like excitement but darker and sharper, as if this tightness in her was almost a blade ready to stab.

"What is it?" asked Joshua shortly. He was still thinking, or being, at the piano, thought Jessie, amazed. Didn't he notice that dread thickened the air in the room?

"Here, I think you should read this," said the house-father, and he held out the telegram. The little yellow paper crackled in his fingers. Joshua took one end of it and Jessie took hold of the other corner. They read it together.

Matthew, Alida Howells missing since 3/18.
Forest abduction feared.
Official notice taken 3/26. Tell children. George Good.

Aie! After that single sound, which came out of Jessie in a kind of whisper and groan, she felt nothing at all. The tightness, cut by the blade, had vanished, and now she was hollow inside.

She stared at the words on the yellow slip. She understood everything that was meant in the telegram, understood how awful it really was, but she was completely calm, empty, without word or thought. She might have fallen asleep, except there was a faint, hurting thud way off in the background. In her chest and not in her chest at the same time.

Beside her, Joshua sighed deeply, through his nose. He sounded like Dad, thought Jessie, and the far-off hurt trembled like a threatening flame. Jessie looked sideways at

Joshua and saw his nostrils flared, white and pinched, with the effort to hold back tears. She had no tears and not the slightest desire to cry.

"What about Cassie?" asked Uncle Walker.

"Ohhh," said Joshua softly. "Oh." It was a little, plaintive sound made in the back of his throat.

"Maybe she'd rather hear it from you," said Uncle Walker gently. "But Aunt Pearl and I will do it if you want."

"No!" said Jessie, with more feeling than she knew she had left in her. That would be too terrible for Cassie to bear. To be told by the houseparents, the not-parents, that Mom and Dad weren't—were . . . that something had happened to them to make them . . . what? What would she and Joshua say to Cassie?

"What about Bible Conference?" asked Joshua, and now Jessie felt something, a long, stinging pang, and she was ashamed of it. She felt deprived—not of her parents, but of being able to show them off to all the other kids. Thoughts—all of them the wrong ones—roiled and slid up against each other inside Jessie now, and as soon as she recognized them, they were stifled. She couldn't hold her mind still.

"Well, I don't know what we should do about that," said Uncle Walker. "I'm going up the hill to Enongal to talk about that. And to tell them about—this." And he tapped the telegram. Enongal was the hospital station. Maybe Uncle Don and Aunt Eleanor would do Bible Conference. Jessie would like that. How could she like anything? Mom and

Dad were missing, gone. What was the matter with her head and her heart?

"I saw her last with Martha," said Jessie dully when Joshua asked where Cassie was. "Maybe they're upstairs together." But along with the great emptiness in her was this new and terrible confusion of what to think next and what not to think, that she was thinking anyway.

Jessie felt enormously tired; the thought of climbing the two long flights of stairs to the second floor, and then walking along both halls on the girls' side, calling for her sister, was so huge and heavy that she couldn't say the expected thing: "I'll go look." What she really wanted to do was read a book, a good Cherry Ames mystery; she'd read all of them over and over, so she wouldn't have to wonder how the end worked out. A book would order the words clashing together inside her and lift the heaviness off of her brain.

"Come on," said Joshua, getting up from the bench. He took Jessie's hand and tugged. Jessie got up slowly, feeling every muscle in her knees and calves and ankles, even to her toes, tensing to carry her weight, as if she were suddenly much more than her blood and bones and skin. Well, this was interesting to think about, Jessie said to her listening mind. What more could I be besides myself? A boat, a canoe, and someone is throwing bales and baggage into me, stones maybe, filling me up and maybe I'll sink.

"We'll go find Cassie," Joshua said to the housefather.

"Let's not worry too much," said Uncle Walker soothingly, getting up from his chair. Jessie released her inner attention, listening to the housefather. She had the idea he was forcing himself to give them this reassurance. "I'm sure Bible Conference will work out. That's the least of our problems. Your worry won't help. And nothing bad has really happened, so far."

As we know, thought Jessie immediately. If only he hadn't spoken. Now that he'd said not to worry, useless concern leaped into life in her. She saw tree trunks crashing over the road, blocking a car—the carryall—front and back, and then dark men with guns, leaping from the bush at the side of the road, leaping over the ditch, arms out to yank the car doors open, to grab Mom and Dad out, dragging them off the road through the bush, through leaves weighted with red dust that closed again immediately behind them and showed only by the dust brushed off the green where the abduction had taken place. And so soon, the dust would have covered over any trace. Then what? Now what? What next?

Let's not worry too much. Right. How was she to stop the run of worry words swarming up and down the scale endlessly, tunelessly, patting and prodding her feelings back into recognition, back up from the thick wadding that covered her heart and kept her from needing Mom and Dad, from knowing how much she wanted them, and always would.

7

*In the Time
of Trouble*

As if he knew that Jessie couldn't do it herself, Joshua asked Elissa Janeway, Wheat's younger sister, to run upstairs and look for Cassie. He let go of her hand after they'd got out of Uncle Walker's office, and Jessie felt him do that, knew the warm pressure of his fingers and then a sense of his absence even though they walked close enough to each other for his arm to brush hers. Joshua walked faster. She seemed to be moving but going nowhere.

Her eyes focused heavily on the gray cement floor of whatever room they were going through, dining room, hall by the staircase, front porch. She kept the backs of Joshua's dirty, fraying tennis shoes at the periphery of her vision and followed him to the chapel. The floor was polished by de-

cades of steady use, packs of shuffling or running feet crossing and recrossing it.

And then there was all the sweeping, thought Jessie.
How many times in the six years she'd been at Hope School
had she swept the hall and the chapel and the front porch
during morning chores? Well, if she took five months of
school in a term and broke it down into twenty, maybe
twenty-two weeks and figured how often the weekly chore
rotation brought her back to sweeping this area . . . She
began the calculation on the fingers of her left hand and
noticed on her palm by her little finger a tiny blob of butter
from the cold pancake she'd just eaten. Her gorge rose, and
she had to swallow hard to quell the urge to throw up.

Everything was making her sick. Thinking of anything
—even the thought of her passport made her sick. She
longed to be asleep. She wanted to talk. But all the words
in all the books in the world wouldn't be enough to say
what she meant. Then she knew she meant nothing. She
had no sense of what was happening that she could put into
words. But even so, she knew she wanted someone who
really cared about her to help her listen to the roaring inside her.

Who would that be? Martha? Not likely. Martha wanted
to listen to Joshua these days. Mendômô? And why on earth
had she thought of Mendômô just now? Jessie warmed a
little to the memory of the sudden, immediate heart sharing
between herself and Mendômô this past vacation. The
warmth brought a longing to be with Mendômô. Then Jessie

had a sense of being imprisoned in the walls of the dorm, clutched and restrained by the simple fact of being fourteen in a boarding school and having nowhere to go.

"I can't find her!" yelled Elissa, thumping down the stairs. "Joshua! I don't know where she is, but she's not upstairs!"

Joshua had gone back to the piano. He sat there without playing anything. Now he swung around on the piano stool and called without energy, "Thanks, Elissa," and then in the same tired voice said to Jessie, "Let's walk around and look outside. Stop pressing your head into the bricks," he added. "It looks stupid."

"Right," said Jessie, and the warmth of her breath startled her as she mumbled the word into the wall. She lifted her head, and the skin on her forehead stung from the rough texture of the bricks. She noticed that when Joshua spoke to her, the curious wordless pressure receded inside her head. Maybe she'd imagined all this. Not the telegram, she hadn't. Aware that she was short of breath, Jessie tried to fill her chest with air and couldn't. Maybe going someplace with Joshua would get her breathing again.

As she watched Joshua walking down the chapel aisle to the place where she stood, Jessie saw one of her daydreams come and go in a tiny gasping flash.

There was a table covered with a white cloth and a slant of afternoon sunshine on Mom's old crystal rose bowl filled with blue and yellow flowers among narrow green leaves. The bowl was set between two small cakes decorated with blue and yellow candles. There were green ribbons trailing across the white cloth under the silver dessert forks from Grandma Howells, marked with the fancy engraved *H*; a ribbon curved around Mom's Wedgwood dessert plates, stacked and waiting for the cake to be served.

In the moment after the image was granted and then snatched from her sight, Jessie knew clearly she had always believed in a time in the future, although she had no idea where it would be, when she and Joshua would celebrate their birthday at home again. Their birthday came in October, and since the first grade, they'd had it at school, celebrating with Mom and Dad at a distance.

Suddenly, as she came out of the dimness of the dorm's porch and covered her eyes against the glaring African afternoon sunlight, Jessie knew they would never get the blessing of that time other families had with each other, stretched out over days and months and years in the same house. That time was spent, gone, in separation.

This was true for everyone at the dorm, but for the Howellses, for herself and Joshua and Cassie, the telegram really meant that no one was home anymore, even for visits. *Ah, Jesus!* she shouted in a great, silent shout. A small flame of sorrow blazed sharp and fierce and high. *We gave it up for You!* shouted her heart.

Jessie was startled by the passion rising and falling in her and held perfectly still, barely breathing. She had a sense that the words of her heart and her fury together were being listened to; and then she was astonished to find she was clean of the whole feeling, with the speed of a single normal breath, in and out. The daydream, too, was gone completely. She couldn't even bring the faintest image of it to mind. Some memory remained, a rounded hard thing in her chest. What was it? Ah, it was yellow on the edges, yellow like the telegram.

Her hands were cold little lumps hanging from her wrists. She pressed her right knuckles into the opposite palm and felt colder. Mom often talked of how cold she felt in her fingers and toes. Was it possible that Mom was dead and Jessie was suddenly getting bits of Mom in a weird, ghostly sort of inheritance?

Mom was not dead. And *that* would be the last time she would think it.

Swiftly Jessie drew herself together, iron in her heart. She felt swept and bare of hope, but she had strength to turn her back immediately on the temptation to imagine anything drawn from death. Joshua had gone on while she'd been standing—how long? Forever and hardly at all, it seemed—on the top step. He was only a few feet away. She hurried to catch up with him.

Ahead of her, she saw a big crowd of dorm kids gathered on the tennis court, where the game of six-square was played. The ball should have been bouncing back and forth, making a round, high *ping!* each time it hit the roughened cement. Wheat was in A-square, as usual, his long legs and arms giving him the advantage over everyone else in scooping the ball from the corners of his territory and sending it beyond reach of whoever was in B- or C-square. He wasn't playing, though. No one was playing.

They were gathered around someone Jessie couldn't see, making a knot in B-square. And there was Cassie, only one braid with a green ribbon on it now. She must have had two ribbons on when she came down to devotions and breakfast this morning. Jessie couldn't remember seeing Cassie this morning. Now Cassie was pushing at the edge of the crowd, with a bunch of other little kids, to get closer to whoever was in the middle. When Jessie and Joshua came to the cement paving of the court, someone gave the warning to hush, and everyone turned to look at the twins.

Apprehension and a greedy kind of curiosity made their eyes round and bright. As if they can't help liking our trouble, thought Jessie, noticing how the kids looked from her to Joshua, Joshua to her. Everyone stared at them, as if, thought Jessie, we were going to do something excitingly horrible, break out in blood from our foreheads or throw up on each other. Maybe they were waiting to see if the Howells twins would start crying. Somehow, Jessie was sure, the kids on the tennis court already knew the news.

Cassie didn't know. Jessie could tell, because she was arguing with some fourth-grade boys about having been sixth in line before Wheat's brother Andrew had started telling everybody something. Whatever he'd said. "What did he say?" Cassie asked. "I didn't hear," she complained. "What's going on?"

"Is it true?" asked Martha, looking over the heads of

most of the kids standing between her and Jessie. Jessie nodded.

"Who's going to come for Bible Conference, then?" yelled little David Brumbaugh. He certainly had a grasp of the important things, thought Jessie.

"My parents are! You know that!" said Cassie scornfully.

"They can't!" said Penny Robertson, a fourth grader with whom Cassie often fought over turns and places at the table and in lines.

"They are too," protested Cassie.

"Hey," said Joshua softly, drawing the word out a little, and everyone looked at him, Cassie included. "They aren't coming," he said to her quietly, just barely shaking his head.

"They're not?" gasped Cassie, angry and disbelieving. And then as Jessie watched, belief came fast and robbed her sister, as though she had all along suspected something would go wrong and her heart's desire be taken away after all. Cassie stared at Joshua; now her face was still, but her eyes filled and then her nostrils flared, her lips tightened and a line of tears ran over her right cheek and dripped from her jaw.

"Oh, Cassie," said Martha in a motherly voice, crossing the court and putting both arms around the little girl. Cassie stood and allowed herself to be hugged without yielding to the comfort. She sobbed, sucking for air, trying to swallow the sounds. Kids moved away, uncomfortable with the weeping, uncomfortable with the whole thing. Joshua motioned with his head, so that Jessie understood he meant they should go over to where Martha was still patting Cassie and talking to her quietly.

All right, thought Jessie. Sure. Why not? She won't want me, and I don't feel like comforting anyone, but it's the thing I have to do, isn't it?

At this, hot resentment stabbed Jessie, cutting through to that thudding ache in her chest that had first come to her in the moments in Uncle Walker's office when he'd given them the telegram. (What had she done with that? She couldn't remember putting it down or giving it back. She patted her jumper pocket—nothing there.) What good was doing the right thing? She had no strength herself. She needed what Cassie needed. And what good was getting comfort? Jessie could see quite plainly that comfort now would not bring the family safely together again.

Oh, Cassie! Jessie heard that little, sad sound of Joshua's in the office, when he'd thought of telling her the news, and then Jessie's heart had hurt for Cassie. But now, now she felt nothing except mean pinching in her chest, which narrowed her eyes and forced her tongue against her lower teeth.

All Jessie could think was wrong to be thinking. Her mind and heart and feelings were in constant disagreement. Somewhere above all this, Jessie watched herself not moving, not doing her share of comforting Cassie and being sisterly, being loving. I don't care. I really don't care, she thought. They can be gone forever—and that thudding ache became something ragged right close to the base of her throat, and she was about to cry. She was lying to herself. Of course it mattered that they not be gone forever!

"Hey, Jess, what happened?" asked Meba Noe. The sound of her voice made the truth seem like just so much gossip. The words struck Jessie as if Meba had thrown stones at her. Jessie shrugged.

Others crowded around her; she'd have had to push them aside to be with Joshua and Cassie. Instead of being the kids they really were, whom she'd known while brushing teeth and doing housekeeping chores and singing hymns together, they now seemed horribly like strangers she was supposed to entertain with her trouble.

Wheat hung back, but he was watching her. When she met his eyes, he moved toward the group gathering around her. Jessie breathed again and knew herself to be not so alone as she'd thought. She thought about Wheat's green seersucker pajamas; he'd had them for three years, until the bottoms were tight against his calves. She smiled at him.

Wheat asked, "What did he say?"

"Who?" demanded Meba.

"Uncle Walker got a telegram, and Jessie and I were in the office when he told me to go get Joshua," said Wheat. "My dear brother Andrew was hanging around under the office windows and heard him talking, but we all know how reliable Andrew's gossip is."

"Oh, yeah, Andrew was the one who told us Uncle Walker was buying a crocodile as a dorm pet," said Lynnie Page. "I remember."

"What did he say?" asked Wheat again, and by his urging her to talk, Jessie was set free from her shocked silence, which made everyone around her seem like strangers. She looked at Wheat as she talked.

"The telegram says that my parents were abducted in the forest, and that means, I think, by the Maquis." Wheat's family lived in Edéa, in the heart of Bassa territory. He knew about the Maquis.

"So what does that mean?" asked Isaac Keller, the only sixth grader in the school that year.

"I don't know," said Jessie. "It means they aren't coming—" And she had to draw breath quickly and pretend to rub her nose hard to keep tears from rushing out. She wouldn't let these kids feel sorry for her! She *wouldn't!* And that's enough, said a dry, steely voice of her own to her softer feelings. The tears obediently hardened in flow.

"What did he say about Bible Conference? Or didn't you ask?" said Wheat, still quiet and calm.

Jessie knew she loved him. He made her feel whole and able to think straight again. "Yeah, Joshua did. He said he was going up the hill to talk about it with someone."

"There he is!" called Phoebe Peel, pointing. Everybody turned to watch the housefather getting into his little gray Deux Chevaux. The group of them faced him in unnatural stillness as he drove by the tennis court and down the lane.

He looked at them gravely, and he did not smile or wave.

The group broke up when Isaac knocked the ball out of Wheat's elbow and claimed A-square for himself. The game reformed itself with lots of arguing. Everyone was louder than normal to cover their confusion. Jessie understood this. It was partly why she ached so to talk, fast and long, about anything at all and nothing in particular.

And Cassie still didn't know what everyone else knew.

As kids milled around, arguing about their place in line, Jessie went slowly over to Joshua and said, staring down at the dirty broken shoelace on his left shoe, "She doesn't really know yet."

Joshua didn't say anything. Jessie wanted to punch him, to get an answer out of him. She wanted something aloud. He sighed as if he agreed with her. This next thing was going to be worse than living with the fact that Mom and Dad were missing, but he glared at Jessie as though it were her fault that Cassie had to be told.

"Come for a walk with us, little heart," said Joshua, and his gentle tone was like a soothing finger laid across Jessie's arm.

"Together?" asked Cassie, sniffling.

"Yeah. Together," said Jessie. "Why? Aren't we allowed to go around together?" Her voice sounded too loud to her.

"You don't like it," said Cassie.

Jessie laughed, embarrassed. "Got me," she said. She put her arm awkwardly around Cassie's shoulders. Cassie shifted uneasily in the embrace, and the little hairs sticking out of her braids irritated Jessie's skin. Even so, they walked in step, following Joshua across the lane to the merry-go-round.

Joshua sat up on one of the old gray plumbing pipes used for the railings, waiting for them with his legs dangling toward the boards of the merry-go-round. Jessie saw an unripe grapefruit rolling back and forth under his feet. When she and Cassie climbed on with him, they also sat on the railings, at the center of the sort of arching web the pipe railings made over the boards. This meant that each of them would face a different direction while they talked. Jessie felt there was something the matter with this arrangement, and she got down to stand on the boards so she could see both Joshua and Cassie. "Listen," she said to Cassie. "We know why Mom and Dad aren't coming."

"They promised! They never really care about us. They only care about those stupid old students at Libamba. Why did they have us if they didn't want to be with us at all! I hate them, and I'm going to hate them the rest of my life for this!"

What scared Jessie about Cassie's words was that Cassie wasn't crying. And then she knew that Cassie's words were her own. Jessie began, "They would have come if they could," and Cassie cut her off.

"We're always second. We're always after their work. If they really loved us, they'd keep their promise."

Joshua moved uneasily on the railing. "But they can't," he said. "Don't you see, Cassie? This isn't about whether they love us or not. This is about the troubles at Libamba. You know. The fighting between the Maquis and the French."

"Oh," said Cassie, puzzled. What did she see? wondered Jessie.

"Mom and Dad got caught somehow in the middle of something—and they're gone. They're missing, some— somewhere in the forest." Joshua inhaled a huge breath and blew it out loudly through his mouth.

"Really?" Cassie asked, swinging around to look at Joshua. She didn't lose her balance, although Jessie had expected that and moved to catch her. "That's all?"

Neither twin could answer. When Jessie met Joshua's glance, she read her own uneasy bewilderment in his quick look away. Then Jessie understood. At first Cassie thought that Mom and Dad had decided not to come; she thought they had done it on purpose, as if they loved her less than their work. Absolutely nothing could be worse than that. So of course Cassie didn't think their being stuck in the forest was so bad, because now she knew they hadn't changed their minds. Cassie, Jessie figured, must think Mom and Dad were only delayed.

"That's all," Jessie said, laughing a little. Somehow Cassie had made it a very simple thing. Maybe.

"What do you mean, missing somewhere?" Cassie asked suddenly, sounding suspicious now.

"How should I know?" Joshua said, irritated. "Beats me. I mean, we know they're in the forest, with some Maquis, but we don't know where. At least they're with somebody."

"The Maquis aren't lost anyhow," said Jessie, wild and awful laughter bubbling up inside her, shocking her. Joshua caught the laugh from her and grinned.

"I didn't even think about that," he said cheerfully, and he picked up the puny hard green grapefruit from the merry-go-round boards, weighed it, and tossed it back up into the grapefruit tree two yards away. The unripe fruit crashed through the leaves and twigs and bumped back out again to fall heavily to the ground. A flock of weaverbirds scattered into the air, scolding shrilly, darting about above the tree and flying off to perch elsewhere.

"I wonder what you can make out of unripe grapefruit," said Jessie, consciously trying to keep her thoughts away from the little black typed words on that crackling strip of paper: "Forest abduction feared. . . ."

"Marmalade," said Cassie, looking at the green fruit and then at the twins. "Mom told me once. Well, okay," she said, as though they'd settled something among them. She slid off the railing and jumped to the grass. "I'm going back to the game. I was sixth in line, but now they'll feel sorry for me. They'll let me be first if I want."

"Where's your other green ribbon?" asked Jessie.

"I dunno. I don't care," said Cassie, looking back over her shoulder.

"You'd better find it!" warned Jessie. "They don't grow on trees!"

"You're not the boss!" yelled Cassie, running off toward the tennis court.

Joshua laughed. "No shame!" he said.

"She'll probably wet the bed tonight," Jessie said glumly.

Joshua avoided Jessie's eyes, although he grunted his sympathy. The mornings after Cassie wet the bed, Jessie usually helped her take off the sheets and rinse them out. Boarders only got one set of sheets a week, and Jessie agreed with Mom that Cassie could not sleep on stinky dried sheets for however many days were left before clean sheets were issued.

It was easy to imagine how awful that smell and feeling would be. So she would willingly help Cassie rinse the sheets and hang them in the shower to dry, and then later in the afternoon help her make the bed again. It was one of the few ways Jessie did help Cassie, and to Jessie's relief, this term she'd only needed to do it in the first two weeks. Cassie had been dry since then.

"I wish I knew what happened," said Joshua, biting a piece of skin from the side of his thumb. Jessie watched him, a part of her mind saying, Joshua doesn't bite his fingers. He takes care of them. The rest of her mind listened to him moving right on to the real topic, because they both knew there was nothing to be done about Cassie.

"It doesn't make sense," agreed Jessie. "I mean, if the army had kicked them out because of that man in the guest room, or if they'd found guns in the house or something, it would figure. But to be abducted by the Maquis doesn't make any sense at all."

"But I can't believe they'd be hurt by them," said Joshua. "They speak Bassa, for one, and they know what's going on and agree with the Maquis, for two."

"And three, they're from Libamba, which counts for something."

"Why?" asked Joshua, looking over at her from his hunched position on the rails.

"Because last year all the teachers at Libamba signed a formal statement to the United Nations, saying that they supported Cameroun's efforts toward self-determination. And the Maquis know about it."

"Where'd you get all that information?"

"Mom told me while we were doing the washing on the last day at home."

"She never told me," Joshua said, indignant.

"Well, I asked," said Jessie. "It isn't a big secret." She breathed lightly, sniffing at the spice of citrus just ripening. It was an ordinary fragrance, but just then it made her throat swell with sadness.

"Oh." They were silent for a moment, and then it seemed all the weaverbirds in the grapefruit tree burst into chatter to fill the space around the twins. Nothing could touch the silence between them. The feel of it reminded Jessie of the time she'd been sitting next to a strange American boy in a transit lounge of the Paris airport three years ago. After finding out where each of them had been born and where their fathers worked in Africa, they had suddenly come upon nothing more to say. Although Jessie began to think of things she might have talked about, she knew the strange boy would ignore her words. She had that awful feeling about Joshua now. It made her want to hit him or pinch him, to wake him up and force him to be someone from her family instead of just another kid in the dorm.

Joshua said, "I guess I'll go play, too."

"You didn't finish practicing, did you?"

"When did you suddenly take over Martha's job?" Joshua got off the railing. He stretched so hard that Jessie heard his bones crack, and then he said, with his face averted, "Tell Martha to back off, will you?"

"What do you mean? She's got to take the dummy pages down to the press this afternoon, and you did say you'd get people's jokes for that last page, you know. Are you still going to do that?"

"I will if I want to. Anyway, that's not what I meant," said Joshua, and Jessie saw his blush stain the edges of his ears and his skin under the short hairs at the back of his neck. He leaped off the merry-go-round with such force that it rocked and bounced half a revolution while he ran to join the kids on the tennis court.

"I see," said Jessie to his back. "You don't want her to know, and she doesn't want you to know, and I'm supposed to be figuring it out for you two. Well, good grief!" She got off the merry-go-round and wandered across the grass, going nowhere in particular, with a vague idea that she would look for Cassie's lost hair ribbon. Cassie would miss it and want to have it back.

Martha liked hair ribbons. She tied them on her ponytail. Jessie didn't think ribbons looked very grown-up. She pushed her hair behind one ear and thought about bangs. Mom hadn't agreed to cut bangs in Jessie's hair, but Jessie wanted bangs before she went to Egypt. Say she had bangs, and somehow her hair had grown long enough to be curled for a pageboy look, and she was sitting in the departure lounge with Wheat and Sam, and they were playing a game of rook or something. Maybe she'd be reading instead. The *Thurber Carnival*, for instance. Say it was the departure lounge in Douala, with those huge green sofas and armchairs. Joshua always said they must be expecting passengers with giant-sized legs and regular-sized bodies. Even Dad's legs didn't comfortably reach the floor if he sat all the way back in the chairs. . . . Where was he sitting now? Was he sitting down now? Or had he already fallen? Maybe he'd fallen in between the stakes, slipped somehow, curving his body so the stakes were on either side, not through him. . . .

Jessie shivered violently. She needed to be around people, but she didn't want to play a running game, or any game for that matter. She wanted to be doing something real. Something that mattered. All she could do was wait. She clenched her fingers into fists, tight, tight enough to hurt the muscles in her forearms, so when she let go, she felt an ache. It was hard to breathe again, and nowhere that she looked could she see Cassie's missing hair ribbon.

At supper, Uncle Walker tapped his spoon against his water glass until kids on his left and right took it up, bringing conversation all over the four tables to a halt. He stood up so everyone could see him, but Jessie kept her head down, refusing to look.

"I know all of you have heard the news about Aunt Alida and Uncle Matthew," said Uncle Walker.

Jessie was sure kids turned to look at her, and at Joshua and Cassie, too. She ate a forkful of the dry, revolting bullet peas she had intended to hide under her salad plate and throw away when she went out to wash her dishes.

"We're all sorry and concerned, kids," said Uncle Walker.

Isaac Keller, sitting on Jessie's left, touched her briefly on the wrist with his fingers. Jessie looked toward him without moving her head, so she wouldn't see the sympathy in his eyes. She didn't want Uncle Walker to say any more. If he did, and if the others told her how sorry they were, she thought she'd shiver into small pieces inside and start screaming at them. They ached for her, and she couldn't ache at all; she could only feel shards and broken pieces grating against each other, and all her thoughts running fast or stopping short, nothing coming to a quietness where she could rest and be herself.

"So of course Aunt Pearl and I can't go away, as we'd planned to. This means we don't get our annual vacation from each other," Uncle Walker was saying.

"We need it!" yelled Robbie Teller from the far end of Jessie's table.

"No doubt," said Uncle Walker, "and no more than Aunt Pearl and I do, but we're going to have to do our best this year, our best for the Howellses."

What can that mean? wondered Jessie. What good will your best do them? She mashed three slimy rings of boiled onion into a whitish pulp on her plate and added three greeny yellow bullet peas and mashed them, too, as Uncle Walker went on talking in a pleasant tone of voice.

"We haven't got anything planned, the way the Howellses would have had, and rather than trying to do something worthwhile in a hurry, we're going to give everybody a kind of miniature vacation."

"No school?" "Nothing to do but whatever we want?" shouted a couple of kids.

What do I want to do? thought Jessie. She stirred a bit of beef gravy into the smash of vegetables in the center of her yellow Boontonware plate. I want to get out of here. I want to be free of everything here, myself, Joshua, Cassie for sure, having to sleep and wake up and everything be exactly as it is now. . . . Airports have long hallways; I'd have to walk fast to get from the lounge out to the gate and the plane; walking fast would feel good. My heels would click on the floor or out on the tarmac going to the stairs up to the plane. I'd like the sassy grown-up feeling I'd get from the sound of heels on a hard floor. I bet I could get Mom to give in and let me buy heels for the trip. . . . Immediately Jessie had a familiar sense of Mom, unyielding on the matter of high heels, and then, just as fast, a sense of no one, neither opposition nor guidance, and sorrow and loss rushed into the void.

Her head was already down, leaning into her palm; no one noticed, it was too late anyway. Tears fell fast, drops of them, not running together but falling separately into the mess on her plate. Jessie shook her head, appalled at the idea that anyone might see her crying. Stealthily she brought her left hand up and pinched her nose and blinked her eyelids fast to clear the tears still left on her lashes. Then she busied herself positioning her salad plate right over the mashed pile she'd made, hiding it from Aunt Pearl's scrutiny. It was a sin at the dorm to throw away food.

"So, this is the shape we'll give the day, starting tomorrow," Uncle Walker was saying, and Jessie could tell by the lift of his tone and the pause he made that he was coming to the end of whatever he was telling them. "We'll come down to chapel as usual, but without talking, and we'll hear the psalm for the day, and then we'll go to breakfast, still without talking—even though it's a Saturday. Okay?"

Jessie looked up, puzzled. How had she missed the explanation for this weird idea?

"I can't do that!" called Meba Noe. "I can't not talk all that time!"

"We knew that already, loopy lips," called Andrew Janeway. Some of the other boys began chanting the name.

"Boys!" called Uncle Walker.

"Well, we'll just try it, okay?" Aunt Pearl looked encouraging. "We've got to do something that's different, even though we're all the same people in the same place this week." She had a pleading note in her voice, thought Jessie, and recognized at once that Aunt Pearl and Uncle Walker were strongly disappointed at not being able to get away from the dorm for a week. Something with tears in it—not sorrow but self-pity—stung the back of Jessie's throat as she wondered if they blamed her parents for this disappointment.

Later that night, on her way upstairs for bed, Jessie saw a scrap of green hanging from a splinter on the railing. Had she not been looking for it, she'd have missed it altogether. She stooped to see, but it was only a scrap of torn cloth. Joshua, coming behind her, said to Wheat, "The rear view is blocking the way."

Jessie whirled around. "I bet lazybones here didn't get his *Hope School Daze* stuff done for the press, did he?"

"It so happens I did, Miss Boss," Joshua said, brushing past her at the landing and going up the rest of the stairs three at a time. Wheat looked at Jessie and shrugged, following Joshua. "And if I hadn't? What would you do? Get

Martha to fire me? Come to think of it, you could do me that favor. How about it, huh, sis?"

"Grow up, Joshua," said Jessie without turning her head. She used to be able to irk him by reminding him she was the elder of them, born twenty-three minutes before he had been. She didn't care for that game anymore.

She walked onto the girls' side, forcing her feet down with exaggerated quiet; it was another sin at the dorm to wake anyone up who'd already gone to sleep, and the punishment for that was going to bed exactly twelve hours after waking the other person up. Imagine being made to get back into bed at nine o'clock tomorrow morning! In fact it had happened to boys in previous years a couple of times, but closer to noon.

Jessie stopped at Cassie's door anyway, wondering if she ought to check on her sister, wondering in spite of herself if Cassie were lying awake and crying alone in the dark. But it wasn't worth it to find out. How could she comfort Cassie when she herself had nothing comforting to offer? She couldn't say, "We'll see them in just twelve more weeks," or "Think about how nice it'll be to get home. Imagine skating on the dormitory porches!" She couldn't say, "It'll be all right, Cassie." She could only hurt with Cassie, and that Jessie didn't want to do at all.

8

Carrying Water

In the darkness, complete and thick without light anywhere, Jessie suddenly knew she was awake. Some cry had pulled her into thought. Its sound was not repeated. If the sides of her ribs had not felt edgy, she might have slid back into rest again. Something was calling her. The voice pulled; she knew this without hearing it.

She sat up in bed. Right now, she had to decide if this was real, if she was going to get out of bed and answer or pretend the normal things were more true—if you didn't hear with ears, you hadn't really heard.

Crying, like a wire pulling taut through her midriff, pierced and strung her heart.

She tuned her ears and heard nothing, nothing but the

light, constant trilling of night insects. Her fingertips reached through the blackness for the tight, invisible screen of mosquito netting around her and then slid down its surface to untuck a short length of its hem from her mattress so she could slip out and close the bed in again, to keep her sleeping area safe from the danger of malaria.

Out in the pitch-black of the hallway, she opened her eyes wide but saw nothing. Feeling for the corners and the turns, she held her hands out on both sides, stiff armed. She put each foot down carefully. The thinly corrugated black rubber matting in the hall pinched the balls of her feet, but she ignored the stinging after recognizing the sensation. She counted the rooms she passed, naming the gaps in the walls and then the folds of the canvas curtains under her fingertips—Meba and Chloe's, Sarah Lynn and Phoebe's, Lois and Jean's, the sewing room. Now a couple of steps, and she should turn left soon—oh, dreadful to have the whole wall disappear from beneath the reassuring touch of her right hand.

In the sudden black emptiness she stopped walking. What was ahead of her? *When* am I? she thought. What night is this? Saturday? Sunday? I don't remember! Why is this taking so long? What's down there in front of my feet? Is it a hole? I'll fall!

Come on. It's just the wide part of the corner. The wall goes on straight, and the hall turns.

There's only empty blacker blackness—with white pointed stakes waiting down inside—

Don't look at that thought. Don't. Go on. Go forward. You're in the dorm, on the back hall. Don't stand still. That was the first step—see? Now the next one. And the next. Step up soon . . . now. Here are the laundry boxes. Good. Turn right; step down. Wait. Wait now. Listen, to be sure.

Jessie waited, rubbing her toes against the worn mahogany flooring of the hall outside Cassie's room. She could see only gentle blackness, wavering a little where she imagined the whitewashed walls to be. Peaceful sounds of steady, slow breathing and light snoring came over the transoms of the three large rooms where the youngest girls lived.

She'd come for nothing, after all. She'd imagined it all and, like a stupid idiot, had made herself believe. Still, Jessie hesitated. The ache she'd felt in bed was growing sharp again right under her ribs, and now the sound came again, this time out loud.

Little, like a kitten's maybe. Tiny, like something pressed into a small space, needing out, scared to move, desperate—

Quick, quick, before it's too late. Jessie hurried and stubbed her big toe on the doorsill to Cassie's room. She barked her shin on the end of Lorayne's bed, bumped into the corner of the girls' dresser, felt in the dark for Cassie's bed net, with both hands clutching only air, and whispered, "Cassie! Cassie! Wait! Hold it! I'm here. I'll help you!"

Fumbling with the bed net, hearing with regret the little rip she made in it in her haste to help Cassie out, she reached for Cassie, who trembled, warm and just slightly sour smelling. Cassie pressed toward Jessie and then grasped Jessie's left hand and came stumbling behind her as they threaded past the furniture in the room, crossed the front hall, and walked carefully on the cold, damp cement floor of the bathroom, trying to judge the distance between them and the first toilet, just barely visible as a pale blob ahead of them in the dark.

Cassie sighed with sudden relief. In perfect understanding, Jessie smiled into the dark.

"I'm not going to wash my hands," Cassie whispered.

"That's okay, the water's too cold. It'll wake you right up," agreed Jessie, whispering back through a yawn. "I'll tuck you in."

Cassie followed Jessie across the hall again and got into bed. Jessie lifted the mattress edge and tucked the hem of the bed net under it. She tried not to make the net taut, because that would stretch the rip, and somehow mosquitoes always found the hole. Cassie wriggled comfortably in the sheets, blessedly dry, thought Jessie. Cassie sighed again, deeply. "Night," she whispered, and then, "Jess? How did you know?"

"I heard you," whispered Jessie, wondering at the fact.
"Night, little heart." On the way back to bed, she remembered that tomorrow would only be Saturday.

Everybody sat in silence in chapel the next morning. At first
Jessie paid attention to it, but very soon she wanted something to happen. She kept thinking of words that could be
read or things that could be said. At least they could sing,
for heaven's sake. Sitting still like this was a waste of time.

Jessie was not the only one edgy and anxious. On the
bench ahead of her Pickles Dill was flicking his thumbnails
against his top front teeth. Michael MacLeod and Donny
Moore were whispering and giggling. Across the aisle, Meba
and Sarah Lynn whispered more successfully than the little
boys. Meba's whisper was slight, enough for Jessie to hear
the little rasp of air but not loud enough for words to be
distinguished. At first all this bothered Jessie, but gradually
she gave up wondering when the houseparents would turn
around from the front bench and start scolding. They
seemed determined to let the silence go on as best it could.
Jessie started to fall asleep in the early-morning sun coming
through the dust-choked screen window on her left.

She dozed, watching odd dreamy pictures float across
her sight: a hole in Cassie's bed net; her own toothbrush
fallen from her water cup onto the windowsill; the chickens
that she saw from her window, chasing each other in the
high bird enclosure down at the back of the dorm; the stone
markers and stock crosses of the little pet cemetery next

to that bird enclosure, where the fourth graders annually dug up the mummy of the monkey Wheat's and Martha's older brothers had buried years ago. Nobody had done that yet this year. When her class had dug up the hard parcel of something wrapped in shreds of cloth and paper, the eighth-grade boys had supervised, and Noah Janeway had made them bury it again without unwrapping the supposed mummy. They'd had a long memorial service, and Jessie had written the prayer for the beast on the back of some blue wrapping paper. She'd been quite proud of that prayer. It had probably been stupid.

Jessie's head nodded, and she jerked herself back into the moment. Aunt Pearl was already standing at the lectern, a worn black-leather-covered Bible in her hand. The Bible had all its corners smoothed down. When Aunt Pearl turned the thin pages, they didn't crackle as new pages would have, they whispered.

Mom's Bible looked like that. Once Jessie had woken up in what she thought was the middle of the night and gone into Mom's room, and then knew it wasn't even ten o'clock yet because the electricity was still on. Mom had been lying in bed, reading. "Do you like reading the Bible?" Jessie had asked, and Mom had laughed—Jessie remembered the sound now as light and watery—and she'd said, "Well, as a matter of fact, I do."

The memory made Jessie smile, just as Aunt Pearl caught her eye. The housemother smiled back. Jessie shifted in her seat and looked away.

"We're going to read the same psalm every day for a week," said Aunt Pearl. "You'll be surprised to hear something different each time."

> "You search me, O God, you know me.
> You know me sitting or standing;
> you read my very thoughts from far off;
> walking or resting, I am known by you,
> and all my life is open to you."

Psalm 139, thought Jessie, recognizing it as Aunt Pearl began. Half of her attention was on the words, and the other half puzzled over the noise of men's voices rising in agitation somewhere at the back of the dorm, out in the courtyard where the dorm's two cisterns were dug beneath the wide covering domes of gray cement rising up from the grass. Aunt Pearl finished the psalm, but everyone—including the housemother as she read—now was listening to the shouts and the peculiar echoing of the voices out back.

"We'll pray now," Aunt Pearl said, glancing at Uncle Walker. He was already at the back of the chapel, making his way to the courtyard. The housemother looked at all the kids, and her face took on the slightly inward focus people get before they begin to pray aloud. Jessie recognized the look and wondered if it happened naturally, or if you learned to do it, the way you learned to stand up straight and speak clearly in front of the class. The expression Aunt Pearl had now was partly from the way her eyes collected everyone's attention and made it drop inward, so that they all prayed together.

Jessie didn't really pay attention to the prayer, although she knew she ought to. She was listening instead to the sound of Uncle Walker's voice raised in question, then to the sounds of the cook's and the wash man's voices answering, and then to the odd echoey sound of all three voices together.

"Be present for us throughout the hours ahead," Aunt Pearl was saying, "and guide and protect all our loved ones far from us. Especially we pray for Alida and Matthew, in their needs of heart, mind, and body."

Hearing Mom and Dad prayed for electrified Jessie. At the mention of her parents, Martha jabbed her in the side with her elbow. It was as though everyone had been in a dark room and suddenly someone had turned a bright light on Jessie, Joshua, and Cassie. Why hadn't she thought to pray for them before this? A cold flow of blame came down over her shoulders. What if by not praying for them Jessie had prevented them from being safe?

Immediately common sense, in the shape of Uncle Don's bright blue eyes and his gently amused smile, brushed this fear aside. I mean, said Jessie to herself as Aunt Pearl went on praying—for rain in drought-stricken areas of Ethiopia and peace in Korea and freedom in South Africa and health for the people sick up at Enongal hospital—I mean, Jessie again said to herself, God *called* Mom and Dad, didn't He? God doesn't pay attention to them only if I ask Him to.

They are important not just because of me and Cassie and Joshua, but because of themselves and what God asks them to do. Of course God is watching over them, and He knows I love them even though I haven't prayed for them yet. . . . Pain pushed straight up from the core of her heart and burned, thin and flamelike at first; then it turned thudding and hard, as if trying to become tears. Jessie pinched her nose to keep from crying, and all thoughts about prayer vanished.

Aunt Pearl was done, finally. Any intentions of maintaining silence on the way into breakfast were lost as Aunt Pearl went out of chapel only a hair away from running. Everybody else crowded along behind, chattering and laughing, gladly released from the stricture of quiet.

Uncle Walker appeared at the back door on the porch. "Don't all of you come out here! In fact, nobody come out here! We'll tell you what the matter is when we know ourselves! Sit down! Wheat! Martha! Eighth graders, get the others to sit down!"

"Sit! Sit! Sit!" yelled Wheat, waving his long arms at the other kids, all shorter than he. He held his palms up like American policemen always did in picture books Jessie had seen. The kids backed away and turned around, knocking over chairs and running into each other, generally making a much louder noise over getting napkin rings and sitting down to breakfast than they would have on other mornings.

"Come on, sit down!" yelled Jessie. "Pickles Dill! Cut out that game of tag and *sit!*"

"Uh-oh, here comes bossy Jessie," said Lynnie Page to the other fifth graders at her end of the table. "Better behave, everybody."

"Let's pray and eat!" yelled Michael MacLeod, his voice much louder than anyone would guess of a third grader.

"All right, all right!" yelled Wheat, again waving his arms. "Shut up!"

"Ooooh, you're gonna get your mouth washed out!" sang Tom Beebe and Andrew Janeway. "Soap, soap, dee-licious soap!"

"We're going to pray!" shouted Sam. And then when the noise dropped slightly, he called, "Jessie?"

Oh, no, thought Jessie, panic rising in her. Not me.

"Yeah, Jessie, pray for us. Let's hear you!"

Uncle Walker always said the prayer before breakfast. At the other two meals of the day, they sang grace together.

"You want to pray?" asked Wheat. The others had gone sort of quiet, interested in the exchange between the oldest kids. Something more than just a yes-or-no question was in Wheat's glance at Jessie. Jessie imagined that Wheat thought she could do it, pray like an adult, for all of them. Jessie knew she could and knew at the same time that if she did, right now, she'd just be showing off.

"Let's sing," she said, relieved and surprised by the suggestion coming to her without her having to hunt for it.

Everybody turned to Joshua now. "Oh, let's do 'The Steadfast Love,' " said Joshua from the other end of the room, sounding bored, wanting to get on with things. And waiting only until everyone had joined hands as usual around the whole U-shaped arrangement of tables, Joshua started the song without even clearing his throat, pitching it perfectly for his own tenor voice and the higher voices of all the younger kids. It sounded funny to be singing at breakfast, but by the second line they were singing the grace in harmony, the way they did it for other meals. Jessie sought the alto because Joshua's tenor was too low, and the soprano was now too high for her. As always, she listened with pleasure to the harmony. And as always, she sang and thought the words at the same time. Before this, she'd been quite sure the words were true. It had been easy to be sure, because everything was okay. Now, she tried the words on her tongue and in her mouth, and she felt herself beginning to cry.

> "The steadfast love of the Lord never ceases.
> His mercies never come to an end.
> They are new every morning, new every morning!
> Great is thy faithfulness, O Lord,
> Great is thy faithfulness!"

The spring on the screen door screeched as Uncle Walker came in from the courtyard. He stood behind Eddie Carter's chair, holding the back of it with both hands, waiting for the song to be over. Everyone stared at him. He looked around the room and sighed immensely.

Jessie listened to the sigh and thought how often she'd

heard grown-ups sigh like that. It seemed to go with some heavy concern. She ought to try it herself the next time she started to get all wound up with worry about Mom and Dad. She pulled breath in right then, at the very thought of their names.

"Kids," said Uncle Walker, "we have no water."

The first thing Jessie did was look at her glass of milk. At the same time she thought, That can't be. There's always water.

"Both cisterns are dry," said Uncle Walker. "I had known one was low, but somehow the second one got a crack that I didn't see. While we used up the water in the first cistern, the water in the other one leaked out, and what's left now is too muddy for us to use."

"Well, now what?" asked Isaac Keller. "First no Bible Conference, and now no water. Should we do a rain dance or something?"

"Oh, Isaac, we'd need something on the order of a forty-day flood to make a difference. Here's what Aunt Pearl and I see we have to do right away. We have to get enough water into the dorm for today's drinking, cooking, washing, and flushing the toilets."

"Euuu, ick, don't talk about that while we're eating!" called Meba.

Uncle Walker said gravely, "Each of us uses at least five gallons of water a day, and most of that goes when we flush the toilet. So only flush after three of you have used the toilet."

"I'm going to be sick!" called Sarah Lynn Stimson, smacking her forehead with the back of her hand.

"Run outside! We don't have enough water to wash up after you indoors!" shouted Isaac.

"Listen, guys," said Uncle Walker in the peculiarly soft and dangerous tone that meant immediate attention or swift and terrible consequences. "Right after breakfast, we're going to start bringing water from the Press House cisterns up to the dorm in a bucket brigade. Everybody helps, everybody sticks with it until Aunt Pearl or I say we have enough to get us through the day and into tomorrow."

"But that'll take all our time!" complained Isaac. "We were going to play little Yaoundé today!"

"Or steal sticks!" argued Andrew Janeway.

"Were we going to play little Yaoundé?" said Jessie to Martha. "We didn't get ready for it."

It was a whole-dorm game that she and Martha had made up at the beginning of last term. They had organized everybody into two cities of two different countries because Jessie wanted an airport as part of the game. Each Saturday everybody came to the "office" the two oldest girls made out of the space behind three huge round starflower bushes by the study-hall steps. Jessie and Martha prepared the countries in advance, looking up cities in the encyclopedia after school, and assigned everyone a profession and a city in one of the two countries. And then everybody traveled, went to market, went to school or church or the bank—Sam insisted there be a circus traveling from city to city by plane—and each week somebody got hurt and had to go to the hospital, or got married and set up housekeeping, only to have one of the children die untimely and be buried. Every week the kids invented a new twist to the game, and each week Jessie and Martha assigned all the professions to different kids, and somehow the kids wove all the twists together, making the game alive and interesting Saturday after Saturday. It was easy to revive after vacation.

"I want to be the owner of the Red Donkey this time!" called Phoebe Peel, leaning over her plate of fruit and turning her head to catch Jessie's eye. The Red Donkey was the popular café in Yaoundé where real ice cream was served. Because beer was served there, too, lots of the missionaries avoided the little restaurant, but Jessie's parents had made a habit of driving through Yaoundé on their way back home at the end of each school year and treating the twins and Cassie to a celebration of ice cream and soda as the start of summer vacation and being home again.

Summer vacation. Home again. Jessie was suddenly reminded that it was all blank ahead of her now, that nobody else would be likely to waste time for the poor Howells kids on ice cream in a beer joint after school was over. She didn't want to go on thinking in this sour, breathless way. Sigh, she said to herself just in time. Make a big sigh right now. She could only manage a kind of panting.

"You okay? Or are you going to cry?" asked Martha,

looking sideways at Jessie. Jessie closed her eyes and shook her head at her plate. Martha didn't ask again, and Jessie stopped trying to sigh.

"I'm sure you all made your beds before breakfast," Uncle Walker was saying. "After you've washed your dishes and gone upstairs to brush your teeth and check on your bed making"—and he paused here so everyone knew their rooms would be inspected as usual—"meet at the front door when I ring the gong. I'll give out pails and whatever we can find for carrying water, and we'll get the brigade in order. All right, everybody?"

"Nooo!" shouted a number of voices. Jessie said it, too, but she wasn't against carrying water. Her *no!* was for not knowing what would happen at school's end, not knowing what would happen next week, even.

"All right or not, that's the way it is," said Uncle Walker. "Here comes the oatmeal. Eat up. You'll need your strength."

At first the work was entertaining. That was only on the first day, when not having enough water was an interesting crisis. When Uncle Walker rang the gong as he had promised, a lot of kids were already down in the chapel area, milling around, waiting for his instructions. Jessie could hear them from the front hall, where she was braiding Cassie's hair into one long plait. "Hurry up!" Cassie complained, and when Jessie braided faster, she said, "You're pulling my hair! Stop that!"

"Then hold still," said Jessie, moving her lips but keeping her front teeth closed. "Give me the ribbon. And where is the other green one?" Jessie sounded cross, as Mom might on that issue.

"I don't know," said Cassie shortly. Jessie thought about arguing and decided it would be too heavy and bothersome.

"I want to go down," said Cassie, walking ahead of Jessie, so that Jessie braided and fastened the plait as she followed her little sister, like the girls followed the goose in the fairy tale.

Only I don't want to be stuck to Cassie, thought Jessie. She pulled the braid just a bit tighter than necessary, and Cassie jerked her head so that Jessie would know it hurt. She looked around to glare hotly at Jessie, and Jessie saw tears gathered in Cassie's eyes, but she ignored them and let Cassie think she was ignoring her, too. They were talking to each other angrily in silence. I'm not really hurting Cassie's feelings, thought Jessie, as long as I don't say anything out loud.

The cook, Amougou, and the wash man, Mvom, had brought as many buckets and kettles and other large containers as they could find to the dorm's front steps. Uncle Walker stood at the door and handed each boarder some container, according to his idea of matched size and strength. He gave Jessie a huge pot normally used for cooking spaghetti. She looked at it and said, "I'll have to carry that on my head."

"I know," said Uncle Walker. "Joshua says you're good at it."

"I am," said Jessie. But she didn't like Joshua's recommending her skills, because he didn't really admire them himself. "Did you give him a bucket or a pot?" she asked.

"I forget," said Uncle Walker. "Really, it doesn't matter as long as we have enough water."

"I need to get a head pad," said Jessie. It hurt too much to balance a container on your head without something between your skull and the bottom of the container. It helped if it was something flat. She went back indoors, pushing through the bunch of kids waiting for their assignments, and got a hot pad from the shelf at the back of the dining room. She turned around as she was leaving and picked up the whole stack of them.

"Here," she said to Cassie when she got to the front door. "Carry the pail on your head, and use this." She gave one to Lorayne and Elissa, too.

Martha was waiting for Jessie by the merry-go-round. "Which way?" she asked, swinging the bucket she was carrying. "The road or the path?"

"The path is shadier," said Jessie. It was a grass track running between and then behind the school buildings, going parallel to the road but ending up in the Press House courtyard. By the huge kapok tree behind the Little School, Joshua, Wheat, and Sam were arguing with Andrew and Isaac.

Jessie noticed Joshua kicking the base of one of the tree's

great wing roots. He usually played the piano for a couple of hours on Saturday morning. Now he had his hands in his pockets. His bucket was on the ground. Every village common she'd ever seen floated through her memory, and all she could remember, suddenly, was how the women and girls were carrying water or wood or the chickens for stew, while the men stood about talking, and the boys rolled hoops.

"Do your share!" yelled Jessie over her shoulder.

"Mind your own business!" Sam yelled back, and Jessie whirled on the path, so furious with him that she knew she was furious with all those unknown little boys she'd seen, playing while the girls worked.

"Getting this water is your business, too! Move it, lazybones!"

"Bossy Jessie!" Sam called.

"Come on," said Martha, who'd been waiting on the path, swinging her bucket in a wide arc around her body. "Let's just get our share over with. They can't get out of the work, Jess."

At the Press House, Uncle Nat, the printer, was showing the fifth-grade boys how to pump the water evenly so it would go on shooting out of the spigot instead of spurting and coughing, then gushing out of control and spraying most of the water on the ground. "This is going to take forever," said Martha. "Maybe we should divide the work, and somebody who's good at it pump for everybody else."

"No, thank you," said Jessie. Her arm and shoulder ached just from looking at the repetitive labor that Steve

Ware, Sam's younger brother, was doing. And then it ached for real. She was out of breath by the time she'd pumped her first kettleful.

In getting the kettle up to her head, Jessie slopped enough water over the edge to soak her shoulders. Irritation rose in her. *"A néga me ngwañ malep ma témi,"* Nléla had said, all those years ago. Don't look straight down. Push strength up from your spine to the top of your head. Don't hurry. Jessie had lost her temper once on the riverbank and thrown the half-spilled pail of water down on the ground, and Nléla had laughed at her. *"N, mut nye ki nye nu a mbem we á wo bé nyu."* Now that water is gone. You are like a three-year-old because carrying water is what a three-year-old learns.

"I wonder what I learned when I was three that I use now when I do stuff," said Jessie when Martha had got her pail on her head and the hot pad adjusted under it. They started up the path again.

Behind them, the pump squeaked and screeched as Joshua flushed water into his pail. Jessie knew he was angry, too, but she didn't have an immediate knowledge of the thing wrong. A kind of thudding resentment rose in her, even with her back turned to him. She dismissed the thought of him; it was more ungainly and heavier than the water she carried.

"I mean," she said to Martha again, "what did we learn when we were that little that we needed to know for everybody's sake, the way little African girls know how to carry water?"

"Oh. Nothing," said Martha, after considering the idea. "I wouldn't want to anyhow. It isn't much fun, carrying water instead of playing."

"Well, wherever Mom and Dad are," Jessie began, and impulsively Martha turned her head quickly and took one hand down from the side of the pail where she was keeping it balanced and put her hand on Jessie's arm, comfortingly. But in the same gesture, Martha's water sloshed, and Jessie cried out, "Be careful! Don't jerk your head like that! You'll spill the water!" They stopped on the path until the water settled.

Martha could put her hand on Jessie's arm because Jessie walked with only one hand up on the kettle, while Martha had to use both to carry her load. Martha touched Jessie again, lightly, touched the spilled water on Jessie's arm, and, putting her hand back up to steady her own pail, she said, "They're all right. I'm sure they're okay, Jessie."

"Yeah, well, you don't know," muttered Jessie, thinking about Mendômô's words: "Even women on their way to the fields can fall into those traps," she'd said. "The soldiers don't care."

"No, I don't know, but I'm sure anyhow," Martha insisted. "If it comes to that, who knows about any of our parents? I mean, the hospital at Metet could have burned down last night and I wouldn't know about it yet. If I went around thinking about all the bad things that might happen, I'd—I'd . . . I don't know, but I'd be no good."

At first Jessie laughed at the idea of Martha's confusion, and then the laugh hurt. "I can't stop that kind of thinking now," she said. "Remember how we talked about this a couple of years ago—"

"Sixth grade," said Martha promptly. "Yeah. And we said that we did it on purpose. We sort of pretended to ourselves that nothing could happen to them while we were away from home."

"I can't do that anymore, because I found out over vacation what kinds of horrible things can happen to people in the forest now." They came out of the shade of the huge primeval kapok and duma trees behind the Little School. The sun was dazzlingly bright in the air and on the grass ahead of them, where the path was shiny with reflections from spilled water.

"Well, what are you going to do? Do you pray?" asked Martha in a practical tone.

"No," said Jessie in a low enough voice to make Martha prompt her for the answer again. "No, I don't," Jessie admitted. "I don't know what to say."

"Neither would I," said Martha after a little silence. "You feel like saying, 'God, it's all Your fault.' "

"Yeah," said Jessie, nodding her head, so relieved that Martha understood this secret, silent urge of her own. Nodding was a mistake. The kettle shifted and water poured down her back. "Eaaah!" she shouted, skittering forward as though she could escape the load on her head. More water slopped down the arm she held at the rim of the kettle to steady it. "Ick," she said, shrugging under her wet blouse. She stopped herself and waited again for the water to regain its level. She thought about the idea of blaming God. "But then you have to say, 'God, it's Your fault that I hurt,' right? And what good is that?"

"What good are parents anyway?" asked Martha. They had come to the front door of the dorm. Michael MacLeod was just coming out. "Hold the door!" yelled Martha.

"Bossy!" Michael yelled back.

Jessie grinned at them both.

The last stretch of carrying was the worst. Jessie climbed the stairs behind Martha to the second landing, where Aunt Pearl had put out three huge laundry tubs. Only one of them was even close to being full. There was a lot of water spilled on the black rubber matting of the stair treads. Jessie lifted the kettle down carefully, and it trembled in her grasp. She poured the water in one beautiful wide fall into the tub and was suddenly, furiously thirsty.

"Only one drink! One cup now, one cup this afternoon," called Aunt Pearl on the stairs. "We're boiling water now, but it's got to cool and be filtered before we can use it, and it won't be ready till tomorrow."

"If she hadn't said that," Martha grunted, "I wouldn't want more than a cup."

"I don't even like water very much usually," said Jessie, tossing her metal cup back on the nail over her name, on the cup rack near the filters. She swallowed hard, because the idea of limited water made her throat dry.

When they were outside again and passing a straggly file of seventh graders carrying water in pails, Jessie said, "I think parents are like airplanes."

"What?" said Martha.

"Well, I think their job is to get you from one place to the next, but when you arrive, you get out and take your own trips after that. See what I mean?"

Martha said, "Sort of," but her voice let Jessie know that she didn't see.

They walked on the path toward Joshua and Wheat, who were staggering lopsidedly with their big heavy buckets, stopping and changing hands, rubbing their palms where the handles bit into the flesh, picking up their loads and staggering a little farther before stopping again. "If you put it on your head," began Jessie, but the fast I'll-kill-you-soon glance from Joshua made her stop. When the boys had gone beyond earshot Jessie said in a lower voice, "That brother of mine is so stubborn!"

"I don't think he should have to carry water," said Martha. "He's got to practice sometime. We all know that."

"He's got to flush the toilet, too," said Jessie. She swung her empty kettle up on her head. "See," she went on, using her free hand for small gestures in front of her without moving her upper body, "our airplane—Cassie's and mine —is stuck—crashed maybe—but somehow Mom and Dad gave Joshua enough to keep going, by giving him the piano, because he's got something he's sure of. But Cassie isn't old enough, and I don't have anything that tells me direction. So we're stuck."

"Why do you talk as though your parents are—are—"

"Dead?" Jessie shot the word out of her mind and mouth all in one effort. "Because. I'd rather think they were dead and find out otherwise than think they're alive now and be disappointed later, too."

"Yeah, but . . ." Martha stopped and blew out a short forced sigh.

Jessie thought of Uncle Walker this morning. There must be something useful in whooshing out air when you were troubled. She herself couldn't find enough room to breathe in that much air. Her breathing was shallow, quick, as though there were too much air in her lungs already, and she couldn't let any of it go.

"My parents could easily be dead this minute, chopped up in little bits and dropped into a hole in the forest, and nobody would ever find them, and I'd have to spend the rest of my life taking care of Cassie," said Jessie grimly, having to gasp a little at the end.

"They aren't—that, what you said—and you know they aren't," Martha argued.

"I don't know anything!" Jessie shouted, and made fists of her hands and threw them ahead of her. The kettle slipped off her head and fell behind her, thunking hollowly onto the ground.

"None of us does," answered Martha, raising her voice.

She went back, picked the kettle up, and held it out to Jessie. "Nobody does! Nobody, nobody, nobody!" Now she was shouting, too.

"It's just the wide part of the corner," said Jessie quietly, and stopped on the path, struck still by the full memory of walking in the dark last night to help Cassie; the full memory included the wondrous, unbelievable moment when she'd heard Cassie without having to use her ears.

"What is it?" asked Martha, stopping on the path, too, looking anxiously at Jessie.

"I just remembered something from last night," said Jessie. She smiled at her roommate. Warmth was spreading inside of her, opening enough space for air, filling her and emptying her all at once. She laughed for no reason at all. She took deep breaths and sighed hugely, luxuriously, as they went on to the Press House courtyard. She felt like running and leaping those last few yards, but she walked sedately, the smile in her and on her face. The odd feeling of something new, something unknown, stretched gaps in the darkness within her. Some light shone through and felt like hope.

So she wouldn't give in to it and be disappointed, Jessie bent all her energies to pumping water, filling her kettle, Martha's, and buckets for the next three kids in line. The burning in her muscles folded over and sealed whatever was happening in her heart.

9

Loving Cassie

In the queer light of the earliest part of morning, Jessie could see by the fair hair and bangs that it was Lorayne beside her bed, even though the film of white netting between them obscured the little girl's face. Lorayne was standing close to the head of the bed, pinching the net between two fingers and rubbing it to make the slight raspy sound waking Jessie up.

Jessie blinked and swallowed and rubbed her front teeth with her tongue. Finally she pushed herself up on one elbow to see the little girl more clearly. "What is it?" she said, clearing her throat and looking beyond Lorayne's shoulder to see if Martha had been wakened by all this.

"Jessie? Can you come help us? Can you come help Cassie?"

Her duty to Cassie clamped hold of Jessie's attention. She dropped back on her pillow, covered her face with both hands, and groaned into the hollow she made there. Tiredness lay in her chest like a sodden blanket. She had to say yes. "Sure," she said, meaning every ounce of resentment in her grumpy tone. She got out of bed slowly, taking all sorts of care with her bed net, hunting fruitlessly under her bed for her thongs, rubbing her eyes again, and stifling another sigh as she followed Lorayne out of the room and down the hall.

Even outside Cassie's room, Jessie knew the worst had happened. She could smell the sweetly sharp reek of urine-soaked sheets from the doorway. "Oh, for pity's sake, Cassie," she began in a harsh whisper, but she bit back everything else when she heard her words as if they were someone else's—Aunt Pearl's or even Mom's—angry with her for something she couldn't help. All resentment drained away.

"Here I am, Cassie," said Jessie in low tones. Her sister stood in the middle of the room, holding her pillow by two corners of the pillowcase. "Did you get that wet?" asked Jessie. Pillows were impossible to make clean and sweet after a bed-wetting. Cassie shook her head. "Good."

Cassie's bed net was pushed back, its hem coming close to the faintly gleaming pool in the middle of the mattress. Elissa was trying to get Cassie's blanket untucked, but she hadn't untucked the bed net. "Do one layer at a time," said Jessie, going over to help. "Bed net first. Lorayne, get Cassie a clean nightgown."

"I don't have any," said Cassie in a little voice. "They didn't do our wash yesterday, remember? Because of no water."

"Oh, that's right. Can she borrow one?" Jessie asked Lorayne, and Lorayne nodded. No water meant more problems right now. Jessie lifted the bed net into its canopy, running the length of the hem through her fingers to feel for wetness. None. Oh, marvel and goodness. She said this aloud, and Elissa, tugging the blanket free, whispered, "What?" Jessie said, "It's dry," and Elissa nodded. The top sheet was wet, though. Jessie held her breath as she worked. The smell burned her nose, and besides, she wished Cassie didn't have this problem. The odor was wholly mixed with Jessie's sense of Cassie unhappy, Cassie lonely, Cassie needing help. Hers was the only help available.

Jessie loosened the top sheet, folded it roughly so the wet spot was on top, and dumped it on the floor. Then more carefully she folded the corners of the bottom sheet in to the soaking center and, turning her head for a deep breath, lifted it away from the bed, placing it on the floor. A wave of the fierce, nose-piercing stink hung around her head. "Give me your hand towel," she said to Cassie.

Working fast, Jessie laid the hand towel on the rubber sheet to blot what urine was left there, and then she picked up the lump of bed sheets. "Come on, and don't forget your towel," she said to Cassie, leading her across the hall to the bathroom.

"It's not too bad," she lied to Cassie. "Let's get you

clean," she added, not urging, not demanding, just telling Cassie what was next. In the predawn blur of light and dark, the rows of wet washcloths looked like black square blots against the wall. Jessie couldn't tell red from green, blue from yellow. "Which is yours?" she asked. Cassie reached out for one and handed it to Jessie. "It's going to be cold," Jessie warned, looking down at the immense laundry tub full of water between her sister and herself.

Carefully, while Cassie held her arms up in the air, Jessie lifted the nightgown by its hem, gathering it as she went so it wouldn't touch and put its clinging stink on too much of Cassie's body as it came off. She moved the garment delicately as she took it over Cassie's head, keeping it away from her hair. "Breathe now," she said, and Cassie let out a little shaky sound, somewhere between a crazed giggle and the beginning of tears.

Then Cassie went over to the damp, moldy cement of the shower floor, and Jessie handed her the washcloth she'd dipped in the water. Cassie used it, wrung it, and gave it back. Jessie wet it again and soaped it. And so they passed the cloth back and forth until Cassie was clumsily washed. "Oh, drat, you forgot the towel!" Jessie spoke more loudly than she meant to; her voice echoed in the bathroom and startled both of them.

"I'm sorry," Cassie said, beginning to cry. Jessie fled the tears and hurried across the hall to get the bath towel.

Lorayne and Elissa were making Cassie's bed. "Where'd

you get the sheets?" Jessie asked, grabbing Cassie's towel
and remembering to take the wet hand towel, too.

"They're our top sheets," whispered Lorayne. "We'll just
use blankets. It's okay."

"I'll help you make your beds back to normal in the
morning," said Jessie.

While Cassie toweled her body dry, put on the clean
borrowed nightgown, and dried her feet, Jessie argued with
herself, even after she'd made up her mind. The water, a
lot of which she'd carried up here herself, was mostly meant
for flushing toilets. So it didn't matter if she rinsed the
sheets in it first. But it couldn't be used for anything else
except flushing toilets after she put the sheets into it, and
what if someone came in tomorrow morning to wash her
hands with that water before breakfast? But she couldn't—
she *couldn't*—leave the stinking sheets to dry like this till
tomorrow, because the stink would never really get out of
them until the next sheet washing, and who knew when
that would be, what with the water crisis. And then Cassie
would have to sleep on dried stinking sheets and the whole
room would smell and kids would start to mock Cassie—
and it was all too awful to wait for. So she was doing the
right thing now, no matter what trouble she made for the
day ahead. Anyway, she'd already dipped Cassie's soapy
washcloth into the water.

Jessie pushed the sheets down into the tub and pulled
them up again, heavy sodden masses with water pouring

off the linen back into the tub and some out onto the floor, splashing on her feet and the hem of her nightgown. She rinsed the sheets, plunging them four or five times, until her arms ached from their weight and she didn't smell the urine as much when she lifted a sheet out. Then she sighed and began to squeeze the sheets, made rough with wetness, hand over hand. Cassie took the end that was slightly wrung and kept the sheet from falling to the floor, piling it nearby on the old wooden dressing table. Then, her forearms stiff from wringing and squeezing, Jessie draped the wet sheets over the two shower heads. Everything in the bathroom had changed in shape, grown more definite and become pale rather than dim, and the room seemed smaller in this earliest of the day's light.

Jessie's hands felt raw and freezing from the cold, heavy linen, and her skin stung from the acid urine. The cloying stink of it was still in the sheets, but there wasn't anything more Jessie could do without laundry soap.

Holding her own soaked nightgown away from her stomach and thighs with one hand, Jessie took Cassie across the hall and helped her get into bed and get the bed net down. Every time Jessie's nightgown touched her flesh, she felt stung and shivered with the chill and distaste.

"I'm sorry. I'm sorry. I'm sorry, Jessie," Cassie whispered, swallowing her tears, trying not to cry. Jessie, burning with regret, knew Cassie was holding the tears down because that's what Jessie wanted her to do.

"It's all right, Cassie. It's all right, little heart," she whis-

pered back, whooshing her breath out not in a sigh at all
but to keep her own tears down. She tucked Cassie in and
wished there was something someone would invent to take
away the brittle, burnt-sour smell Cassie had to sleep in—
all three girls had to sleep in. "Thanks, guys," she said to
Lorayne and Elissa, who now lay in their beds again, sealed
inside the hanging white walls of their bed nets.

"Night," they whispered back.

The unpleasant smell of stale urine clung to Jessie's
hands and arms even after she'd washed them several times
with lots of soap, rinsing them in the sink in the back
bathroom, using her water cup. That meant she'd have to
get the cup boiled clean tomorrow—to kill the bacteria from
the Press House cistern water—so she could drink from it
again. Bird song was so loud and thick that she wondered
how she ordinarily slept through the noise day after day till
six-thirty. It must be about five-fifteen now, judging from
the grayness of the light in the window.

She couldn't get back to sleep. Her nostrils widened as
she sniffed along her arms, hunting for lingering odor on
her skin. The houseparents hadn't told the kids how the
dorm was going to manage showers. There weren't any bath-
tubs. Suddenly, all the turmoil of Friday and Saturday rose
up and overflowed in her, and she began whispering so hard
that her throat hurt.

"What about *me?* What about *me?* I'm in *trouble* now.
What about *me* some of the time?"

·   ·   ·

Uncle Don came down to the dorm for Sunday school as usual. Jessie was nearly on time, but as she and Martha went by Cassie's room, Cassie called out, "I can't find my hairbrush!" and Jessie remembered her nighttime promise to the other two little girls. She went in to help make their beds. Martha found Cassie's hairbrush in a shoe, and when the two beds were made up neat and tight, Jessie checked the sheets hanging in the bathroom, but they weren't even close to dry, and they stank. Cassie's bed would have to wait, and Jessie would be late again.

As she came into the study hall, Uncle Don looked up and said cheerfully, "You are so consistent, Miss Howells, that I begin to think it is we who are early rather than you who are tardy." Jessie smiled at him and took her seat feeling quite even rather than at her usual disadvantage of being the last one to arrive.

"Now," said the doctor, "I hadn't really prepared a lesson for today, because of Bible Conference"—and the thought of Mom and Dad whispered across Jessie's mind but didn't call out for attention—"so we're going to read what I read this morning in my own devotional. I happen to be in the Revelation of Saint John the Divine, this time of year. If you will all turn to that book, please." Bibles thunked open on the study-hall table, the full measure of the pages falling to the left.

Jessie opened her Bible to the end; because the pages were so few there, the back cover hung down awkwardly, making a right angle between the book's spine and the tabletop. Jessie flicked a pencil into the hiding space there. She didn't much like Revelation. It was a frightening and mystifying book, hard to read, as impossible to understand as other people's dreams and nightmares. There was an urgency in the passages, a sense of having her mind put just on the edge of something alive and coming true, that made considering them an uneasy thing. It wasn't a book she read by herself anymore.

"For most of us, this is the most mysterious book in the Bible," said Uncle Don, tapping the pages lightly with a short, pinkly clean forefinger. "There are brief passages of clear beauty. One I read today made me think of a question I want to ask you. Uh, Joshua," he said, looking around the group, "will you read verses three, four, and five of chapter twenty-one for us?"

Joshua turned the pages, breathing lightly as he looked for the place. Jessie watched him as he read. He opened his mouth and touched his lips with his tongue before he started. His Adam's apple moved up and down, and his chin—narrow and squared off at the end—looked like Mom's. She'd never noticed that resemblance before. Seeing it now, she saw more than something curious about inheritance. Maybe that's the only way I'll remember what she looks like, thought Jessie, and pressed her lips together hard and pinched her nose again, thwarting her sudden urge to cry.

" 'And I heard a loud voice, out of the throne, crying "Lo, God's dwelling place is with men; they shall be his people, and God himself be with them. He will wipe away every tear from their eyes, and death shall be no more, for the former things have passed away. Lo, I make all things new," ' " read Joshua in a clear, untroubled voice, looking up at Uncle Don when he was finished.

"Thank you, Joshua. Now, it's obvious that Saint John knew something about life's general misery. And it seems clear that life's general misery—about which you all know something specific, I would guess—is shared from one century to another. Agreed so far?"

Everybody nodded. Jessie assumed all this was leading up to some statement about heaven. The class had had a Sunday school teacher two years ago who had used this same passage and had told them what a wonderful place heaven would be. Jessie hadn't cared at all then. Now she cared, but she didn't feel like waiting until she died to have the present misery pass away from her and Cassie and Joshua. She certainly didn't care for the idea of Mom and Dad in heaven right now.

"It seems to me that this passage is about God caring for us, exactly where we are, at this moment. And it's about God wanting new beginnings, freshness, starting over in His Presence."

Hah, said Jessie, though the word was quite silent. I don't believe it. Alarm tingled through her and made her sit up straight, because she knew suddenly she was speaking directly, and in cold, hard anger, to God All right, she would do it again. Dull excitement throbbed in the back of her throat as she made her challenge: You mean that? Then prove it to me!

Now, it was known to be dangerous to test God, even though people in the Bible had done that and lived. Jessie backed away from her demand, leaving it hanging in the air between herself and God. People who tested God and lived, like the prophet Gideon, Jessie remembered, had been called by God. She didn't think she'd been called. Don't be angry, she said silently. I just want to know. It was quite all right to want knowledge of God. Feeling relieved, as though she'd escaped bringing disaster on herself, Jessie pulled her attention around to Uncle Don.

He said, "Now take a moment to think, and then each one of you will tell us what absolutely new thing you have done this year, which you couldn't have imagined yourself doing before you did it. Is that clear?"

Nobody nodded this time, but Jessie liked the assignment and after a moment's consideration, knew she could do something with it. When she did this sort of work, she was most sure of herself. It made her feel like singing. Somehow she'd forgotten that she liked using her brain. Since Friday everything had seemed different, every good thing lost and ruined. Goodness, but Friday seemed ages ago!

Sam groaned, and Martha grumbled, "I don't know what you mean."

"Don't make it hard on yourself," said Uncle Don,

laughing a little. "This isn't terribly serious. Just look for the new thing you've done in the past year—anytime in the past year."

Jessie smiled at Uncle Don while she thought through the year just gone by. After some moments, in spite of her first impression, the assignment appeared hard. She couldn't think of anything. Really, there hadn't been anything new since last April. She'd gone home and come back to school, gone home and come back. There was this thick, discouraging dark business with Mom and Dad, but that wasn't anything she had done; it was being done to her.

What had she been thinking about just as Uncle Don finished telling the assignment? She'd seen a quick picture of Ngo Masé's dim, smoky village kitchen. But Jessie had been there plenty of times and had seen many plucked chickens in her life, even chickens being killed. And trucks with soldiers weren't new, exactly, although she wasn't used to them as normal.

Jessie snaked the pencil out from under her Bible cover and on a scrap of paper idly began sketching a clump of palm trees. She realized she was thinking about the foundations of the new house being built for the Essams. That was it!

She had made real friends with Mendômô. She couldn't think of any other kid in the school who had made friends with an African of the same age. But how was she going to say this? Mendômô wasn't some kind of prize, and she herself hadn't even been very willing to make friends in the first place. But the friendship was a completely new thing. New and lasting and heart satisfying. Suddenly, sharply, she wanted to see Mendômô, be with her right then.

"And Jessie? What new thing did you do that you couldn't have imagined doing before?"

She'd missed whatever Sam had said. Uncle Don had started on his left instead of his right. She wasn't ready to speak, but everyone waited, and the longer they looked at her, the more curiously they stared.

"All right," she said, and blushed as the bottom of her stomach sailed away from her. "Before Christmas I couldn't have imagined being friends with an African kid my own age. I couldn't have imagined being alike enough to be real friends, like I am with Martha. But this Christmas a Bulu family came to Libamba to teach, and they have a girl my age, and—because Mom made me—I made friends with her." Jessie stopped. She meant to go on, but she had a sudden image of herself through everyone else's thoughts. Crazy. Dumb. But then Mendômô's warm, open manner and laughter were present to her; immediately the rest of what she meant to say came in the right words. She slowed down and spoke deliberately, but she kept her eyes on the table and the edge of the sun swatch warming the wood under her fingertips.

"It wasn't like going to the circus, which you remember later. And it wasn't like tasting a new food. Making this friend was something about the future, like leaning into it. I mean, I think the two of us make a new thing, together.

Oh, I don't know." Jessie looked up, first at Joshua, then over at Martha. "I didn't know we would be friends, the kind that last. We are. And that's a new thing I did." She finished fast, feeling everything she had said was very stupid. She glanced quickly at Uncle Don.

No one said anything. Jessie felt her blush tighten inside her chest as well as on the skin of her forehead, her neck, her ears. The lines around Uncle Don's eyes softened as he looked at her. He didn't call on Martha right away, and Jessie thought, Now they're going to start laughing at me, and I don't care if they do.

"Thank you . . . very much," said Uncle Don, and Jessie knew suddenly that he had been completely surprised by the answer given. "I think, Jessie, that your parents have every right to be proud of having you for a daughter. All right. Martha?" he asked, going right on, and Jessie breathed again over a fiery gladness rising in her chest and throat. It felt like tears but without the urge to weep. She held that tiny, clear truth of Mendômô's friendship in her heart, brightened by the glow of Uncle Don's praise. Thinking about it, she realized that he hadn't been speaking about the friendship. He'd understood her sense of the future together with Mendômô. That was a new idea, and he hadn't expected anything like it before she showed it to him.

As she and Martha were going upstairs after Sunday school, Aunt Pearl came out of the houseparents' apartment on the top landing and said, "Jessie, I want to see you a minute."

Martha went on while Jessie waited, her heart beating hard as though she was about to be caught. "I notice that Cassie wet her bed again last night," said Aunt Pearl, folding her arms across her waist. Jessie nodded and kept her mouth closed tight against any word that might betray her sister's shame by commenting on it. "It's the water, Jessie," said Aunt Pearl. "You rinsed the sheets in the tub of water, didn't you?"

"Yes, because I didn't know what else to do!"

"Well, I wish I didn't have to say this, Jessie, but you're going to have to replace that water. As things stand, we can't afford to lose that much water to one kid. So you'll have to be responsible for replacing it."

"Yeah, but . . ." Jessie had brought up three full containers of water for that tub alone, and each load had barely raised the water level. It would take her forever, alone, to replace all of it.

"I don't mind if you have others help you," said Aunt Pearl. "This isn't by way of punishment." But Jessie thought it was. "I can fit one more tub in that bathroom, and we'll label it for hand washing only, and the other one for flushing only. But I'll depend on you to get the second tub full, all right?"

Jessie stared at the third button on the red-and-white checked blouse Aunt Pearl wore and swallowed against the painful soft swelling in her throat. Nothing, nothing, in-

cluding hearing the news about Mom and Dad, had made
her as angry, or hurt as much, as this demand of Aunt
Pearl's.

"All right, Jessie?" Aunt Pearl said again, warningly,
clearly expecting Jessie to answer before leaving.

Jessie barely got the words out. "Yes, Aunt Pearl," she
said, looking from the red heart-shaped button to the floor
and the pointed toes of Aunt Pearl's red high heels.

"You can do it and still be ready for vespers this afternoon," said the housemother, leaving her in the hallway.

Jessie dragged her feet along the floorboards until she
came to the black mat runner down the back hall. Then
she hit the chipboard walls on either side with her fists,
and slammed her heels down on the floor, and screamed
each time, "I *hate* her! I *hate* her! I *hate* her!" until she
reached her own door and no longer knew whether she was
speaking of Aunt Pearl or Cassie or Mom, or even herself.

And Joshua wouldn't help. Instead, he practiced the
piano, even though Jessie had asked him and implored him
and finally yelled at him to do his share. "You said that
yesterday, too," he reminded her quietly. "You could have
waited and taken her sheets down to the washhouse.
There's some water there. Wheat and Sam and I filled the
tub yesterday. No. I'm going to practice. I've gone two days
without it already. I can't go another one, and I won't have
time to get a full hour in if I help you. No."

Every time Jessie carried a pail of water through the front
door that afternoon, she had to grit her teeth and push her

feet along to keep from marching over to Joshua and pouring the whole pailful over his head. He sat with his back perfectly straight and ran scales for forty-five minutes. Then he played the same Czerny warm-up piece for the next fifteen, until Jessie heard kids in the living room begging him to change to another song.

"I hope you all go deaf listening to him!" she yelled as she went by with her empty pail, and then, giving in to hot fury, let go and threw the pail to the cement floor.

"Jessie!" called Aunt Pearl from the dining room. "For shame! Pick that up right now! And control yourself!"

It helped a little that Cassie and Lorayne and Elissa were carrying water, too, and that Martha joined them. After a while, Meba and Sarah Lynn carried water for the tub as well. It took all of them about an hour to walk, pump, carry, and fill the tub with water. And then they had to carry their ordinary share of dorm water, and that took another hour of the day. Even Joshua had to carry water then.

When Jessie finally took the empty pails outside and around back to put them away in the washhouse, all she could think of was shaking Joshua by the shoulders until his teeth rattled. He was standing in the light shade of a papaya tree, facing the hearth of the school fireplace, poking the ashes of that day's wastepaper, when Jessie went by.

On her way back she went up to him and punched him in the upper arm with her fist, as hard as she could. He whirled around and shouted, "What did you do that for?"

"I'm telling you, you have to do your share!"

"I am doing my share! What are you talking about? Why'd you hit me?"

"Because I'm mad at you, Joshua Tyndale Howells!"

"Leave my name out of it!"

"I won't leave anything out!" shouted Jessie, swinging at Joshua again.

He dodged her and yelled back.

"You haven't helped at all!" screamed Jessie. "Who's been getting up at night with Cassie? Who's been paying attention to her all the time? I have! And I'm sick and tired of it! I won't do it the rest of my life!"

"Who's talking about the rest of your life?" demanded Joshua, whacking the ashes with a stick and making the soft, hot pile of them jump into a little cloud of gray dust.

"I am! I refuse to be stuck alone, thinking about Cassie, taking care of Cassie, giving my life over to Cassie from now on."

"What *are* you talking about?" asked Joshua, in scorn.

"I'm talking about having to go back to the States this June instead of getting to go to Egypt in September. I'm talking about having to live with relatives in the U.S. until we're adults. I'm talking about not leaving Cassie by herself until she's grown-up!"

"Oh, for Pete's sake! You're going crazy." He turned away. "That's not going to happen, and you know it."

"Who says? How do you know? You're just not paying attention, Joshua Tyndale Howells. That's all. You're letting me do everything—the worrying, the caring for Cassie, *everything!*"

"Two days and you're loopy about this! You've had to pay attention to her for two little days!"

"Twelve days! Twelve they've been missing. It's only been two for us!"

"Stop making such a big deal out of it!"

"Why? So you won't feel bad for not helping me?"

"I am helping!"

"Oh, yeah? How?"

"By not turning into a cowardy custard at the thought that Mom and Dad are somewhere in the forest we don't know about. Somebody in the family's got to keep his head, and it isn't going to be you!"

"Mom and Dad gone forever maybe and us stuck with Cassie—and you're just pretending everything's all right. That's keeping your head? What are we going to do if it's true?"

There was a sudden cold silence between them. Jessie heard the things she'd said, listening to her thoughts for the first time.

"What *can* we do about it, Jess?" said Joshua, his voice quiet and threatening. "*What can we do about it?* What can *you* do about it, Jess? Nothing, and you know it! So what's the point of getting all upset?"

A lump of despair rose in her chest to meet and accept the truth of his words. Still she argued, just to keep the realization at bay a little longer.

"I'm not upset about that. Stop changing the subject! I'm saying I'm doing the whole share of taking care of Cassie, and you have to help! You're as much related to her as I am."

"How do you want me to help? Anyway, you shouldn't make her into such a big deal either," said Joshua.

"She is a big deal if I have to get up every night to wash her sheets and then carry water to make up for it the next day. She's a huge deal if she cries herself sick going to sleep at night. You think because you're a boy and can't come over on the girls' side you can't help at all. Well, we're stuck together, like it or not."

"Jess," said Joshua, "I don't have to feel exactly the way you do just to prove I love them."

Jessie heard him, but she had to make sure he remembered just as precisely as she did the things she'd learned last vacation. "And what about the fact that when the French army searches the forest, it shoots whatever moves? And what about the people who've had their heads cut off in the forest? And what about the pits where—"

Joshua put his hands over his ears. "Stop it!" he yelled. "Don't talk nightmare stuff *anymore!* It's not good!"

"All right, then, fine! Why couldn't you help me today? Even one trip for water would have helped!"

"You know why, Jessie."

But she didn't.

He was sucking in air to be able to speak, and he began to cry through his words. "If I give in to everybody saying,

'Do this, do that,' I won't keep practicing, and I won't be any good *and then what!*" He screamed the last words at her. "Only Mom and Dad really care that I play the piano. It isn't really important to anybody else. If I don't have them—"

Jessie was appalled. She'd never known that practicing was hard for Joshua to do. She'd had no idea how fragile a thing was his determination to use his gift; but she could see it now. If he treated the piano as though it were just an extra thing, everyone else at the dorm, grown-ups especially, would treat his time for music the same way, and he'd lose his claim on practice time over everything else. And then he'd lose the gift.

"I can't stand it. It feels like this will go on forever," Jessie said, dropping her own voice now, wanting to make up the quarrel with him.

"Yeah, well, it won't," said Joshua. The moment she took on his discouragement, he switched to hard optimism. "Feeling like it isn't being it." He dug the point of his stick hard into a spot between the bricks of the fireplace where the mortar was cracked. When he got out a piece, he tossed it into the hot ashes.

"You're wrecking that wall," observed Jessie.

"So what," Joshua muttered.

"So don't." Jessie waited a moment longer, thinking he might say something that would bring them together. She'd put it all out in front of him—the dread and fear, and even the shame about resenting Cassie's needs—and he'd blown everything to sensible little bits, and then made her feel sad for him. He hadn't taken his turn listening to her at all.

"Forget it," she said bitterly between closed teeth, and pivoted so hard that her heel dug through the grass and exposed a little sore of red dirt on the lawn. She marched to the dorm and slammed the study-hall door twice after she went inside.

Raw from the argument with Joshua and trembling with regret and fury when she thought of him, she couldn't find distraction in any of the games and conversations going on in the dorm. She wanted to go back out to Joshua and push their argument all the way to some agreement. She ached to be in balance again with him, with Cassie, with Mom and Dad. She needed something, something certain, but she didn't know what.

That afternoon, after the vesper service, which all the missionaries in the area attended, the other dorm kids dashed about, hanging off the frangipani tree across the road from the little church and playing freeze tag on the grass. The adults stood talking in small groups on the porch and the steps. Jessie and Martha walked slowly around the edge of the rectangular rose bed planted beside the church. There were no roses on the tall thorn-spiked plants.

Martha said nothing as they walked. Jessie was grateful to her for knowing when not to talk. On their second lap around the skinny, disappointing garden, Jessie saw Uncle Don leave a group of adults and cross the grass toward them.

"Hello, girls," he said. "I've a notion to go over to the cemetery. Either of you want to come along?"

"No, thanks," said Martha politely. She looked at Jessie and signaled with eyes and eyebrows that she thought Uncle Don wanted to talk privately with Jessie. Jessie returned an exasperated expression with her eyes and eyebrows and shrugged her shoulders. Martha wandered off to pick up a conversation with the seventh-grade girls.

The cemetery was a ways from the church. Jessie and Uncle Don walked with a matching rhythm. His legs were short, and hers were long. Wind sprang up and tossed the palm fronds in the trees they passed. Jessie watched this, thinking how palm trees looked like heads of hair. Under that thought, she wondered what Uncle Don wanted to talk about. "Are we going to be back before the dorm kids start walking home again?" she asked.

Uncle Don took out his pocket watch and held it in the palm of his hand, so Jessie could see its face. "Walker plans to start out in fifteen minutes. That's plenty of time," he said.

An idea came swiftly, and as swiftly, Jessie worded it aloud. "Are you going to tell me my parents are dead?" she asked, and thought that forever she would remember the moment by the grating sound of a pied crow's startled cry as it flew up from the road in front of them. It had been picking at a dead frog in the ditch. Waiting for Uncle Don's answer, she was amazed to feel nothing at all. She was numb.

"No," said Uncle Don, making the word small and quiet. He was not denying the possibility of Mom and Dad being dead. It hadn't come to that yet, is all he meant. "But—" And he cleared his throat. A sign that he wasn't at ease with the subject. Jessie watched the road dust rise up in little reddish puffs each time she put her foot down deliberately hard. She looked back, and her footprints were clear in the dust behind her. So were Uncle Don's.

"There is the feeling among the adults that some plan is needed for the three of you, just in case. If you were all Cassie's age, I don't think anyone would consult you. But you and Joshua are old enough to journey across the continent by yourselves, and you can't be moved about like sacks of flour." In his definite tones at the end, Jessie heard the tail of an argument he must have had with other missionaries. Since he was talking with her now, he must have persuaded them. He knew she was old enough to be treated as responsible. In spite of the gravity of the moment, Jessie was flushed with an odd kind of pride, and then immediately felt stupid and young.

"What's supposed to happen?" she asked, carefully keeping her voice even, not betraying her self-doubt. She most certainly wanted to have a say in what happened to her life.

"Well, your parents made a will before they left New York. We all had to. The suggestion now is that Sam's father, since he's the executive secretary on the field, write the Presbyterian offices there about your parents' absence and at the same time find out the terms of their will for you."

"So soon?" asked Jessie, thinking of Joshua's remark earlier. Twelve days didn't seem long enough to panic over, after all.

"We'll wait another week at the most," said Uncle Don. "The French government is looking for them, and when they report to us, we'll have to telegram New York."

"Won't we get to finish the term here?" Jessie asked, not only her stomach but her heart flying out from under her in dread.

"You do have some say in this. I want you to know that." Uncle Don stopped in the road and looked directly at Jessie. "You more than the others your age have an understanding of direction. In effect, Jessie, I'm asking you what you want."

"I want us to go to Schutz, just the way we planned," said Jessie. For a moment she entertained the vision of everything happening right anyway, even though Mom and Dad weren't part of the plan's working. They faded out of the picture, but otherwise the picture was the same. She would go on growing up just the way she'd imagined it. No matter what.

"But what about Cassie?" said Uncle Don.

Cassie! The hope swooping into Jessie so wantonly, so fast and many colored, of traveling with the group, of living in Egypt, of being free and on her own and away from every adult she'd ever known, that hope fell and was wasted, shattered like a glass falling on a bare cement floor. It wasn't worth picking up the pieces. Throw them away! Never let her have anything good that she wanted! Nothing she wanted was good anyhow, probably!

In anger and despair, Jessie no longer watched her words. "It's not fair of God to ask me to give up everything I've wanted and hoped for before I've gotten anything!" She kicked a stone savagely and scratched the toe of her good Sunday shoe in the dirt.

Uncle Don said, "Whatever gave you the idea God is fair?"

"Isn't He? I mean, that's what God is all about, I thought. Everybody mattering just as much as everybody else. None of us cheating on each other. None of us stealing from each other or hurting each other, so everybody mattering can come true. All that! The Commandments. Aren't they fairness?"

"No," said Uncle Don, sounding surprised. "They're not. They're justice. Doing right. Fair is everybody getting the same amount in any division. God is not fair. You see that for yourself, Jessie, anywhere you look. Merciful and just, yes, but fair? Fair is a concept invented so one person in authority can control a lot of people without using violence. Fairness isn't made for encouraging people to grow inside. It just keeps them from fighting. It keeps them from maturity, too."

"Am I supposed to decide things just so Cassie will be happy?" demanded Jessie.

"Is that what you think?"

"It doesn't matter what I think! I don't get to choose!"

Jessie could feel tears coming and decided she didn't mind crying in front of Uncle Don. "Don't you see? I *have* to stay with Cassie."

"Why?"

"Because you think I should," muttered Jessie, resenting him as she spoke.

"Why do you say that?"

"Because you asked me about her. You want me to think of her first, because that's the sisterly, loving thing to do." Jessie didn't bother damping the sarcasm in her voice.

"I did ask you about Cassie. You're not an only child. You have to think of three people at once. Your brother and your sister can't do this as well as you can. You have the ability to do it, to see us all in balance as we should be, Jessie. But it takes tremendous courage to be the one who chooses to re-create that balance. Do you understand that?"

You, you have courage. You hear its voice.

"I don't have that courage," said Jessie. She hadn't wanted to cross the bridge and the snake's blood alone. She had wanted Nléla to come get her, too, but Nléla had taken care of Joshua instead. "I need something for me, too. I can't keep loving them if no one loves me."

"Don't your grandparents love you, Jessie?"

Jessie had a quick vision of Grandma Howells, small, curly haired, talking to her as they worked in her garden, her voice rich with laughter. Yes, Grandma Howells loved them all. And she loved Grandma. That would be all right, if it had to be.

"But why don't I get what I want?" cried Jessie.

"What do you want, Jessie?"

She thought of the passport. She thought of the airplane trips she'd imagined. She thought of Joshua, helping her carry water. She thought of Cassie, dry every night and free of that old urine stink forever. She thought of walking around Libamba campus with Mendômô. All that was possible somehow, even if Mom and Dad were really dead and the Howells kids had to go back to the States to relatives, but Mendômô and Libamba—friend and home together— would be lost forever. The new thing in her life would be impossible now.

"I want not to lose—" But Jessie couldn't finish. She'd meant to say *everything*, but at the thought of never coming back, not having any of this life in her future, she was dissolved in grief. Never to be here, never to be in Africa again! Never to hear or speak Bassa, not to live with anyone from the dorm anymore, not to have Martha as a daily friend, not even knowing Uncle Don after this, not to have Mom and Dad in her life or Mendômô in her future—with every thought, Jessie's sorrow rose higher and the sobs came harder.

Uncle Don turned to her on the road, in front of the little wooden gate by the cemetery, and put his arms around Jessie. Being hugged was such great relief to her that her tears came faster, and the pain lessened. In the middle of it she thought, Cassie needs a hug. Then Uncle Don pulled a large blue handkerchief from his pants pocket and unfolded it for her. "Here, blow," he said.

"Thanks," said Jessie, making a little laugh out of the shakes in her voice. "Can I ask you something?"

"Of course," said Uncle Don.

They stood looking over the pipe-and-cement-post fencing around the cemetery. There was a frangipani tree in the northeastern corner in full blossom. The four- and five-petaled flowers covering the tree were thick, creamy white with peach and gold centers. When the breeze moved, the perfume from the tree was lemony and delicious, but if the breeze dropped, Jessie could smell nothing from the blossoms, as if she'd imagined the scent.

"Remember that lesson you taught last term, about Stephen, and about calling?"

"Yes."

"Do you think—do you think it's awful if someone doesn't hear a calling? I mean, does that mean the person isn't called, or isn't listening right, or maybe isn't old enough, or something?"

"You can hear with your heart as well as with your ears and mind," said Uncle Don.

"What do you mean?"

"Calling isn't restricted to knowing you'll be a preacher or a doctor—"

"Or a pianist or a banker or an artist," said Jessie.

"Yes. Calling is what makes the best people so good at

their work," said Uncle Don. "But most of them forget they were called. We all tend to forget that we work not just for ourselves but for God, and when people forget their calling, they rely on their gifts alone. The work isn't as good then."

"But what if you don't have any gifts? I don't," said Jessie. "I don't know what they are, anyway."

You see patterns in people. You understand others. That had been Mom's answer that day of the picnic down by the river.

"Oh, Jessie, you are so full of gifts all wrapped up and waiting to be opened. You listen with your heart. Many people who want to do that spend all their lives learning how. You do it. It's one of your greatest gifts."

"How do I do that?" Jessie was disbelieving.

"Think of Cassie."

"Oh, her again," Jessie growled.

"Yes, her again," said Uncle Don, laughing a little. "You hear her with your heart even when you don't want to. You can't help it. And Jess, you should never block your heart from answering the call you hear. You shouldn't resist just because you know that doing the right thing won't be easy or convenient for you."

"What do you mean?"

"I mean," said Uncle Don slowly, "I mean that your *choosing* to help Cassie is in itself doing as much as the actual help you give her."

"Really?"

"Yes, really."

Jessie considered this. It was true that deciding to go to Cassie took as much effort from Jessie's will as doing the work of helping her. Jessie had never thought the decision itself counted as much as the work. "Why does the choosing matter?" she asked.

"That's part of the truth in the parable Jesus told about the father who asked his two sons to go out and work in the field."

"Oh. You mean the story in which the first son said no to his father but changed his mind and went after all, and the second son said yes but didn't go. That one?" asked Jessie, knowing she was right.

"That one," said Uncle Don. "And when he was done telling the story, Jesus asked a question. Do you remember it?"

Jessie hunted in her memory for the shape of the parable they were discussing. "Jesus asks, 'Which son did what the father wanted?' "

"Right. And why does Jesus ask that?"

Jessie stared at the peeling silvery gray bark of the frangipani tree, followed the line of its graceful trunk up to the delicate twisty branches and on out to the thin, fragile twigs holding up the elegant blossoms. "I don't think Jesus cared about who worked in the field," she said slowly, putting that detail aside. "I think he told the story so we would look at the kind of answers people give when they're asked to do something."

"And just answering will do?" asked Uncle Don, pressing her.

"No," said Jessie. "Of course not. You have to give the right answer."

"Ah," said Uncle Don. "And what is the right answer?"

"Do you mean the right answer is changing your mind?" She knew she was being flip and was suddenly embarrassed. "Well, I don't know!" she said impatiently. Something in this conversation was hunting her heart, chasing her out of anyplace where she might hide and feel comfortable and safe.

Her answer made Uncle Don laugh, and the little amused sound brought her attention back to him. "You can change your mind either way, can't you? But Jesus is saying only one answer is right, and that is what God wants us to do. It isn't like tossing a coin, with either answer being okay. Only one answer is right."

"But how do we know which one?"

"Through calling, Jessie," said Uncle Don.

"What do you mean?" What had Dad said that night during Christmas vacation? Calling is hearing your gift.

Uncle Don frowned a little, looking down at his surgeon's hands, which he now held out in front of him, palms up, fingers spread. He turned them over, flexed the fingers, and looked up at Jessie again. "Calling is in the answers you give when you are needed. It comes first in your willingness to give, and *then* in what you do. And you aren't answering yourself, or the other person. You are answering

God. You see, Jessie, the parable means that you get to *choose* to love, to *choose* to do what is right. God won't force us to do what is right, because He wants us free."

Jessie felt her heart caught and imprisoned as he spoke. How could God want her to be free and then cut off everything good ahead of her?

"There isn't any best time for answering God, or a time that is easiest for doing what is right," said Uncle Don. "The time to decide is the time you're in."

"It's hard," said Jessie, and tears stung her nose. "It's really hard."

"Yes, it is," said Uncle Don quietly. "Listening with the heart is just as hard for adults as for children. But that's how you know you're choosing the right."

They stood by the cemetery gate, and three black-and-yellow butterflies flickered out through the bars, hovered over the grass between herself and Uncle Don, then followed each other back through the gate into the cemetery. Jessie, breathing slowly, caught the delicate fragrance of frangipani again and longed for the moment to last, so she could stay at rest in this time of companionship.

"Well," said Uncle Don, turning to her, meeting her eyes with respect in his own. "Well?"

"Do you think," said Jessie, fishing for some way to prolong the conversation but also because the question came to her right then, "do you think that if I go back to America now, I can stay friends with Mendômô—the African girl I talked about this morning?"

Uncle Don stepped through the long grass around the cemetery gate and made his way back to the road. Jessie reluctantly followed, hurrying a little to keep pace beside him so she could hear his answer. Ahead of them, where the road forked, she could see kids gathering and starting off in the line, two by two, returning to the dorm.

It took Uncle Don a long time to answer. He cleared his throat twice before speaking. "I don't know," he said. "That would be a grievous loss. I don't know." He touched Jessie on the shoulder. "Don't fear it," he said. "Wait and see."

"Well, then," said Jessie, "I want us to go back to Libamba before we leave. I don't want to go away to America straight from here."

"I'll make sure of that," said Uncle Don. "But, Jessie, let's wait and see, all right?"

"All right." The words, as she said them, were empty and dark.

10

The Forest and the Letter

Owl calls, made by birds, came insistently, now close by, now far off. Sometimes after a long stretch of no calls at all, Jessie's mother would begin to fall asleep. Then she would jerk awake again, her heart pounding as the bird called, perhaps right over her head or in a tree beyond her feet. Her mind swooped from floating rags of bad dreams to unfamiliar hard edges where she lay on the ground. Slowly she sorted out the birdcalls from remembered calls that men made. She lay rigidly still, wide awake, listening to the quiet, constant rustling of forest creatures going about their business in the dark.

Night in the forest was cold, much colder than either she or Jessie's father had ever imagined it could be. The chill was of dampness rising through earth that never absorbed enough sun to dry its top layer. High overhead, the treetops whispered together as nocturnal animals moved across the branches in search of food. Down on the forest floor some little thing snuffled and lightly scrabbled its way around the temporary camp made by the three Maquis and two missionaries.

How long, thought Mrs. Howells, how long, O Lord, will we be in this?

It seemed they had been walking forever, for days, for weeks. During the light of day, while the walking had to be done, she sometimes caught herself believing she'd never done anything else, because of the sameness of the bush through which they walked, hour by hour. During the night, when they could not move, she wanted to rush forward, run through the forest and come out among the trees into the clearing where the dorm was, where she would see Cassie and Joshua and Jessie, or perhaps they would see her first, it didn't matter, as long as they saw each other again.

That afternoon twelve days ago, when her husband, Matthew, had come back from his last class, he'd called cheerfully, "Come to Môm with me to deliver the school payroll! We'll have an hour to ourselves!" And she'd squared the stack of exams she was grading and gone gladly, not even stopping for a sweater, because Môm was just half an hour away. They would be home again long before sundown, when the air cooled.

That brown sweater folded lengthwise, laid across the back of the easy chair in the office, was the single thing

Mrs. Howells thought of most often. Sometimes she thought about her toothbrush, and every morning she wanted a comb for her long hair, but if she were warmer by the thickness of that one layer of wool, she'd be ten times stronger in hope right now, she thought, shifting on the layer of banana leaves between her and the chill in the ground.

The Maquis, with their long rifles pointed at the missionaries in the carryall, hadn't been as frightening as the two tall forest trees flashing down in front and behind the car, almost simultaneously. Now that she went back over the memory of that afternoon, she could hear the *crack!* and the huge tearing sound of the trunks going over. But at the time, she had imagined unnatural thunder, and the trees flailing the air as they came down had made her think of immense ocean waves rushing forward. She hadn't known what the sound meant. She hadn't known what the Maquis meant either, except they meant to threaten. Why? Why the Howells? Why people from Libamba?

For days there had been no answers given, none at all.

Mr. Howells had called to the men while he still sat in the car with the motor running, but they made short, choppy motions with their rifles, clearly telling the white people to get out. He could not drive forward or backward over the trees now blocking the road. So they both got out. Immediately three Maquis had leaped from the forest banks onto the road, aiming guns at herself and Mr. Howells.

One of the Maquis had prodded her with his rifle barrel

and told her in French to get off the road into the forest, in the direction he pointed. She followed her husband, who was pressed by another Maquis in the same dangerous way, rifle tip grazing the spine. When she heard the car motor turn over, she looked back, in spite of the man with the gun behind her, and saw that a third, older Maquis was driving the carryall down into the ditch and then up again, crashing through the smaller branches crowning the fallen tree.

Perhaps they were driving it beyond the barriers in order to hide it off the road somewhere else, to distract any search party by removing clues. The longer searchers tried to find out who was missing and why the trees had been cut into barricades, the longer they might wonder if anyone was missing at all.

Mrs. Howells sighed into the darkness; there was no doubt now, twelve days into captivity, that they had been missed. By now, someone had scrambled to put together a substitute Bible Conference, and by now, Jessie and Joshua and Cassie knew.

The ground where she lay was hard. She shifted slightly to let her bones rest on a piece with fewer bumps under her hips. Beside her, her husband moaned lightly in his sleep. In the complete blackness, she could not see him, but she raised herself and leaned on an elbow to touch his forehead with the back of her hand. His fever was receding. Soon he would get the chills again. He was suffering the worst attack of malaria she'd seen in all her years in Africa. In spite of herself she remembered the ominous warning old-timers gave about Cameroun. It was called the White Man's Grave, because of malaria.

On that first night, darkness had fallen about an hour after they had entered the forest, stumbling along over un-cleared ground, brushing branches out of their faces so they could see to take the next step. The Maquis took them a long ways before they stopped at last, outside a small make-shift hut walled and roofed with palm branches laid so thickly that barely a single beam of light from the lantern inside showed through the fronds.

There had been answers of a sort, she thought, now moving closer to her husband to give him some of her own small warmth. Both of them had wondered how the Maquis managed their strategy, inside the forest. Now they saw for themselves. Still at gunpoint, they had stumbled into the small, green, leafy room, blinking in a sudden glare of light. It was only a single lantern, but after so long in the dark, the little flame seemed very bright.

The lantern stood on a small wooden table; maps were spread out around it. On the other side of the table was a man a few years older than they. The dense black of the skin on his oval face was marked with tribal scarification in dark blue arrowlike hatch marks over the cheeks and in two delicate beaded lines across his forehead. In his ordinary khaki-colored pants and shirt, he looked like any of the teachers in the elementary schools around Libamba. Mrs. Howells began to relax when she saw him.

But he had been angry to see them. They were evidently not the right people. He had expected someone else to be caught in the trap. When she and Matthew handed over the identity cards required by the French of every adult in Cameroun, the man had read their professions and place of residence carefully and then looked up at them in fury. He began spitting questions at them in French.

"What are you doing in this country? Where were you going today? Whom were you going to see? Tell us his name! Why are you carrying so much money? Where are your weapons?"

When their interrogator paused for breath, her husband had said very quietly, *"Men me ye Matthew Howells."* I am Matthew Howells.

And at the first words in Bassa, a change came over the leader's expression. Something happened to his eyes, some hardness and deep bitterness were considered and then removed. He looked at her and at Matthew as though he were willing to see them for themselves now. French government workers rarely bothered to learn the African languages of the areas where they were stationed.

Mrs. Howells thought again about that curious silence falling after Bassa had been spoken by a white man. Everyone seemed to listen differently, to be less angry and frightened. Mosquitoes had whined about the little shelter. Someone slapped at himself to kill one of the insects. Then the African began talking again, in Bassa this time. He asked all the questions over, but without the ragged edge of a threat in his voice. She and Matthew answered the questions in turn, speaking calmly, though they both trembled with exhaustion and hunger and the effort to keep fear down.

They had been given water to drink—and she hesitated to drink it, knowing full well all the deadly parasites in unboiled, unfiltered water. Mr. Howells had calmly drunk three dipperfuls before handing the dipper to her. She thought, What happens to him, happens to me, and she drank, too.

They had not seen the leader again after that night. When they left him, they were put into a low leaf-and-branch shelter. They huddled together on the bare earth and tried to sleep. Neither she nor Mr. Howells deceived themselves. This was not a friendly place. This was a war zone. Had they been the ones the trap was meant for, they'd have been questioned and likely shot. Outside the hut, they were guarded by a Maquis who sat by the entrance with a gun on his knees.

Early the next morning, one of the younger Maquis— perhaps two years older than Joshua—had called them out. "Go a little ways into the forest for your private needs," he'd said softly. "We will eat and begin walking." And when they started out, after each eating half of a dry, flat, spicy piece of ntumba and swallowing two mouthfuls of water, the same man had ordered them, "Walk without sound. Do not talk. Do not break off leaves or branches. When we can, we will let you go."

They had walked the boundary of Libamba, some ten kilometers square, for three days, stopping at every possible place in the forest where she and Matthew might have simply come out of the forest and onto the edges of campus. They had walked toward Makak and toward every village the Howellses had ever heard of or been to, but at each point, there had been soldiers of the French army in force, waiting for them, so they had turned back into the forest.

The rescue of the missionaries was of much less importance to the French than the capture of the Maquis, Mrs. Howells knew. Were she and her husband to go out in the open, they would not be hurt, but the young men behind them would be chased; some would be shot, and others caught and tortured, likely even killed. So no attempt was made to come out of the forest. The Maquis wanted to keep all their number safe, and the Howellses were unwilling to be freed at the price of any young man's life.

On the fourth night in the forest, while the two of them sat close together on the ground in the darkness of the second small leaf-and-branch hut, they heard the voice of the leader again. They tried to discern his words, but the distance was just great enough to prevent their understanding. The conversation in the palm shelter next to them went on a long time, and Mrs. Howells fell asleep with her head on her husband's shoulder before the talking was finished.

The next day they began their trek through the deep forest.

No one told them where they were going or what would happen to them, or why they were no longer walking the edges of Libamba or Makak. Each succeeding day there was less to eat, and every night was colder.

The jungle they walked through was dense, deeper than the Howellses had ever known. The path was difficult to find. After half an hour of walking, Mrs. Howells had a headache from looking constantly for the Maquis ahead of her. In the thick overgrowth she often found herself alone and choked by the green. Then, in terror, she would clamp her eyes on the heavy screen of grasses and crowded saplings growing from the jungle floor, but she could see no one through it, even though the leaves ahead of her moved. The wide, glossy greenness had swallowed the person in front of her whole, and would swallow her and each one behind her as well.

Somewhere in all that sun-bright greenness, and somewhere in the dim brown gloom under the trees, there were soldiers. *Tirailleurs*, they were called, men who shot as they were told at anything that moved. Mercenaries. Mrs. Howells hurried to keep up.

Occasionally the path led them through tiny sun-catching clearings caused by long-dead forest fires kindled by lightning. Tender new greens grew in splashes across the black charcoal of burned trees. Jessie would have liked to see this, thought Mrs. Howells, longing for her elder daughter's conversation and company. What was she doing now?

And oh, what did she feel? Lost? Abandoned? And could she love Cassie as Cassie would need? Would Joshua have the courage to turn to his sisters in his time of misery?

Mrs. Howells was swept by a wind of desire so great that she doubled over on the path. Ah, hold them in the palm of Your hand! she cried out, in the pain of her heart.

It began to rain as they walked. At first they knew it by the light fingertip tapping of raindrops on the thick roof of leaves high overhead. The rainstorm gathered, and the light dimmed below just before the storm swept in force across their part of the forest, pouring itself upon them. For a time they walked in a waterfall. Then the rain passed over and continued west, the way behind them. Now every branch, every bush, and every palm frond held and dripped cold water. Even though they were already drenched, the sudden sprinklings and splashes from the leaves above and on either side were cold and uncomfortable, and each surprise wetting made Mrs. Howells angry.

They walked in the true primeval forest, where no one had ever cut the ancient trees. Sunlight fell in pieces through the forest roof, moving fluidly over the browns and grays of shade on the forest floor when the wind ruffled the green canopy overhead. The trees rose up, huge and smooth, white of trunk, forest columns straight and silvery, crowned hundreds of feet in the air. Sometimes when Mrs. Howells looked up, she saw a breeze stir the distant branches, and minty green and pale red leaves made graceful lacy patterns, revealing glittering chips of blue sky. When she saw these things, the walking was easy.

One afternoon they came to a small river. The air in the open was hot, bright, yellow. The light hurt Mrs. Howells's eyes. The riverbanks were high, and there was no formal bridge. A log had been flung across the water from bank to bank. It was old and well traveled. The ground on either side had been smoothed by many feet. Sucking and gurgling, river wavelets reached up and slapped at the banks, sending foam into the air.

Mrs. Howells waited for the signal from the Maquis who had crossed ahead of the others. She thought about the day in June, some years ago, when she had heard about Nléla and the new baby. Oh, the waste! she thought, and cried for the first time since the horrible adventure began.

When it was her turn to cross, she balanced her way a short distance out on the log. It was broad, and going carefully, she should have crossed easily; but she looked down and stopped, caught by the glistening, slippery brown tumble of water four meters beneath her feet.

Behind her, the last Maquis, the one who had angrily prodded her into the forest with the gun on the first day, called softly and urgently, *"Kenek mbeñel, u bege bañ malep, nun ndik bisu."* Mrs. Howells understood him quite well. Look up. Look ahead. Go forward.

She tried to move, but she jerked herself slightly off balance and stumbled. Her heart swooped downward. The

Maquis was behind her immediately and steadied her with his right hand. He held her elbow firmly until they were safely across the bridge.

About midmorning the following day, moving along in as great a silence as they could manage, Mrs. Howells heard a birdcall that didn't quite carry as pure and light a sound as the others in the air around them. Suddenly both her elbows were grasped from behind, and a Maquis clapped his hand over her mouth.

The Maquis in front of her reappeared among the trunks of the trees just ahead, his eyes burning with urgency. He held a forefinger against his lips, and the Maquis behind her slowly took his hand away from her mouth. Mrs. Howells swallowed, and her throat grated against its own dryness.

Everyone stood absolutely still. And then, without a sign perceptible to Mrs. Howells, it seemed safe to move again. The man who held her by the elbows let go of only one arm and guided her forward a ways. By pressure of his fingertips, he told her to go down into a hollow off the path. She slipped and sat down hard, slithering along layers of dead leaves carpeting a steep incline.

The trees in this dip were as tall as the trees on higher ground. The bush and scrub were dense. Everyone sat, wedged between roots and woody stalks and thin, doomed saplings. They waited. Mrs. Howells sighed once, and a Maquis glared at her. She sought her husband's eyes, but he seemed to have fallen asleep, his head back, resting against a slender tree trunk.

Mosquitoes came and feasted. Mrs. Howells brushed them off her ankles and neck, but they returned immediately. One of the Maquis shook his head at her. She was to make neither sound nor motion. The Maquis all held their guns, cocked, on their knees. Birds around them gradually resumed their song and chatter.

And then there came unfamiliar, harsh noise in the forest, the sound of heavy-booted feet pushing through the undergrowth. The ground, even in the hollow where Mrs. Howells was, reverberated with the trampings. Though she could not see them, she knew many men were moving through the forest, following the path the Maquis and the missionaries had just left.

Here it was, the French army, a Frenchman at the head, certainly, but otherwise columns of mercenaries gathered from other French colonies on the African continent. It occurred to Mrs. Howells then that these men were her rescue. At the same time, she felt something hard pushing into the small of her back and slowly reached around to shift what she thought was the sharp end of a branch. She felt the cold metal barrel of a gun but did not turn around to see who held it.

The soldiers stayed in that part of the forest for more than an hour, searching thoroughly. The hollow was overlooked. Mrs. Howells felt and heard her muscles creaking when the Maquis finally let her stretch and get up. They walked on, stopping frequently while all three Maquis carefully turned over the leaves and branches on the path ahead of them, using long pronged sticks. They poked at the ground when it was too smooth, too leafy, checking for hidden tiger pits. They looked under the leaves for land mines the soldiers routinely left concealed on the paths they searched, making the forest a dangerous place to walk.

They went around one pit, after the Maquis had carefully and entirely uncovered it. It was freshly dug. The sharpened points were still white. Mrs. Howells listened to the whispered argument between the Maquis, who concluded they hadn't time to pull the stakes out now and would come back this way to do it, after taking care of the missionaries.

On the seventh day, her husband had collapsed on the path. He had been walking ahead of her that day, and she came upon him suddenly, nearly falling over the Maquis who crouched beside him. He felt the skin of Mr. Howells's forehead and arms. "Fever," said Mr. Howells faintly, in Bassa. His eyes were closed. "Malaria."

And then Mrs. Howells could not disguise the fact from herself any longer. One or both of them might die here in the forest.

Two of the Maquis had stripped off their own sweaters and put them on Mr. Howells. They had given their rifles and machetes to Mrs. Howells and the third Maquis to carry, and made a chair of their arms to carry Mr. Howells. They went more slowly now, resting often, changing shifts and weapons among the four of them.

They had no quinine to help her husband counter the sickness. But when they made camp that night, one of the

Maquis hunted off the path for a certain tree, and, when he found it, stripped the bark and ground this between two stones. He mixed the rough powder with water and gave it to Mr. Howells to drink.

"The forest medicine will work," he had said to her in Bassa, "but in a few days." He looked at her, and she felt her lips pressed tightly together against worry and distress. "Do not be afraid," said the man gently. "It is a thing I have taken myself against malaria."

Together and with great, silent speed before complete darkness fell, the four of them made a stretcher of poles cut from saplings and the pagnes, the clothes the men wore over their shoulders. In the morning the band had started out again, filled with frustrated urgency. They kept moving; they couldn't stop; they had to stop often. At least once each day they had waited, silent and hidden, while their path was crossed ahead and behind by the army, searching, searching for them. Now they had finished the fourth day of walking after her husband fell sick.

Today, Mrs. Howells had heard a high, distant wailing, a sound she remembered but now found unfamiliar because it was so clearly not a thing of the forest. And then when she heard it again, she knew the cry was a train whistle, far off. By that sound Mrs. Howells thought they must be going toward Mbalmayo, toward the edge of Bassa territory. The Maquis must think there would be less surveillance at this place than around Libamba. Maybe—maybe they would be out on a road tomorrow.

They had been walking for eleven days, and carrying the stretcher now for three. Mrs. Howells was afraid for her husband, and she was often nauseous with hunger. They were all hungry. She needed to sleep to walk well in the morning. She needed to stop imagining soldiers and gunfire and blood on the road when they did come out at last.

An owl called again, three low hoots, and then a little farther away called once more. Mrs. Howells looked up into the dark, able to see nothing in its soft blackness. In need of something to do lest fear overtake her, she began writing a letter in her head to Jessie. And as she thought of Jessie, she was able at last to move into prayer.

During the silence of Thursday morning prayer in the dorm chapel, Jessie sat still, almost falling asleep in the warm bar of sun lying over the chapel benches. Cassie sat close beside her, and Jessie didn't take her hand away when Cassie reached for it. Jessie didn't want to hold Cassie's hand, but she pushed her irritation aside, grimly. She let Cassie fold both hands around her own. Unexpectedly, she knew a strange sense of comfort. Odd, that Cassie's touch should be comforting to her. She thought that was her job for Cassie.

Behind her in chapel, where she couldn't see him, Joshua was sitting with Wheat and Sam, Hal Brumbaugh and Isaac. As Jessie thought of him, anger and frustration twisted together in her, pulling her right out of Cassie's embrace. She turned around to glare at Joshua and caught him watching her. He looked away immediately, pressing his lips tightly together in a sullen expression of frustration and resentment.

He must know the same sense of imbalance as she. Well, she would not be the first one to reach to the middle this time. He would have to speak, or do something, to right things between them. As Uncle Walker rose to read the psalm to them, Jessie was conscious of Cassie next to her, not next to Joshua. She felt selfish, having her little sister warm and sweetly affectionate beside her. Well, she'd worked for that balance with Cassie. Joshua could work, too.

Really, thought Jessie as Uncle Walker began Psalm 139 again. This business of making sure we get along together is like trying to get the gold chain of a necklace untangled. You almost think you'd rather have the knot than keep picking at the tiny thing to get the links straight.

"Where could I go from thy Spirit,
where could I flee from thy face?
I climb to heaven—but thou art there;
I hide in the depths of the world—and thou art there.
If I flew with the wings of the dawn
to farthest reach of the ocean,
even there thy hand would hold me,
thy right hand would reach me.
If I say, 'The dark will cover me,
night will hide me in its curtains,'

even darkness is not dark to thee;
the night is as clear as the daylight."

And as Uncle Walker came to those words in the psalm, and Jessie heard them for the sixth time that week, for the sixth time she thought, Of course this is true for Mom and Dad if it's true for me.

But today, as she listened to the words, she had a new thought: The person talking is running away from God. Mom and Dad aren't—they go toward God. So even more, God should cover them. This doesn't say anything about their danger, only that they won't be without God. And suppose that's all we have? God, but no parents? What's the worth of that? God, without being happy? *I won't have God, if that's the way God is!*

She almost shouted the words. Cassie must have sensed something pulling Jessie out of the moment together; she sat up straight, away from Jessie, and Jessie withdrew her hand, because she was clenching her fists. *I won't have You!* she yelled at God, with all the voice in her heart. *You let anything happen! It isn't right! It isn't fair! I don't want You, God!*

In the perfect, empty silence after that, silence in the room and utter silence inside her, Jessie knew she had nothing at all. Nothing.

I can't! she cried. I can't do it! You don't give me anything but hard words! But I can't let go of You! Why aren't You fair!

She felt tears on her cheeks as she finished speaking to God and came awake, aware of everyone around her, bowing heads to pray at Uncle Walker's urging. Well, she wouldn't. She'd prayed already and that was that. No holy words that fit everybody all at once were going to make a difference to her now. As she listened to them praying, Jessie felt a burning inside her, some heat emptying her heart, and then a heaviness floated in her.

She tried to ignore it by moving fast, talking loudly at breakfast, working hard while she made her bed and did her dorm chore of straightening the living room with the other kids on her team. The sensation refused to be ignored. The heaviness became a restlessness not to be soothed with busywork. Jessie longed to be outside in the morning light.

Thursday was mail day. Wheat's special job at the dorm was sorting the mail when Uncle Walker had other things to do. Today, Uncle Walker had gone back into the town of Ebolowa to work on the matter of getting water supplied to the dorm. When her share of the living-room chore was done, Jessie passed Wheat without saying anything. His back was to her as he slipped letters into the pigeonholes in the old secretary. She went out the front door into the blue and golden morning, intending to stay clear of any further reminder of letters—letters that weren't coming from home to her family anymore.

She wandered over the short grass of the playing field toward the large straggly liana plant between the field and the road. There was no breeze, but the air was dry and the smell of dust from the road sharp in her nostrils. The pressure in her chest hung along her spine now, made her heart beat thickly. She moved slowly, came to the bush covered with yellow trumpet-shaped flowers, and stopped. She looked around, wondering what to do next, and poked her right index finger down the lemon-colored throat of one of the thick satiny-petaled blossoms.

Liana flowers were beautiful, but Mom had never let her or Joshua or Cassie pick them, because their stems oozed drops of milky white juice, and even one drop would leave a permanent ugly brown stain.

Mom. Jessie had a sudden image of Mom at home, her dark head bent over a sheet of thin white letter paper, covering it with long, even lines of words written in blue ink, words about the garden and the broken washing machine and the student who fell asleep in Dad's class last week and sometimes the price of eggs or oranges; she made remarks about Jessie's letters, the pleasure of reading Jessie's descriptions of other dorm kids doing ordinary things, thoughts on the ideas Jessie had tried out in an essay she'd sent home, words about Jessie's discouragement over grades or Cassie's homesickness or Joshua's too-short letters.

The pressure evaporated.

Jessie had seen and felt the whole picture of Mom at home in the office, writing her a letter, before she could stop herself from letting the image come. And that was all. She touched the place in her where she'd been feeling dread at the merest reminder of Mom and Dad and felt nothing, no swelling of tears or soreness of heart. Nothing but the idea of Mom writing a letter. She didn't feel cheerful, exactly. It was more a relief from feeling awful.

"Jessie! Jessie Howells!" yelled Wheat. She heard him calling, his voice floating out into the air through the high screens along the porch. He shouted again, but her name was muffled this time. He had probably turned and begun calling for her inside the dorm.

She didn't want to scream back. She walked, not hurrying. He was still calling, "Jessie!" toward the stairs when she opened the front door.

"Yes! What?" she said to his back, coming inside. "What do you want?"

"You've got a letter," said Wheat, spinning around to face her, his tennis shoes squeaking on the cement floor. He held out an envelope. "Just you," he said quietly.

Jessie looked at him rather than the letter, because she was suddenly, coldly afraid of the oblong folded paper in his hand. She took it from him, held it between her fingertips. Wheat said, "It'll be okay, Jess," and she broke away from his gaze because he seemed to think he knew what she was thinking.

Having that idea of Mom at home in the office just now and having a letter immediately appear in the mail made Jessie feel like hiding all her thoughts. Then Martha came to mind; Martha would say calmly, "Jess, that letter's been coming through the mail to you all week. Don't get all weirdy-weirdy on me. Things like that happen all the time.

There's a word for it, if I could remember it." Jessie laughed at herself and Martha, and Wheat smiled back at her.

Fortified by that smile, Jessie looked down at the letter.

She did not recognize the firm, careful French script. She turned the envelope over. It had only the postbox number common to everyone at Libamba. Little Michael MacLeod rushed past her, hanging on to her as though she were a post as he dodged Pickles Dill's grasp in a game of tag. Jessie looked around at the kids running wild in the chapel, through the dim living room, in the hall. She needed quiet and the out-of-doors again.

Nobody was on the merry-go-round. Jessie went over to it and sat down, putting both feet firmly on the ground to keep it in one place. She still held the letter carefully between her right thumb and forefinger. The paper was smooth and soft. The edges of the envelope were marked with blue and red dashes, the sort used on airmail. She put the letter on the boards beside her.

Her heartbeat was so strong that she felt sick. Because she was so stupidly, terribly afraid of what was in that letter, she had to find a way of making herself open it. Jessie imagined Martha next to her. Martha would say, "Come on, Jess. If it was bad news about them"—and Jessie could not name her parents, even in Martha's voice—"the letter would have come to all three of you, right? It would have been like last Friday, with Uncle Walker in the office." Jessie shivered in the warmth of the sun. Just open it, she told herself.

She used a sliver of wood to cut the envelope and drew

out a single sheet of French school notebook paper, the sort lined in a grid. Her hand trembled, and she watched the edges of the paper flutter in a rhythm she recognized as that of her heartbeat. Then suddenly she knew this letter was from Mendômô.

Jessie flicked the folded sheet open and grinned when she saw Mendômô's signature at the bottom of the page. Immediately everything righted itself, inside and out, and she felt in tune with the world. The noisy chatter of the weaverbirds in the grapefruit tree overhead almost had melody to it. When Joshua began practice for the day, playing scales, Jessie recognized the sounds and thought of him without rancor. She had a letter from Mendômô!

"Ma chére amie Jessie," it began. My dear friend Jessie. "I am sick at heart when I think of your parents taken into the forest. It is not right. It is NOT RIGHT!"

Mendômô's outrage expressed in thick blue capital letters on the page let Jessie hear Mendômô's strong contralto voice raised in righteous anger. As they walked on the road around Libamba, she would raise her hands, too, and chop the air as she spoke. No one else had admitted out loud that the abduction was a terrible mistake, not justified, not to be accepted.

Since Mendômô could be angry with the Maquis, so could Jessie. Those stupid idiots! Couldn't they see who Mom and Dad were? She hoped those Maquis were good and ashamed of themselves. In the dorm, Joshua stopped playing scales and went into chord progressions. Jessie remembered him saying, "Well, they're with the Maquis, anyway. That means they aren't lost."

Jessie laughed aloud, tipping her head back to let the relief flow out of her and over her shoulders. The sun was warm on her skin. She laughed, as if with Mendômô. The Maquis could make stupid mistakes, but above all, they knew the forest. They would bring Mom and Dad back.

She looked down at the letter in her hand. "I am sure we will always have much to say to each other," Mendômô wrote. "This was true when we were together during vacation. I am waiting to see you when your school is finished, but I hope you will send me a few words soon. I want to have a letter from you." Reading this, Jessie had an urge to write back immediately.

The letter went on. "Today while I remembered you, I thought of my grandmother in my village and of the verse she read to us at my second uncle's funeral. It was this one."

Jessie paused. She could read French without trouble, but Mendômô had switched to Bassa; in Bassa, many words were spelled the same way but had different meanings according to their tonal pronunciation. Slowly, Jessie read the verse aloud.

> "Kon me ngoo, a Nyambe, kon me ngoo,
> Inuyle ñem wem u nsolbene i weeni;
> Ñ, m'a solbene isi titii i bipapai gwoñ,
> Letee bilim bi tagbe.   Hiembi 57:1"

The words seemed to fall out of Jessie's own heart. Be merciful to me, O God, be merciful, for I have taken refuge in you; in the shadow of your wings will I take refuge until this time of trouble has gone by.

Jessie thought about the young man lying dead on the board outside Mendômô's grandmother's house. Broken and pierced by sharp stakes, killed for his belief and his calling. She thought about Mendômô's grandmother looking upon the ruin of her son's life and still calling on God, not out of anger but in need. God, not fair, not safe, but a refuge, a place of strength in the time of trouble.

Somehow Mendômô had known that Jessie needed a sense of this strength. Mendômô had been remembering her all this time. Jessie had not been alone in trouble. Mendômô had carried some of it for her. Jessie read the rest of the short letter: "I am sure God will bring your parents out in health. Your friend and African sister, Mendômô."

Almost before she was done with the letter, Jessie got up and went into the dorm, through the study hall. Swiftly and smoothly, to match the narrow flow of hope moving in her, she got her fountain pen and some dorm stationery with the palm tree in the upper left corner, printed down at the press. She went to sit at the study-hall table, where sunlight came in through the dusty window screens and fell in diamond shapes on the table's dark, scarred mahogany surface.

Then she sat still, looking down at the clean white sheet

of paper. The tip of the beautiful green fountain pen was glistening with black ink, ready for the first word. In that moment, some great joy seized hold of Jessie, pleasure and light and gladness mixing in her, sounding through her as music. She trembled deep within, below thought. Sparks shot through her blood. What *was* this?! She couldn't stop smiling. She breathed slowly, holding quiet. Now she waited, listening as the fizzing, swooping sensations settled gently.

She knew what it was then.

She was truly and absolutely happy. It amazed her. Here she was, doing something for herself, wanting and choosing what she wanted. She was looking forward again—and some saltness moved in the very bones of her spine. Jessie stretched her shoulder blades apart to let the wonderful strong sense of purpose have room in her.

When she wrote any letter, Jessie looked forward to a response. This letter really mattered. Mendômô wanted to hear from her, Jessie. She was more than her parents' daughter, more than Cassie's sister, more than Joshua's twin. She was Mendômô's friend. They were friends of the heart. Whatever happened, wherever she would go, Jessie knew this truth would not be hurt. This friendship was a thing she and Mendômô would make strong between them, all their lives long. They both wanted it so.

She bent her head and began to compose the French for her first letter to Mendômô.

11

In the Shadow of the Wings

The shower at the Press House had no roof.

Looking up through a stream of water at the blue sky overhead, Jessie was in time to see two black patches—pied crows—fly over the square of azure and gold made by the tall shower box in the yard behind the Press House kitchen. What if she were imprisoned in a space this small? It might not be so bad, if she could lie down, as long as she could see the daylight, that bit of the green arch of a palm branch, those birds. It would be hard, learning to live patiently, but the openness above would be her comfort. Jessie stretched inside of the bleak daydream. She would have the strength for such an imprisonment.

Martha, next in line for a shower, yelled, "Hurry up!"

"Okay! I'm almost done washing my hair!" Jessie called

back. She stretched with one arm, reaching up to touch the sky. Water collected during previous rains sat warming in the barrel high on the kitchen roof. The water was spouted into the bucket over her head, and when she pulled the release chain it splashed into her open palm and ran richly between her fingers. Rainwater sluiced down her back. As she rinsed the soap from her hair, Jessie imagined both sky and rain washing her body. It was lovely to be clean again. It felt like a crust had been lifted from her skin.

She pulled on the handle at the end of the chain, and a little tin circle slid over the holes in the wooden bucket overhead, cutting off the water. When Jessie opened the door and stepped out of the shower box, tugging her clean blouse and jumper into place on her slightly damp back and shoulders, Martha said, "Did you leave any water for the rest of us?"

"Don't be grouchy." Jessie rolled her dirty clothes into her towel. "There's plenty for all."

"I don't know. I heard the little kids took a lot yesterday, and it didn't rain last night."

"I only took my fair share," said Jessie. "See you back at the dorm!" She passed the line of fifth- and seventh-grade girls waiting their turn for the shower. All the older girls were showering this morning; the older boys would follow suit this afternoon.

Jessie brushed the fingertips of her free hand along the right side of her face, from her cheekbone down along her jaw to her collarbone. Her skin was soft and smelled lightly of the flowery scent in the soap. She couldn't remember a shower ever feeling so delicious.

It had been six days since she'd been clean, really clean, and washing under the sky like that instead of in the old, moldy cement shower stalls at the dorm had been a perfection. Relaxed and content, Jessie looked ahead at the great brick square the dorm made, sitting on a rug of brilliant green lawn, glowing orange in the morning sun. Then, without warning, the inner shadow of dread moved over her again, darkening her sense of delight.

"Let's wait and see," Uncle Don had said last Sunday. It was Friday now, and the extra week he'd promised was almost up. Sam's father and the other missionaries in charge would have to make a decision about her, Joshua, and Cassie. They probably already had decided what they would do. Jessie sighed hard, not with any deep release of breath, but just letting loose a tired, worn-out sound.

Joshua was right after all. There was nothing she could do about anything important. They would be sent back to America, and everything would be different, everything would be lost. Jessie could already feel herself gone from here and walked the path between the school and the playing field as though it were distant, on a map she looked at, not right under her feet.

"Jessie! Jess-ie! I want to ride my bike and the tire's flat and Lorayne won't let me use her pump and—"

"Oh, get away from me," said Jessie in a low tone Cassie couldn't hear. Her sister was out in front of the study-hall windows, next to her bike, which was parked on the grass. Cassie and Lorayne each had hold of the ends of a long aluminum bicycle pump, wrangling over it. Lorayne was yelling about the pump being hers and Cassie not getting to use it first. Jessie altered her direction slightly, away from the front door, toward the little girls. The corners of her lips tightened impatiently. "Oh, come on!" she said to them both. "Can't you two stop fighting?"

Lorayne started to tell Jessie what the argument was really about, and Cassie interrupted her. Jessie didn't even bother listening to the details. She said, "Cassie, Martha's got a bike pump in her book box. Climb on a chair, borrow it, use it carefully, and *put it back!* Then you can both be ready together, if you can still stand each other. Good-bye!"

This was the third time today she'd stopped a fight between Cassie and Lorayne. Every day it got harder to be thoughtful of Cassie. She'd been hanging on Jessie constantly since the morning she wet her bed. That hadn't happened again, thank goodness, because each night before she went to sleep, Jessie went back to Cassie's room and woke her up just enough to walk Cassie to the bathroom and back.

Now she sat next to Jessie at meals, in chapel, at night during evening prayer. She found Jessie wherever she was and whined about everything. She didn't want to play the baby games that the little girls played—she wanted to play big-kid games with Jessie. She didn't want to be it when the whole dorm played field games before dark unless Jessie was it with her. She didn't want to eat the tapioca for dessert or the Spanish rice for lunch. She didn't want to brush her teeth. She didn't want to brush her hair. She didn't feel like cleaning her share of the room.

Her whiny voice, thought Jessie, was like the planer the men used to cut logs into boards in the work hangar at Libamba. *Weeeeeeeeeeeee.* The sound cut sharply, sliding down and rising up again, going on deafeningly and forever. Not once had Cassie asked Joshua to help; not once had Cassie sat next to him at table or during prayers. In fact, Jessie herself hadn't spoken with Joshua since their argument out by the school fireplace.

Jessie let the front door flap closed behind her, and Aunt Pearl, coming down the stairs, called automatically, "Make sure the door latches! Keep the flies outside!" Jessie reached back and pulled the door shut.

Aunt Pearl paused in midstride to pick up her kitchen notebook from the secretary and said to Jessie as she opened the front door herself, "I'm going to market. Uncle Walker's down at the press this morning. They're having some difficulty running the last part of the Bulu hymnal. Go and get him if there's trouble."

Jessie nodded. Her day had nothing but trouble, but she knew the housemother meant a dorm emergency. Aunt Pearl went out the door, latched it, and drove off in the houseparents' Deux Chevaux. The car raised a cloud of red dust behind it as it went away down the lane.

Jessie breathed in deep and sighed. This sighing was

coming more easily. Martha was already complaining about it. "Quit that. You sound like a bellows!" she'd said this morning as they went downstairs to breakfast. Jessie thought about stopping the next sigh but didn't. Breaking the habit would take too much energy. She dragged herself slowly upstairs to hang up her towel and put her dirty clothes in the laundry basket.

Everything was taking forever. Waiting was taking forever. Here it was Friday, but it might as well have been last week or next week for all the sense she had of time passing. "I can't look forward to anything, that's what," she whispered to herself, leaning into the mirror while she combed her dark wet hair. "I'm sure if I do—" *What then?* I know if I do, she silently answered herself, it's going to be a disappointment. I don't want to go to America. I don't want to play Cassie's mother for the rest of my life. I don't want to be stuck in the States from now on, either. I wanted to go to Egypt! I wanted to use my passport and find out all about that. . . .

She thought about that maturity and responsibility that had been promised because Mom and Dad had needed her to be independent and able to spend a whole year away at school so they could stay here and do their work. They wouldn't need her for that anymore. Now she and Joshua —the wretch!—and whiny Cassie would have to go back to the States, and all their well-meaning relatives would hover over them and pity them and take care of them as if they'd been reduced to babies by Mom and Dad's—

But Jessie could not make herself say the word. She would not. The iron in her heart and soul turned on her self-pitying whimpers and pushed her away from the mirror and from the thought of death.

Yet she couldn't keep herself from throwing the hairbrush, though she aimed it carefully at the edge of the mirror, where it would hit the wood frame. It clattered to the floor. Jessie looked down her nose at it and said, "Lie there!" It was as though she were speaking to someone—someone important who was in charge of things. "I don't care anymore!" she announced, chin high, and then she turned her back.

But feeling so doesn't make it so, Joshua had said. And then Mom's words, quiet and swift: Love is more than a feeling; love is something you do. "Well, do it for *me*, then!" Jessie yelled aloud to God, and with both hands she banged hard against the chipboard walls of the narrow back hall. "Oh, what's the use," she said to herself, but she kicked the wall as she turned the corner.

Cassie was at the bottom of the stairs on the first floor, arguing with Michael MacLeod. Pickles Dill was pulling Cassie by the left arm, and Cassie kicked Pickles as she yelled at Michael, "It's not fair! You already had your turn!"

Jessie considered turning around, waiting upstairs until the quarreling group had moved to another part of the dorm, but Cassie looked up and saw her before Jessie could go back. "Jessie! Jessie!" The plane saw whined and buzzed, slicing through all of Jessie's patience.

"I don't care!" she said loudly. "Do you hear me, Cassie? I don't care anymore! Fix it yourself or just *be* in trouble! I'm done trying to help you! You don't try to stay out of trouble afterward. Now get out of my way!"

She stomped down the last flight of stairs and pushed through the knot of little kids hanging around the three having the argument. They'd been trying on Uncle Walker's hip boots, which was against the rules anyhow. Jessie glared at her sister as she reminded everybody of that. Cassie looked stricken, her face blank but her eyes showing that this rejection, of all things, was not what she'd expected of Jessie.

Jessie knew quite well she'd hurt Cassie, and badly. She'd meant to; she'd said all those hard, heavy things—I don't care! I'm done helping you! Just be in trouble! Get out of my way!—and meant every one. And they were all true; whatever Mom had meant about love, she had been wrong. Jessie couldn't feel any love at all for Cassie now and couldn't do anything more for her. She had used up everything she could spare.

"Pig!" someone said behind her. Jessie turned around. It was Michael, calling Jessie a name. "Pig!" he said again. "You made her cry!"

"So did you!" said Jessie crossly.

"Yeah, but I'm not her big sister. Pig!"

"Shut up!"

"I'm telling Aunt Pearl! She'll wash your mouth out!"

"She's not here, and I'm in charge," said Jessie, pushing

her head forward at the little boy, scorn and power pouring through her tone and gesture. "So there!"

From up the stairs, where Cassie had fled to her room, the thin sound of her lonely, hopeless crying arrowed its way straight to Jessie's heart, calling for Mom. No, calling for Jessie. Mom wasn't here. Jessie rolled her eyes at the ceiling, brushed by Michael and the others watching her, and climbed heavily, dutifully back up after her sister. But as she went, she knew that something more than duty pulled her.

"Go away!" sobbed Cassie when Jessie sat down on the bed. "You said you don't care! So get away from me!" She shoved angrily at Jessie and kicked her thigh. Jessie got off the bed immediately.

"All right," she said harshly, "be that way." She crossed the room. There wasn't any more she could do if Cassie was going to shut her out. But when Jessie got to the door, a kind of warning—a sense of needing to wait for a moment—flopped in her heart and stomach and sounded a single note in her head. It was something like that floating pressure she'd heard and felt the other day, before Mendômô's letter came.

Now there was a pressing of weight and strength against her lungs, on her shoulders, in her heart. It kept her from moving off anywhere with any speed. Wait, thought Jessie. *Wait here a minute. Listen to her.*

Cassie went on sobbing into the pillow. Jessie could hardly stand the pitiful sound. Stop it! she wanted to say, hard and loud. But why should Cassie stop crying? Wasn't the loss of everything—home and hope—something worth crying for? Didn't Jessie know the same loss? Don't, Jessie wanted to plead. Come on, Cassie, it'll be all right. But Jessie didn't know that it would be all right, and she wouldn't pretend with Cassie anymore.

Listen to her.

Cassie was so lonely all bunched up on the bed, with her back to Jessie and her arms tight around the pillow, the crying coming out in long thin wails now, not in sobs anymore. She was crying for Mom, Mom not there.

Even though Jessie was standing in the room, Cassie was alone. Maybe, thought Jessie slowly, maybe Cassie was so lonely because Jessie was just standing there, ready to leave. Maybe she was lonely because Jessie wouldn't touch her.

Jessie remembered lying in her bed on her first night at Hope School, when she was seven. Long after Martha had fallen asleep, she lay on her back and held her pillow tight against her body, crying because she needed someone she loved—someone to touch; she needed Mom to touch her. If she could even have simply held her mother's hand— Mom would have held her hand till she fell asleep if she'd been there. But she couldn't be. Jessie had wept until she was sick with tears. She had wept until that hard knowledge had entered into her mind and heart that night, and there it was still. Now she was on her own; Mom couldn't come get her and take her home, or come for Cassie either.

Jessie hesitated in the doorway. Touching Cassie was no good now. Cassie already knew that Jessie didn't want to care. But if she left, and Lorayne or Elissa or Martha came because of Cassie's weeping, Cassie would never really trust Jessie again. And with shame Jessie knew she would not have cared for her own sister—because she didn't have enough love for Cassie. She could never love Cassie the way Mom and Dad would have loved—any of them.

Listen to her.

What does she want?

Oh, for heaven's sake, thought Jessie, suddenly understanding. She just wants to know she's not all by herself.

In that moment of listening to the dark silence in her, strong even against the sounds of Cassie's bitter crying, Jessie's spirit moved. It was as if she'd been in that shower-box prison but with a roof on it, and suddenly the roof vanished, and in the light she saw the door, and all she had to do was open it. She knew quite simply that she wasn't afraid of comforting Cassie anymore. Jessie couldn't wait for someone to comfort her first so she could comfort her sister. Cassie needed her right now. There wasn't anyone but Jessie. And she knew she had the strength required.

All the same, her tongue and lips were stiff when she said the words. "I'm sorry I said those things, Cassie. I'm sorry I hurt your feelings."

She didn't feel sorry. She felt nothing at all, except Cassie's awful loneliness, which burrowed into Jessie's. She knew, though, this forced apology was the only way they were going to come into the middle of the immense space between them.

She remembered, then, the mud hole on the trip home during Advent. She remembered standing at the edge of the huge mud sea, with Cassie's hand in hers and Joshua standing on her other side, as they watched Mom drive the carryall away from them, around and among the trees at the rim of the hole, toward Dad farther ahead, out of sight, picking out the way. Then the three of them had been alone, and they had managed to find their way.

Jessie went all the way back into the room again and stood near the bed but out of reach of Cassie's legs and arms. "Cass," she said after a moment. Cassie softened her sobs but didn't stop crying. "Cassie," said Jessie. "Listen to me."

Cassie rolled over on her back and put her hands over her ears, but she turned her head to glare at Jessie.

Jessie went closer to the bed. "If this were happening at home, with Mom, do you know what she'd say?"

Cassie stopped crying; she closed her mouth and relaxed the pressure of her hands over her ears. Jessie went on, knowing these were the right words for this moment, even though she'd never felt less like using them in her life. "Don't you remember what Mom always said when we argued like this with her? She said, 'Can we begin again?' " She knew Cassie was listening. "Let's begin again, Cassie. Okay?"

"I'm sorry! Oh, I'm so sorry, Jess!" Cassie rolled off the bed and flung herself at Jessie, hugging her, crying afresh, full of regret. She snuffled into Jessie's middle.

Jessie hugged Cassie and closed her lips tight against the burning soreness thickening her throat. "I'm sorry, too, little heart," she said softly.

They held on to each other until Jessie's arms ached. She patted Cassie's shoulders and turned away to look for a handkerchief in one of the dresser drawers. She helped her blow her nose. "It's all right," she said. "It'll be all right, Cassie," she repeated, and wondered now if she was lying. No. It would be all right somehow. *That's Your job*, she said silently to God, between her closed teeth. *You'd better do it, and soon!*

"Come here," said Cassie, suddenly revived, talking through her stuffy nose. She pulled Jessie by the arm. "Come with me."

"Why?" Jessie followed reluctantly. "Where are we going?"

"Just come," Cassie ordered, and held on to Jessie as she went all the way down the stairs and into the living room, where there was a rook championship series going on among the big boys. "Joshua!" said Cassie imperiously, standing across from him on the large oval hooked rug. He looked up, distracted from his hand of cards.

"I need a trump! Give me a trump!" pleaded Sam. He groaned when Hal put down a card.

"Joshua!" said Cassie, demanding his attention. He

looked at her, and his glance flicked to Jessie and away again. He probably thought she had put Cassie up to this interruption.

"Play, Howells!" said Wheat. "We've got them with this trick!" He leaned over and slapped Joshua's last card as it landed on the rug, covering the other three. "Former and undefeated champeens, still holding the title!" he crowed, shoving Joshua's shoulder.

Joshua leaned back and shook hands gravely with Wheat and then with Sam and Hal. Then he said, "What is it, stars?" He did not look at Jessie again.

"Stars" was his own term of affection for Cassie, who was named after the constellation Cassiopeia. Jessie hadn't heard him use it in ages. Cassie beckoned to him. "I need to talk to you," she said importantly, and dropped Jessie's hand.

The two of them went off to the back porch, where Joshua sat on the brick window ledge and bent over, listening to Cassie whispering in his ear. Jessie watched his smile come, fade, then come again until he laughed aloud at their sister. Looking at the light brown color of their hair, the straight lines of their eyebrows, the same chin, and the same long curves of their cheekbones, Jessie saw once again how much more the two of them looked alike than did she and Joshua. Trying to imagine what they were talking about baffled her.

The little girl stood arms akimbo, waiting for Joshua to

answer her. "Please," Jessie heard her beg. "Come on. For me? Please?"

Joshua looked over at Jessie and rolled his eyes. "All right, all right," he said, but he didn't sound really irritated. He beckoned Jessie and, when she came to him, said, ducking his head almost shyly, "She wants us to be twins for her."

"Oh, good grief!" said Jessie, letting Joshua think she was as unwilling and embarrassed as she expected him to be.

Instead, Joshua shrugged as he said, "It's all right. I don't mind. If it's okay with you."

When Cassie was much younger and they'd come home from Hope School for vacation, she hung around them as though they were curiosities or new, living toys arrived just for her. She knew that they had the same exact birthday, but she didn't understand why they didn't do everything the same way. To get her to quit bothering them, Joshua had begun a sort of game with her.

"We'll be twins for you now," he would say to Cassie, "but then you have to leave us alone for a while. Okay?" Then he and Jessie would do something exactly synchronized—repeat three Mother Goose rhymes while lifting their knees and arms in unison, or sing a song in harmony, or stand opposite each other, making precisely opposite gestures, as if they were looking at themselves in a mirror.

The one Cassie liked best, though, was her own version of the game. She would push Jessie to the piano while Joshua was practicing and demand that they be twins for her right then; so they played what Joshua called junk pieces, requiring coordinated timing. They played four-handed twiddles, usually "Heart and Soul" or "Chopsticks." Cassie especially loved "Chopsticks."

"Which part do you want?" asked Joshua, waiting for Jessie to choose the left or right side of the piano bench.

"I'll do the bottom hand," said Jessie. Whichever part she played, she did it straight. When Joshua played "Chopsticks," he wanted to improvise, and Jessie liked providing the steady bass line for the different complicated things he came up with on the top hand.

"Joshua's playing 'Chopsticks'! Joshua's playing 'Chopsticks'!" screamed Lorayne, announcing the fact to everyone on the first floor. Everyone could play "Chopsticks," and Joshua never did. Joshua made an embarrassed face at Cassie, but Cassie said, "You promised!"

"All right, then," said Joshua, "let's go." Jessie slid onto the left side of the piano bench and held her fingers above the bass G octave and the G seventh chord, and Joshua said, "Start together and hold the octave. After I've done the fancy intro, we'll go into the regular stuff. And listen to the count. Okay?" Jessie nodded. Joshua didn't think she had a keen enough sense of timing. "One, two, three . . ."

The beginning was like making an announcement. Jessie held the octaves while Joshua did fancy stuff that sounded like a parade starting. Then he nodded, and they began playing ordinary "Chopsticks." On the second time through, Joshua began to sing to the usually wordless tune.

> *"Here we were*
> *Two of us*
> *Now we are*
> *Three of us*
> *Three of us Howells—*
> *Oh, where are the rest of us?"*

Shocked, Jessie laughed. "You're awful!" she said, looking over at him, her eyes wide, mouth open.

"So are you. You laughed," said Joshua.

"I know! But it's awful!" she insisted. And the words were so easy and free, so blazing and simple, as if calling out and making fun of danger. Joshua, never looking up from the keys, made a sort of Mozart sound out of the doggerel music. When they came to the plaintive, sweet refrain, his fingers came down the keyboard and her right hand brushed his at middle C.

Joshua said, still looking at the keys, "Are you mad at me?"

Jessie thumped the bass chords hard and said, "You've been terrible so far."

"How could that be? I'm such a nice guy," said Joshua. "Ask Martha."

"Yeah, I am mad at you," said Jessie, and knew she wasn't anymore.

Joshua looked sideways at her briefly and said, "Sorry, Jess."

And that, Jessie knew, was all the apology she would get from him. It was enough. He'd already begun listening to Cassie. Being twins for Cassie was a beginning again for all of them.

As Joshua went through another intricate variation, this time using a lot of minor notes, Jessie thought about what she'd wanted from Joshua that he wouldn't give. She'd wanted the kind of strength from talking about the trouble that she could have from Martha and had gotten from Mendômô's letter. This sense that Joshua knew they were still a family, which he gave her right now, was enough to keep her from feeling alone when she thought about leaving for America. He wouldn't talk about it much, but he would do things with her.

Raising his voice, Joshua said, "Cassie, come play regular top hand, two octaves above me," and when she did, standing at his right shoulder, the three of them filled up the whole piano, from one end to the other. Jessie looked along the keys at their six hands moving at different speeds, all in the same rhythm, and said to Joshua, "Isn't this *great!*" and Joshua said, "Take your foot off the sustaining pedal! Then it'll be great!" Jessie kept the pedal down, though; she thought all the notes running together in harmony sounded glorious and triumphant.

"Ohhhhh, look!" called Phoebe Peel, behind them. "Look!"

The twins and Cassie were in the middle of a full run, and so synchronized that Jessie thought she could turn quickly to see whatever it was without losing place or time. What Jessie saw, though, made her stop playing altogether. Joshua and Cassie trailed off behind her.

There was a man standing in the back of the chapel. Everyone who'd been hanging around there moved away from him, so that he was in plain view. He stood perfectly still. As the Howellses lifted their hands from the piano keys, a tremendous quiet filled the room. Jessie imagined it had come in with the man and spread from him to everyone else.

He was African and much taller than most southern Cameroun men were, even taller than most of the American men Jessie knew. His face was long from temple to jaw and deeply lined in the cheeks, where most Cameroun men's faces were slightly oval and rounded. His forehead was high, his eyebrows thick with grizzled, unruly hair jutting out and shadowing his dark eyes. His skin was neither brown nor black; it seemed a curious reddish gray, as though he were ill. He had a long, long beard; curly gray hair lay matted midchest. His mouth was heavy lipped, unsmiling. Not grim, but serious and grieved.

He wore a long robe of rough light brown material, almost like a gunnysack, open at the throat, unbelted; the hem just grazed the man's ankles. On his feet were sandals fastened with black rubber straps cut from tire inner tubes. In his left hand was a long rusting iron rod, something he'd salvaged from a construction site, thought Jessie. In his right hand he carried a Bible, printed in English, she could see by the words on the spine in faded gilt.

There he stood in the cool light of the front porch, not moving except for the rise and fall of his chest when he breathed. He looked straight ahead at all of them, looked straight through them, not caring that they stared back at him. The quiet was eerie.

Jessie remembered Aunt Pearl's injunction to get Uncle Walker if there was trouble. She didn't think this wasn't trouble, exactly. Martha was on the other side of the chapel arches, in the living room, and she stage-whispered to Jessie, "Where's Aunt Pearl?"

"Market," said Jessie in a low voice, watching the man as she spoke. "Uncle Walker's at the press."

"I'll go get him!" said Hal, squeezing through the bunch of kids in the archway and loping off through the living room. Jessie heard the study-hall door slam. She felt Joshua moving carefully next to her on the piano bench. He cracked his knuckles, and Jessie knew he was nervous.

Though this man in the chapel was very strange indeed, he did not remind her of the peculiar stretch and slip of power and presence that had made her sense the snake man as crazy. But everyone on the porch had moved as far away as possible without actually leaving. He stood alone on the gray cement, in an odd, watchful, unhurried stillness. Jessie found herself staring at the man as if listening to him.

"How did he get in here?" whispered Joshua to Wheat.

"I don't know. He just opened the door and came in, I guess," Wheat whispered back.

If the man read an English Bible, he could understand what they were saying. Jessie got up slowly and went a little ways toward him. The man seemed exhausted, asleep on his feet, and yet his eyes stayed steadily open, looking at something behind her. Jessie turned to see what he stared at and noticed as if for the first time the large wood-and-rope cross her class had made during Bible Conference three or four years ago. Uncle Walker had fastened it against the bricks of the chapel wall. She'd seen it so often she'd forgotten it was there.

Jessie looked back at the man. "We're calling the man who lives here, who takes care of us," she said, speaking slowly, enunciating every word. The African leaned a little on his staff but said nothing, didn't even look at Jessie. "Would you like to sit while you wait?" she asked, going three steps closer to him. The man made no response.

"Be careful, Jess," said Joshua from the piano bench.

"We can't just ignore him," said Jessie. "Are you hungry?" she asked the man. Now his eyes moved from the chapel wall to her face, and Jessie felt a brief shock at the sudden intentness of his focus on her. "Do you want something to eat?" she asked, thinking of the bread cupboard on the back porch by the water filters, where Aunt Pearl kept the bread left over from the previous meal.

When he said nothing, she tried once more, feeling that he had come here because he needed something, feeling that she must have something to give him, even if it was the simplest habit of hospitality. "Would you like a drink?" she asked. It was the only thing she could think of to say.

"I would take water," said the man, looking back at Jessie. She hadn't expected him to answer, and his deep voice and deliberately pronounced words made her skin jump. Her heart beat in hot spurts in the fierce light of his attention.

Jessie ran down the aisle, skittered on the smooth cement, got past the man into the hall, and hurried into the dining room. She took her water cup from its hook, held it under the little spigot on the first water filter in the row of three, tried to hurry the trickle of water into the cup by carefully tipping the almost empty filter, thinking all the time, Mom, I hope I'm doing the right thing, I think it's the right thing, I hope it is.

She went back quickly and held the cup out in both hands, because it had no handle and because she was trembling. He leaned the iron rod carefully against the secretary, took Jessie's cup, tipped his head back, and poured the water down his throat, swallowing it all in two gulps. He licked his lips. It seemed as if Jessie had brought him one drop rather than a cupful. He was dry, dry, dry.

Jessie ran back to the water filters and filled her cup

again. On her way back to the front porch, she passed Lorayne and Cassie and Elissa, all taking down their water cups. Just as the man finished drinking the second cup Jessie brought him, Cassie held up her cup, and he took it and said gently, "My thanks." He took one cup of water after another from the little girls, from Sam, from Wheat, from Michael and from Pickles, from Martha and Joshua, drinking each one down the way he had swallowed the first. Boarders gathered around him, stretching their arms out to him with their full water cups.

Suddenly the man took a full cup and instead of drinking it, he poured it over his head. Jessie was shocked. It seemed he had wasted the water. Everyone was astonished. Then, a moment later, Wheat gave him another cup of water, and the man poured this over his head, too. He took as many cups as were offered now and poured each one onto his head. The precious filtered water ran down through his hair, streamed over his face, dripped from his eyebrows over his closed eyes, along the creases in his cheeks, between his closed lips, onto his neck, along his collarbones. Droplets glistened on the close curled surface of his hair.

Jessie stood back, watching this strange and astonishing thing. The kids had lost fear of the man as they brought water to him. Without second thought, they gave away the water they had with pain and difficulty brought to the dorm for themselves. Nobody said a thing about that. Jessie knew for sure this thing wouldn't have happened had there been an adult there to prevent it.

The man's robe was soaked, changing to a dark brown at the neck and shoulders. When she looked at his closed eyes, Jessie saw the red dust of the road caked in the creases of his eyelids. The dust was washing off his face in rivulets. He put the Bible down on the secretary, took a cup from Phoebe Peel, and poured the water into his large free palm. Then he splashed this on his face and rubbed his skin.

He smiled and shook his head so droplets flew out from his gray-and-black hair and fell on everyone around him. He looked over at the cross on the wall again and, as if by accident, met Jessie's eyes. "The blessings of the Lord be on all of you," he said quietly, and reached for his staff and Bible.

He turned around, opened the door, and walked out.

Jessie began to shake in her midriff. She couldn't hold all parts of the moment at once—the sudden emptiness where the man had been; the huge puddle of water on the floor as proof that he had been there; the mess of kids standing around with their empty tin water cups, just beginning to let chatter fill up the great silence they'd been in; and that silence itself, the man's strange, peaceful quiet. And then the urge in her to offer something to him. It was all bigger than it seemed.

Uncle Walker came in the door. There hadn't really been time to move between the strange man's departure and Uncle Walker's return. He stopped short when he saw everyone standing around. Then he saw the great puddle of water on the floor. "What happened here?" he demanded. "Where's this man Hal was talking about?"

Lots of the kids began to explain. "You should have seen him! He was a crazy prophet! It's Jessie! Jessie did it! It was Jessie's fault! She talked to him, to the crazy prophet."

Uncle Walker shushed the others. Then he looked at Jessie. She told him briefly what had happened, how the man had appeared, how she'd asked him to sit down.

"What possessed you to pour water on him?" asked Uncle Walker.

"We didn't," said Jessie, getting ready to argue.

Then Joshua, without defensiveness in his tone, said, "The man wanted to drink, and later he poured the water on himself."

Uncle Walker wet his lips with his tongue and waited, Jessie thought, to consider what he would say next. He'd either be angry with Jessie or angry with everybody. She didn't care. The stranger had been parched and then had gone away looking the way she had felt after her shower this morning. That was good. She'd known the right thing to do and done it.

"All of it filtered water?" asked Uncle Walker, and by his despairing tone, she knew he was certain of the answer as he spoke.

"Of course," said Jessie reasonably. "He said he would like a drink. We couldn't give him unboiled water. We didn't know he'd pour it on himself."

Uncle Walker groaned. "Clean it up," he said shortly. "I'll see to getting more water boiled. At least ten of you had better start refilling the water supply. It'll be another day before I can use the hospital pickup to get water here in large amounts."

Jessie was on her knees, wringing the mop cloth into a bucket for the last time, when she heard the unfamiliar truck motor. "Who's that?" she asked, almost automatically. Martha got up and peered through the dirty screen in the front door.

"I don't know," she said, dropping down to the floor again and swiping at the cement under the secretary. "It's a small truck. He looks Greek to me—you know, black eyebrows, black hair." She and Jessie laughed. They knew Frenchmen with black eyebrows and black hair, and Uncle Nat, down at the press, had black eyebrows and black hair. All Jessie had to do was look in the mirror to see the same thing.

Then Cassie started screaming. "Jessie! Jessie! Hurry up! Jessie!"

Jessie leaped up from the floor, knocking over the bucket of water she'd just helped collect. She and Martha collided at the door, and Jessie shoved Martha aside to get out to where Cassie stood. No, she wasn't standing there, she was jumping, flinging her arms up and down in the air, shrieking for Jessie, pointing to the truck.

A woman was inside. She leaned out of the open window, holding on to Cassie's hands, and Cassie nearly walked up the side of the truck and climbed through the window. The man—the Greek man—was running around the front of the truck, tangling with Cassie, trying to get her either in or out the window. Finally he got the door open, and, grunting and speaking—in Greek—he helped the woman and Cassie get down.

And the woman was Mom.

Cassie wasn't screaming anymore. Mom could hardly move because Cassie was so tightly pressed to her neck. Gently loosening Cassie's arms, she looked up into the crowd of dorm kids boiling around her, around the truck, hunting among them all for Jessie, for Joshua.

Mom saw her. She opened her mouth and said something, calling.

Jessie couldn't move. This couldn't be. Her chest hurt as if something sharp were turning in her lungs, striking sparks on her ribs.

"Mom! I saw Mom!" shouted Joshua, running toward the dorm. "Jessie! I saw her!" He was still dragging his water bucket, most of its contents spilled. He put it down on the path and ran toward Mom without it. Jessie looked back at the truck. She could not touch what was happening. She felt dream-bound, limb-heavy, barely breathing.

"Oh, Mom!" Joshua's cry was huge, louder than every other voice there, carrying in it all the belief and joy that Jessie wanted for herself. Other kids, and now Uncle Walker, hurried out of the dorm behind her, bumping her, shoving past her, yelling and shouting their excitement.

"Go on," screamed Martha in her ear. Jessie rubbed her ear and did not look at her roommate. She didn't let herself move from the step either.

The Greek man was helping someone else out of the truck, some terribly thin bearded man. Mom was terribly thin, too, but this man—Dad?—was even thinner, paler. Jessie could hardly see him, could hardly see Mom either. She blinked and understood that her eyes were full of tears, and she couldn't blink them away. *Listen to me! Listen to me! I can't make this real!* she cried desperately, all in silence.

"Jessie!" called Mom.

Jessie heard her. The sound was real. It tangled in all the other voices swirling around her and was lost. Then it came again. When Mom said her name, Jessie was able to move in spite of not being able to see. Her name in Mom's voice was the sound Jessie knew best, the one she had rehearsed in hope at night and learned by heart all these years of going apart and coming together again.

Almost without stepping the distance, she was across, her arms tight around Mom's neck, Mom touching her face, pushing back her hair, kissing her forehead. Beside her Dad said, "Oh, Jessie!" and she threw herself on him, crying and knowing it. She let go of her tears, and from somewhere deep inside her, a warmth began to burn through her.

Jessie reached out to hug Mom again, and she had to hug Cassie, too, because Cassie hadn't let go of Mom's waist.

Jessie believed at last when she put her head on Mom's shoulder and smelled Mom's hair and heard Mom's voice saying her name, Joshua's name, Cassie's name, over and over.

They had come back. They had been brought out. They had been kept safe in the shadow and the unknown. They were *here*. She still could not make it real.

It went on being unbelievable, because it was suddenly so normal to be standing next to the Greek man's truck, knotted together in those first crazy, glassy moments when Jessie couldn't let go of Mom's hand because she thought she'd slip and swoop back into nightmare, out of the good dream. And then she saw Joshua crying when he hugged Dad, and she laughed when Cassie reached up to him and said, "It's all right now, silly," and Mom had laughed too, in that beautiful way that sounded like bells.

And everything seemed as if nothing bad had happened at all.

"Where were you?" Cassie demanded.

"Oh, we just took a little unscheduled trip in the forest," said Dad. His voice was the same, but without as much strength as before; Jessie looked closely at him and saw that he looked ill.

"Were you with the Maquis? How did you get back here?" Joshua asked. Everybody pressing around the Howellses asked questions. Jessie couldn't take her eyes off of Mom. Over the heads of most of the kids, Mom looked for the Greek truck owner. She spoke to him in French, thanking him. He reached out and shook her hand, shook Dad's hand, shook Joshua's hand, shook Jessie's hand. Cassie held her hand out, and he shook Cassie's hand, too.

"I am delighted to have made this reunion possible," he said, smiling broadly through his Greek-accented French.

"He stopped on the road near Mbalmayo, where we came out of the forest. He was going to Yaoundé, but he put off his own trip to bring us here," said Mom. "We'd better get Dad to sit down. He should go up to Enongal and see Uncle Don," she added. "We'll eat lunch here and go up after that."

"Is he all right?" Jessie asked, all the shades and tones of the fear she'd come to know echoing under her joy of having the family together again.

"He's had a very bad attack of malaria, but he'll be all right, Jessie. We're all right." Mom held Jessie's eyes with her own, reassuring, probing. "We're all right," she said again, and her eyes filled with tears.

"So are we," said Jessie. "We are, too."

Upstairs in the bathroom before lunch, Martha dipped and poured water so Jessie could rinse her soapy hands. She said, "So, you're not going to have to be a Christian martyr and take care of Cassie the rest of your life."

Speaking before she thought, Jessie said, "It wouldn't have killed me." Then immediately she remembered that prison she'd imagined in the shower this morning—confining and hard to bear, with only a tiny part of the sky always in view, almost in reach. Now she rubbed her hands under the stream of water Martha poured, watching a huge pile of thick, white, shining clouds move slowly across the blue sky. She had been given the strength for loving Cassie, no matter what. It wouldn't have killed her, but it would have been very hard without Mom and Dad. She touched this knowledge lightly, to be sure she remembered these things. A sudden quick breeze passed through the palms outside the window, tangling the dark green fronds, gracefully lifting and crossing the fingered branches and letting them settle gently again.

Martha poured the last drops of water over Jessie's hands and said, "My turn."

And in that moment, the whole of her life came flooding back into Jessie. Breathing was easy and ordinary again. She was filled with delight. Everything she wanted, she would have. The first thing she wanted, thought Jessie, was to get home to see Mendômô, and then she and Joshua would go up to the consulate at Yaoundé with Dad for their passports, and she would help Mom make her travel suit and sew Joshua's palm-wood buttons on the jacket and—impulsively she brought her hands to her face. The water was cold against her cheeks, cold dripping down her neck and her arms. It made her feel wide awake and absolutely real.

Thank You. Suddenly moved into heart silence, the words came simply, singing in her. *Thank You for not leaving me alone. Thank You for bringing them back. Thank You!* She flung her arms out in a hard stretch and clapped her hands overhead. The sound echoed and was glorious.

ACKNOWLEDGMENTS

I was fortunate to have eyewitness accounts of the events in Cameroun between 1955 and 1960. Among those, I am especially grateful to Martha and Robert Peirce, to Elisabeth and David Gelzer, and to Ruth Engo-Tjega. Without their memories, I could not have written this story.

Reuben Um Nyobe, who is mentioned in these pages, lived from 1913 to 1958. A political leader by calling, he came from the Bassa tribe of Cameroun. In 1944 he founded Cameroun's first legal political party, the Union des Populations Camerounaises (UPC). He was among the outstanding African leaders of that period who began the work of ending French colonial control on the continent. Of those first leaders, Um Nyobe was the only one who did not live to see his country's independence.

On November 13, 1958, soldiers and officers of the French army ambushed Um Nyobe and a number of his supporters in his hometown of Boumyébel. The French killed Um Nyobe and exhibited his body throughout the Bassa territory, hoping thereby to crush any further Bassa nationalist movement toward Cameroun's independence.

On January 1, 1960, only a little more than a year after Um Nyobe's death, France ceded Cameroun her independence. Ahmadou Ahidjo, the first elected president, was able to unite the country by adopting the political platform of independence, reunification, and amnesty first articulated by Um Nyobe in 1955.

GLOSSARY

BASSA A major Bantu tribe. Cameroun Bassa territory borders the Douala tribe on the west, the Ewondo on the east, the Bulu on the south, and, crossing the Sanaga River, the Bafia on the north. The Bassa tribe provided strong, consistent political resistance to French colonial control of Cameroun. Bassa is also the name of the language of the tribe.

BOBOLA A Bassa word for a food made of cassava, a potato-like tuber, ground and dried into flour, then mixed with water or palm oil into a stiff dough, which is formed into thin lengths, tied in steamed banana leaves, and then fermented in the running water of a streambed. A staple food in all of tropical Africa.

BULU This Cameroun tribe is part of a larger grouping called Fang. Bulu territory is in southern Cameroun. This tribe raised resistance to the Germans, who colonized Cameroun in the late nineteenth century. For their resistance (from 1895 to 1906) the Bulu experienced brutal punitive action from the Germans. Most of the tribe did not join the later political resistance to French colonial control.

BUSH The bush is the common term for the second growth in the forest, coming after the great trees of the primeval forest have been cut. Those trees will never grow back. The lesser trees and thick undergrowth replacing the primeval forest is the bush.

CABA A traditional women's dress worn at home in the village. It is a comfortable, roomy dress, the material fully gathered to a straight yoke and falling to ankle length. The sleeves are long and loose.

CAMEROUN Portuguese sailors were mapping Africa in the fourteenth century, inching down the west coast of the continent, trying to find the way to the Indies. They came to an area rich with shrimp, and they gave the surrounding land the name *Camarones*, Portuguese for "shrimp." Starting in the north, the climate and geography are those of the sahel, the near desert. Then there is the grassland, and below that, in the southern region, the tropical rain forest. In Cameroun are all the climates and all the terrains to be found in Africa. In 1884, the land became a German protectorate (in other words, a colony, a land settled and governed by people from a distant country). At the end of World War I, the French and British appropriated Cameroun as victor spoils and divided the land between them as they desired, with the French using the spelling Cameroun and the British, Cameroon. In the 1930s, by order of the League of Nations, lands that were victor spoils became mandates, that is, the nations in charge were given the direct responsibility to bring those lands to eventual national independence. The United Nations renewed this arrangement in 1946. In 1955, Um Nyobe, officially representing the UPC and the Cameroun people under the French mandate, went before the UN commission on decolonization, calling the French and the British to account for their mandates, asking for reunification of the country, and claiming independence. In 1960, national independence was achieved, and in 1963, reunification was accomplished. Official languages, French and English; eleven regional languages; over one hundred seventy tribal languages.

CISTERN   A large, deep cement-lined hole in the ground with a domed cement cover. Cisterns are filled with rainwater collected from the roof. Springs and streams are the other leading source of water in Cameroun, and that water has to be carried to the dwelling in a bucket on somebody's head. As the dry season progresses, one must go farther and farther to find water. All missionary stations routinely dug cisterns to store water during the rainy seasons.

DUMA TREE   Bulu name for a tropical-forest tree growing more than a hundred feet high, with immense wing roots extending fifteen or more feet up the trunk. The wing roots have curving edges and make spaces resembling small rooms around the base of the tree. These spaces are wonderful for playing house and hiding games. On cleared land, the duma and the kapok trees are remnants of primeval forest.

EBOLOWA   A Bulu town one hundred twenty kilometers south of Yaoundé, in a hilly and heavily forested area. Ebolowa was the French colonial seat of government for all of southern Cameroun. The town was a commercial crossroads for southern Cameroun, and it had shops run by Greeks, Lebanese, and eastern Camerounians. Because of the commerce, the schools (both government and church) in the area, the Presbyterian medical facilities, and the great Elat church, the population of Ebolowa varied from nine hundred to about two thousand at any given time in 1958.

ELAT   The largest Presbyterian station in Cameroun, located between

Ebolowa and Enongal, with a cathedral-sized church; the church press; an industrial school, an elementary school, and a secondary school for Camerounians; missionary residences for seven families; a chapel for Sunday evening worship in English; and the little campus for Hope School, an elementary school for missionary children. In 1958, the total boarding population there was forty, with three teachers for eight grades.

ENONGAL A hilltop station, two kilometers east of Ebolowa, that is the site of the Central Hospital for the Presbyterian Church in Cameroun. Central was the first hospital in the interior of Cameroun and is still noted for its school of nursing. Also site of a leprosarium and, in 1958, one of only two dental clinics in Cameroun. Enongal had missionary residences for six families.

FOREST Meaning the primeval rain forest. True forest has a floor as bare as a table and great trees growing more than a hundred feet high, with leaves making a dense canopy that shuts out the sun. The light inside the forest at midday is as dim as twilight, and the temperature is always cool.

FRANGIPANI TREE A small tropical tree noted for its highly perfumed flowers, which are often strung as garlands of honor. The petals are pure white through yellow to deep rose, and the tree has milky sap and fragile branches. The tree is not good for climbing.

KAPOK TREE A tall tropical-forest tree with wing roots, much like the duma, but thinner in girth and having seeds embedded in silky fibers that float great distances on air currents. Also known as the cottonseed tree.

LIBAMBA Site of Le Collège Évangélique de Libamba, ninety kilometers west of Yaoundé. The school was established for students from Cameroun, the Congo, and Gabon by five Protestant denominations. The faculty came from the United States, Italy, Sweden, France, Germany, and Cameroun. In the whole school population of about two hundred fifty in 1958, about forty languages were spoken. At that time, the college owned about five thousand acres, with only about twenty acres cleared for buildings and roads. The rest was primeval forest, bush, and some banana and palm-oil plantations.

MAKAK A Bassa village twelve kilometers west of Libamba, with, in 1958, a French government administrative post, a post office, a train station, a weekly market, and a police militia barracks. Makak had a population of about two hundred fifty people at that time.

MAQUIS   A French word meaning *hidden in the bush*, and also meaning *disguised*. During World War II, Maquis was a term of honor for the armed French resistance to German occupation. Throughout the last six years of French occupation of Cameroun (1954 to 1960), Camerounians used this term of honor to describe those who fought in the guerrilla war against the French colonial government.

NGONT   Bassa food painstakingly made of cracked melon seeds ground and mixed with water, salt, and shredded fish or chicken, then wrapped in fresh banana leaves and tied in a sort of ball and steamed in a pot. It is food to be served at a celebration.

NTUMBA   Bassa food made of cassava flour (see bobola) mixed with palm oil, salt, and hot pepper, then dried in flat cakes over the fire. This is the Bassa traveler's food, and would have been carried by the Maquis.

PAGNE   A width of cloth, the length of which indicated how rich a man was. A pagne is the traditional garment for a man at home in the village. It is worn wrapped around the hips and rolled at the waist, with the length of cloth reaching the man's ankles.

PALM WOOD   This wood comes from the densely fibrous trunk of the palm tree, which has no grain; to cut a palm is to ruin the saw. Palm wood is unsuitable for construction or furniture.

PÔGA   One of the many green leafy vegetables used in Africa to supply calcium. It is a good substitute for spinach, but the leaves are never eaten raw. Like mustard, from the smallest of seeds pôga grows into a tall, bushy plant.

STATION   Land belonging to an institution, either government, business, or church. In this case, land belonging to the Mission of the Presbyterian Church, USA, in Cameroun. Mission stations, most often in the bush, comprised a church, a school, often an outpatient clinic, sometimes a full hospital, and missionary residences (usually not more than three or four).

TIRAILLEURS   Marksmen, and, among the Bassa in 1958, a word used for the mercenary sharpshooters employed by the French army to kill people in the forest on the suspicion of belonging to the Maquis.

WATER FILTER   A large glazed covered ceramic jar with a spigot at the bottom. The jar held impure water inside a lining and filtered it through a slim, porous clay cylinder called a candle. Every missionary residence had at least one water filter, containing about a gallon of drinking water when full.

YAOUNDÉ   The principle seat of the Ewondo tribe, upgraded during the German colonial period to a central military post, and later made the seat of the French high commissioner and his administration. Yaoundé became the capital city upon Cameroun's independence. The city's population in 1958 was about seventy-five thousand.